BILLION
DOLLAR
DREAM

THE
BILLION
DOLLAR
DREAM

DEEPIKA N

Notion Press

Old No. 38, New No. 6
McNichols Road, Chetpet
Chennai - 600 031

First Published by Notion Press 2017
Copyright © Deepika N 2017
All Rights Reserved.

ISBN 978-1-947498-08-2

DISCLAIMER

This book is purely a **work of fiction**. Names, characters, businesses, places, events and incidents are either the products of the author's imagination or used in a fictitious manner. Any resemblance to actual persons, living or dead, or actual events is purely coincidental.

ACKNOWLEDGEMENTS

I would like to take this opportunity to thank God Almighty for blessing me with the gift of writing. I would also like to thank my very good friend Reshu Tandon, without whose invaluable inputs and assistance this book would not have been possible. And lastly,thanks to my family for all their ssupport.

CHAPTER 1

Warm rays of morning sunshine filtered into the spacious, thickly-carpeted cabin through the Venetian blinds. A man was seated at his large, finely-polished teakwood desk. He was leaning forward in his plush leather chair, intently studying something on the computer screen, muttering under his breath. The desk faced the door, and a huge window which provided an unhindered view of a beautiful, landscaped garden some distance below, was located right behind the desk. The door led to a smaller outer office occupied by the man's secretary, an efficient, attractive woman in her late thirties. A little to the right of the desk were a few couches and coffee table arranged in an orderly manner. A mini-bar which contained an assortment of snacks and soft drinks was located on the wall next to the couch. A door on the opposite wall led to a small, private washroom.

The huge desk contained all the paraphernalia which one would expect to find on the desk of any senior executive of a large business organization in the present day and age. A state-of-the-art personal computer with a sleek, twenty inch touchscreen monitor, two telephones, a satellite phone, an all-in-one scanner, printer and copier which hummed and whirred softly in the background.

The desk also contained a framed photograph of a family of five; the man behind the desk and his lovely, elegant wife with their arms around two beautiful teenage girls who were identical twins and a slightly younger, cherubic-looking boy with a mischievous gleam in his big, brown eyes. All of them were sporting wide, happy smiles.

Presently, the sound of the door opening caught the man's attention. Shashi Kiran, the Senior Vice-President of Human Resources at InfoSoft MicroTech, an India-based IT MNC, looked up from his PC as his two young colleagues, Riya and Shalini entered his spacious domain hand-in-hand, identical broad grins threatening to split their lovely faces in two. "Looks like some folks are cheerful this morning," Shashi smiled at them. He was a distinguished-looking man in his mid-forties, with thick black hair lightly flecked with grey, a tall, lean, athletic figure and fair skin. Though he had an easy, friendly manner, there was an air of authority about him which commanded respect from everyone he came in contact with. He gestured the two young women to be seated in comfortable chairs scattered in front of his desk.

"Good morning sir," said Riya Batra in a sweet, sing-song voice. She was a classic beauty in her mid-twenties, slim, tall and sharp-featured. Her long, curly dark hair, which was streaked blonde at the tips, was pulled back into a neat bun and her big brown eyes set beneath thick, well-shaped eyebrows, were sparkling with merriment.

"Well, the 'thank God it's Friday' effect is at play here, so yes sir, in your words, some folks *are* cheerful this morning," chimed in Shalini Samuel, a soft-spoken, petite, pretty girl also in her mid-twenties, as she took the seat next to her colleague and close friend. The two girls couldn't be more different in appearance if they had tried. Where Riya was tall, willowy and lissome, with long, slim legs, slender waist and full, firm breasts, Shalini was short and barely came upto Riya's shoulders. She was fine-boned and petite, with a slender, curvy figure. Where Riya's hair was long and curly and came down to her hips, Shalini's was short and wavy and she wore it in a stylish layered cut which fell a few inches below her shoulders. Where Riya's complexion was pale and creamy, Shalini's was light wheatish. Riya's face was oval while Shalini's was round. Shalini's elfin, doll-like beauty was a stark contrast to Riya's high cheek-boned supermodel good looks. Their contrasting, yet flawless beauty could create quite an effect when they entered a room. And they shared two more, very vital characteristics. Both of them were very smart and creative. And they both had a dry, sardonic wit which others found difficult to comprehend. They were in perfect sync with one another, pushed each other's limits and brought out the best in each other. The two girls were both brilliant in their own right. As a team, they were peerless and unbeatable because they constantly kept striving for perfection in everything they did and achieved it more often than not.

The two girls had joined InfoSoft MicroTech Ltd., at the same time, right after they completed their respective master's degrees in business administration over three years ago. Shashi Kiran had been their manager and mentor ever since they had joined. Initially, they had had a team lead to report to, but he had been transferred shortly after they had joined and they had been directly reporting to Shashi ever since.

He was a genius at what he did and he had the knack of getting people to follow his instructions without question. He also had the ability to discover others' latent talents and bring them to the fore. He had been recently promoted as senior vice-president, Human Resources, and had come up with a brilliant scheme for which he needed the smart brains of his two young protégés. Moreover, the two young ladies could be counted on to approach the issue from different angles and finally converge on the same plane and the results were always mind-bogglingly astounding and highly effective as well as cost-efficient for the company. But this time, he needed them for a project which was very personal and if they could pull it off, all three would stand to profit immensely. What he had in mind had the potential to make all of them very wealthy. But it wasn't the money which stimulated him so much as the prospect of challenging their intellect. And of course, the money too would be most welcome.

Shashi personally thought that if the girls ever went into business for themselves, they could easily end up as multi-millionaires. Riya's natural flair and flamboyance, combined with Shalini's effortless diplomacy and quiet tenacity, made them the ideal foils for each other. Shashi sometimes saw himself in the two girls and shared a special bond with them. And that was the reason why he had chosen to include them in this very special endeavor. Not to mention the fact that Riya and Shalini were among the select few in the company who he considered worthy of his trust. Another factor which had made him choose them was that neither girl saw the other as her rival. They were team players, through and through and complemented each other perfectly. This was important to him because he simply did not have time for silly behavior in the name of competition and one-upmanship. For this endeavor, he needed people who could trust each other implicitly and whom he could also trust completely.

Looking at the girls' outward appearance and proud carriage, people would be hard-pressed to guess what they had been through in life. Both of them had a fighting spirit and never-say-die attitude that helped them through tough times. The adage "When the going gets tough, the tough get going" could have been tailor-made for the two gutsy young ladies. As their professional advisor, Shashi was immensely proud of them and prouder still to have them on his team. They were joint team leads now, after only three years in the company. He gave them a mysterious smile. The girls looked at each other knowingly.

"Uh-oh, I know that look," Shalini grinned cheekily at him. "Spill sir," she said in her most wheedlesome tone. "Something's cooking. I can smell it. So c'mon." She opened her eyes as wide as they would go for good measure. This made Shashi smile despite himself. *Hitting the nail right on the head as usual,* he thought. *Some things never change.*

"You can't ever stop thinking about food, can you?" Riya gave her friend a look of exasperated indulgence. The other girl just shrugged and grinned, as if Riya had said something very amusing. Shalini was one of the few people who could get away with talking to their boss in that way. She had a child-like face and an innocent air about her which could melt the hardest of hearts. But Riya and Shashi knew better than to be fooled by the fragile damsel look, which camouflaged an iron will and nerves of steel. It didn't however, stop Shashi from giving in to her petulance most of the time and it didn't now.

"Yes," he said ruefully. "Something's cooking, to use your own phraseology. The language you kids use these days..." he began.

"Awww sir! Enough of that now. Please tell us what's going on and we'll listen to your complaints about our language all day long," said Shalini interrupting him before he warmed up to his favorite tirade, looking remarkably innocent, head cocked to one side and a slight smile on her full, pouty lips. "Archana said it was urgent," she went on, referring to Shashi's secretary. "What gives?"

Shashi gave up trying to prolong the suspense He knew he would never win. "We're going to make a billion dollars, the three of us. That's the urgent matter I wanted to discuss with you." He then sat back and waited to see how they would react to his announcement.

For a long moment, the cabin was filled with a deafening silence. The two girls looked at him, mouths agape. "Did you say a billion dollars?" Riya finally managed to choke out.

"Yes," said Shashi, trying hard to maintain a poker face. He found the look on the two young women's faces quite priceless. They looked shell-shocked, as if a bomb had just exploded in front of them. However, the girls regained their composure quickly, as they were quite used to his unusual "surprises."

"And how exactly are we going to achieve this miracle?" queried Shalini calmly. She wondered for a moment if her boss had suddenly gone bonkers. "Rob a bank perhaps? Or are we gonna print counterfeit currency?" Riya sighed. She wondered if her dear friend could possibly squeeze any more sarcasm into her words. Shashi was a man of many moods and Riya DID NOT want to be on the receiving end of his wrath thanks to Ms. BigMouth's "helpful" comments.

She shot her a look whose meaning was unmistakable: *shut up Shalini*, which the smaller girl chose not to notice. But Shashi did not seem to be offended by the sarcasm in Shalini's words. He only smiled. "Come now Shalini. You know that's too easy. I won't be needing you if I was planning to rob a bank or become a counterfeiter. That would be an insult to your intelligence. This plan calls for daring, subtlety and thinking way out of the box. In fact, we may have to think out of the entire universe, if it comes to that."

"I don't know about Bandit Queen here," said a relieved Riya, giving Shalini a sideways glance, which earned her a withering look from her dear friend, "but I'm all ears. Lay it on, cap'n."

"Yes, my curiosity is piqued. Is this a company project or do we get to keep the money?" Shalini asked in the most unsubtle of ways.

Shashi stared at her in wonder while Riya tried to hide her smile. *Leave it to Shalini to say out loud what everyone's thinking and not wanting to say!* And all done oozing awestruck innocence too! Both the girls were forthright and straightforward, but Shalini could make even murder seem merciful. Combined with Riya's resourcefulness, this was quite a potent weapon.

"Er, it's our own personal project and we get to share the money equally," Shashi managed to say at last.

Shalini clapped her hands and did something vaguely resembling a tap dance while remaining seated in her chair. Riya looked at her mentor questioningly. "Say what? Does the company know about this?"

"Of course not, silly," her friend looked at her as if she had suddenly grown two heads. "Right sir?"

"Shalini's right," Shashi confirmed. "What the management doesn't know won't hurt them. We won't be working on this project during company time, so I don't see how that should matter."

"You're right. It shouldn't matter. But what if word leaks out and Rajesh and Sanjana come to know about this?" asked Shalini, referring to members of one of the software development teams who considered the trio to be their arch-enemies for reasons best known only to the two of them.

"Only the three of us know about this," said Shashi sternly. "So, unless one of you is thinking of selling us out, I don't see how they can find out."

"Right," said Riya briskly. "That's settled then. And may I suggest sir, that we hold no further discussions about our billion dollar secret inside office premises?"

"That's a very sensible suggestion, Ms. Riya," Shashi smiled at her. "With my two enlightened young colleagues backing me, I feel I can conquer the world."

"Sure you can," said Shalini impishly. "And if you wanna dispose off any bodies, you know where to find us." Shashi's jaw dropped when Shalini uttered these outrageous words and Riya hastened to say something before any more macabre and damaging utterances could spew out of Shalini's mouth.

"Speak for yourself, Ms. Body Snatcher," she retorted. "I have far more important things to think about, like how to turn this fantastic dream into a reality."

"No quarelling girls," he admonished gently. "I don't particularly want to see a ladies' wrestling match or a cat fight for that matter, in my office."

"If not for you sir, I'll rip her little throat out right here," said Riya matter-of-factly, as if she was placing an order for tandoori chicken. What Shashi never realized in all the years he had known the two girls was that their so-called quarrels were mostly for his benefit. Just as Riya intended, her words had distracted him from the latest macabre deluge to stream from Shalini's deceptively innocent mouth.

"Calm down girls. We'll video-conference later. Get back to work, both of you," smiling, he tried to shoo them out of the room.

"Sure, sure. We know when we're no longer wanted," said Shalini with an exaggerated sigh and a full pout. Both the girls exited the room, Riya quietly shutting the door behind them.

CHAPTER 2

"Looks like some early birds have caught plenty of worms," said a throaty, sultry voice behind the two girls as they were heading toward their respective cabins.

Riya's good mood evaporated and she scowled in irritation, but Shalini squeezed her hand in warning and she relaxed once again. With an effort, she arranged her features in a semblance of pleasantness and turned to face the speaker, a fair-skinned, well-proportioned young woman of medium height in her late twenties who could have been pretty if she stopped frowning and scowling constantly at everyone. "Hello Sanjana," Riya said in her sweetest voice. "Now what's all this about worms? Having trouble with your PC perhaps? Maybe we could help," she offered, tongue-in-cheek, trying to smile in her sincerest manner. Shalini cheered silently. Riya's face was the very picture of innocence at that moment.

Sanjana Agarwal glared at both the girls. Even her short, stylishly bobbed hair seemed to bristle with annoyance. "Don't try to act smart with me," she snapped. "You came out of the senior VP's cabin looking as pleased as punch. I demand to know what's going on."

"You can demand all you want, but since it has got nothing to do with you sweetheart, why don't you do everyone a favor and get lost?" Riya bit out. She had a dangerous, untamed side to her, much like a beautiful tigress waiting to be unleashed. Her suave exterior camouflaged it most of the time, but people like Sanjana somehow managed to rub her the wrong way almost all the time.

"In other words," drawled Shalini, "take a hike, love."

"I bet both of you were just being naughty in there," Sanjana's voice dropped to a hoarse stage whisper, as if she'd just had an epiphany.

Riya turned to Shalini, feigning bewilderment. "Excuse me Shalu, I thought I was speaking in English only?" When her friend nodded sagely, as if Riya had spoken the gospel truth itself, she continued, "Even if Ms. Goody Two Shoes is correct in her assumption, how is it any of her business? Maybe she's feeling sore at being left out from the alleged party she seems to believe we were having?"

Sanjana shot her a look that could freeze a raging forest fire, but it had no effect on Riya, much to her annoyance. "You think you're so smart. Just you wait. Something fishy's going on and I'll not rest till I find out what it is!" she was ranting now and failing to make any sense.

"Bring it on, smartypants! You're most welcome to fish all you want," grinned Shalini. She could never keep a straight face and was finding it a struggle to stop herself from bursting into hysterical laughter. Riya was doing a spectacular job of winding up their arch-rival and the poor girl had taken the bait, hook, line and sinker!

"Sanjana, *angel*," purred Riya, her voice dripping honey. "Let me explain in simple terms so that you can understand.

You're part of the software development team." When she saw that Sanjana was about to make a retort, she rushed on, her tone hard and uncompromising, "Human Resources is ancient history for you. Shalini and I are HR team members. Mr. Kiran is senior Vice-President, HR. We have been in and out of his cabin countless times for the last three years and will continue to do so when the need arises. Tell me what part of this you don't understand, what you think seems fishy. Please tell me you are not that dense." Other employees around the three young women stopped what they were doing to pay attention to the drama taking place in front of their eyes.

Sanjana said nothing, realizing she was being made to look like a fool in front of the entire office. She resolved to get to the bottom of whatever was going on by herself. She thought Shashi Kiran's "preference" for the two girls was so obvious, and she could not understand why others were not inclined to believe her. Except of course, Rajesh Tiwari. Oh, how she wanted to get back at the notorious trio! She was sure they were planning something big and curiosity was eating at her from the inside like acid. She hated feeling so......insignificant. With a last venomous look at the two girls, she turned on her heels and stomped off to her own floor.

Shalini shook her head at Sanjana's retreating back. "That one walks around with a giant-sized chip on her shoulder. I thought things would maybe change one day, but with her, it just seems impossible. What a massive ego! It's like she thinks she's the only good and pure one around here and the rest of us are constantly conspiring to bring her down."

"Bring her down?" snorted Riya derisively. "What's to bring down? She doesn't stand a chance against either of us and she knows it. Hence the constant animosity. Classic case of wanting to be the center of attention all the time. Well, she's not as important as she thinks she ought to be and for someone like her, it's a bitter pill to swallow. Besides, she doesn't deserve our sympathy. It's not as if she gave us an easy time when we were both new here. Let's not waste our time on her. We have to conquer the world as it is and we don't have the luxury of throwing away precious minutes dealing with Sanjana's tantrums. Come on."

Both the girls headed off to their respective cabins, which were situated adjacent to each other. Though their cabins were quite small and had open doorways, they afforded them some measure of privacy and much-needed peace and quiet to go about their jobs. Riya sat down and let out a deep sigh. What a way to begin a Friday! What a topsy-turvy day it was turning out to be already! Fabulous, fantastic schemes and a cat-fight. Not to mention, Riya rolled her eyes, Shalini's incredibly big mouth and smart-ass comments!

In her cabin, Shalini was grinning to herself. As far as she was concerned, it was an invigorating start to what would have been an otherwise dull day. Sure, Sanjana was a thorn in their flesh, but such altercations with her always seemed to energize both the girls. *Maybe we are twisted weirdos*, she thought wryly. Then she shrugged. The day's work still needed to be done and she did not want to drag her heels over it. After all, their billion-dollar scheme had to be planned in elaborate detail and the sooner office work was finished, the better.

In a short while, the two girls were completely engrossed in processing joining forms and supporting documents of new employees, drawing up schedules for upcoming induction programs and updating the list of colleges for the next campus recruitment exercise. Shalini had to look into a dispute between two team leads in Quality Assurance which had resulted in a physical altercation inside office premises. She talked to both the parties separately through telephone, but neither was willing to give an inch. She rolled her eyes at their elephant-sized egos and added a few comments to the file on her computer and mailed it to all the Ethics and Discipline Committee members. It looked like the matter could be resolved only through an official inquiry.

In addition, Shalini and Riya were besieged by their co-workers with various queries, which they handled with aplomb. Since both the girls had charming and pleasing personalities, even irate employees calmed down after talking to them for just a few minutes. Before they knew it, the morning had flown by. They still needed to plan the latest campus recruitment drive, but it could wait until after lunch.

Both of them headed down to the office cafeteria for lunch along with their friend Samyukta, an older woman in her early forties who was part of the company's treasury team. They were engrossed in their conversation and were not really paying attention to where they were going. Suddenly, there was a loud crash and Shalini cried out. "Owww!"

Riya turned to look and was met with the sight of Shalini and a man in his mid-thirties sprawled out on the floor, a couple of chairs strewn around them. The man was trying to scramble to his feet, shooting a death glare at Shalini. "Watch your step next time, Barbie!" he snarled. "That cane of yours not guiding you properly?"

"I wasn't paying attention and I apologize," said Shalini in as calm a voice as she could manage as she slowly got back on her feet. "No need to make an issue out of this Rajesh. And don't call me Barbie. Ever."

"Oh?" Rajesh sneered. He was a stocky man of medium height. He had been chasing after Shalini since the day she had joined the company and all his attempts at wooing her had been snubbed. The outright rejection had not gone down well with him and he'd been wanting to get back at her somehow ever since. "What will you do if I call you Barbie, *Barbie?*"

Both of them were back on their feet now and were glaring at each other. Hands on her hips, Shalini smiled sweetly, too sweetly. "You know Rajesh," she said with deceptive nonchalance. "The next time you call me Barbie, I might, just might decide to crush your dream of carrying on your lineage." The unpleasant look on his face told her that Rajesh had received the message, loud and clear. She was quite pleased with herself. "Wanna take the chance?" He shot her a mean look, but turned on his heels and walked off without bothering to reply.

Riya was immensely proud of her petite friend and said as much when Shalini joined them and they continued on to the cafeteria. "Darn good, short stuff," she said. "You gave that creep just what he needed—a shot where it hurts most."

"Thank you," sighed Shalini. "First Sanjana and now Rajesh. What did we do to have them wished on us?"

"I guess the two of you had been too good to them and they just couldn't handle it!" Samyukta was smiling at the two young ladies. She was a slim, dignified woman in her mid-forties. She had taken an immediate liking to the two firebrands and championed their cause whenever and wherever she could, much to the annoyance of Sanjana. Those close to the two young women approved of their relationship with the older woman and felt she was a steadying influence on both the flamboyant firebrands. Being in her company made them happy and when the two were in good spirits, it was always pleasant for those around them.

Presently, Shalini appeared with a plate laden with parathas, kadai paneer, stir-fried vegetables, grilled chicken and pulao. Riya's plate was similarly heaped. Samyukta looked at them wonderingly. "You eat all that and still manage to look like knock-outs. What's your secret?"

Shalini grinned mischievously, "Oh well. We watch what we eat," she picked up a chicken leg as she said this and looked at it intently. "Looks good." Then she bit into the flesh and started chewing. "See? We watch what we eat."

"I think what Smarty means to say," said Riya with a cheeky grin of her own, "is that we eat what we like and then work out like maniacs in the evening."

"Whatever. I envy both of you all the same," sighed Samyukta. "Oh how I miss being young and carefree!"

"Relax, you're not doing too badly you know," said Riya reassuringly, looking at her slender, distinguished-looking friend. "I hope I age as well as you have, right Shalu?"

"Of course," agreed Shalini. "You don't look fortiesh and people won't believe you if you say so."

"Flattery does feel good sometimes," smiled Samyukta. "Especially from really good friends. Come on girls. Let's eat quickly and head downstairs for a short walk."

"You don't have to ask us twice," said Shalini between mouthfuls. "But you have to wait till I finish dessert."

"Of course," said Riya standing up. "What shall I bring you? Ice cream or gulab jamun?"

"Both," answered Shalini without looking up from her plate. Riya shook her head at her as she headed towards the dessert table. Presently, she returned with a tray laden with bowls of ice creams of two different flavors, glasses of fresh fruit juice and bowls of gulab jamuns. Samyukta gave her a strange look. "Are we celebrating something? Have I forgotten any important occasion? Or is someone joining us?"

"None of the above," said Riya matter-of-factly. "I just thought Shalini here required something extra after the morning's exertions."

"Oh really?" retorted Shalini. "Does that mean you won't be touching any of this stuff?"

"Hah!" hissed Riya scornfully. "As if I collected all these yummy goodies only for your sorry self!"

"Calm down and finish up your dessert girls. Please," implored Samyukta. She didn't want crockery to start flying around. The rest of the meal went on in peaceful silence and the three ladies headed downstairs once they had finished.

In the spacious, landscaped garden, they spotted Sanjana, who was deep in conversation with one of the senior associates from finance. They circled around her and headed to the other side, where they would be out of her line of sight. The move was strategic rather than out of fear. Sanjana was a sore loser and could never get over the fact that she had been usurped by the two girls because they were more talented and competent than her. She always thought they were hatching conspiracies against her and for Shalini and Riya, this got tiresome beyond a point. After such a splendid meal, neither of them was in the mood for another catfight.

The trio walked in companionable silence for a while. Soon, they were joined by Arvind Rajan, Sreeja Ravishankar and Anup Sharma, their friends from other departments of the company. The group were soon engrossed in a serious discussion about their upcoming quarterly performance review when Arvind's friend Derek Mathews joined them. He was a tall, handsome young man with an athletic build, big brown eyes and thick, dark wavy hair in his late twenties from Mumbai whose attraction towards Shalini was a secret known only to him, or so he thought. Arvind, a stocky man of medium height in his early thirties, had frequently caught Derek following Shalini around with his wide-set brown eyes with deep yearning during his visits to InfoSoft MicroTech, but had never questioned his younger friend about it. Derek was a child prodigy with an incredibly high IQ, a marketing whiz who had passed out of Wharton School of Business at the age of twenty-one and had worked in England, France and Gernany for a while, then returned to India when he was twenty-three to set up his own advertising agency. Within a few short years, the agency had grown at a phenomenal pace and now had offices in Bangalore, Chennai, Mumbai, New Delhi, Kolkata, Pune and Hyderabad. He had come to InfoSoft MicroTech to discuss a new nation-wide advertising campaign for one of their upcoming products. If it had been any other company, he would have sent one of his underlings for the negotiations, but had decided to make this trip in person for a variety of reasons, the main one being to catch a glimpse of Shalini if he could. He wanted as many images of her as he could get to add to his memories. And besides, he grinned to himself, he would grab any excuse to run into her and stare at her pretty face and bewitching eyes with both hands. She couldn't resist his charms for much longer, he reasoned. He'd keep chasing after her, as he had been doing for the last two years. He was confident that soon, he'd catch her and she'd be his forever. Shalini sat as far away from him as possible, not wanting to deal with his advances, but he was content just glancing at her from time to time.

In contrast, Anup's fanatical devotion to Riya was legendary around the office. Riya liked and respected the tall, fair-skinned, blue-eyed young man with an athletic body and intelligent mind immensely, but couldn't bring herself to take the next step with him. Anup was not unduly worried about Riya's reticence. He was a very patient young man and felt confident he would eventually break down the walls she had built around herself, and earn her trust and love. She wasn't going anywhere. He would wait. He was a perseverant young man who had gone to MIT on a full scholarship and passed out at the top of his class and had worked for a top conglomerate in the US for a while, but his yearning for India brought him home in a few years.

Sreeja was a studious-looking young lady in her late twenties. She was a mathematics genius, an IIT alumnus whose IQ was off the charts, and at the young age of twenty-eight, was number two in the company's Encryption department and head of the section at the Chennai branch. She reported directly to the senior Vice-President of the Encryption section at the company headquarters in Mumbai, an incredible achievement for one so young. However, she had a self-deprecating manner and refused to take herself seriously, which endeared her to her friends and colleagues. And she did not fit into the stereotype of a genius either; no milk-bottle spectacles, no egg-shaped head or a receding hairline or conversely, a head full of shaggy hair. Sreeja was slim, nicely toned and well-proportioned. She had a clear, light-brown complexion and shoulder-length straight hair which was highlighted with blonde and red streaks. Her clothes were always stylish and top-of-the-line, and she gave no one the chance to call her a math geek.

She grinned at Shalini. "So, we hear you had a run-in with the Dragon Lady and King of Jerks. What happened?"

"Oh, just the usual," sighed Shalini. "I ran into Rajesh, literally, by accident. And of course he had to make a scene out of that. And Sanjana is Sanjana. One look from her and fresh milk will turn sour in an instant!"

The group burst into laughter. "Besides," continued Shalini. "It was not all my doing. Ms. Batra here was the one to put the

Dragon Lady in her place. And a splendid job it was, too." At that, Riya grinned wickedly.

"That goes without saying," chimed in Anup, stealing a surreptitious glance at Riya, admiring her ethereal beauty when he thought she wouldn't notice. "And Sanjana should know better than to tangle with the two of you again and again. Smart as she is, I'm surprised she hasn't received the message yet. Right now, she's being a major nuisance in my team. Tried to tell me how to do my job yesterday. Granted, she's a good software developer, but her attitude is just too much to bear. She better watch herself. One of these days, I may decide to issue her a reprimand if she tries to act oversmart."

"She's a weird one," agreed Arvind. "Such a fabulous brain and look how she's using it. Plotting and planning and all the useless stuff."

"If we don't look out, she would probably become Lady Bin Laden," laughed Shalini. "Poor Sanjana! How she must be cursing us right now!" Derek couldn't take his eyes off her. With her head thrown back, mouth wide open and eyes crinkling in mirth, she took his breath away. He knew she was twenty-five which made her four years younger than him, but she could easily pass for a teenager, especially when she looked happy and carefree as she did now. She was beautiful, smart and intelligent, yet she seemed not to be dating anyone as far as he could tell. He couldn't help but wonder why. Not that he was complaining, he admitted to himself ruefully, but it mystified him that such a wonderful young woman had seemingly closed herself off from the dating scene.

CHAPTER 3

If only Shalini knew how right she was about Sanjana!

Sanjana was still smarting from the altercation in the corridor that morning. It would have never occurred to her to believe that all the so-called conspiracies she kept seeing were only in her mind. She longed to take down the two girls who in her view, had so cunningly and unjustly snatched away her prized position as sole team lead in HR and ousted her from her rightful place as the self-proclaimed, uncrowned queen of the company's Chennai branch. She had been with InfoSoft MicroTech for more than seven years now. Sanjana had been offered a software development post with an attractive package immediately after she had graduated with a bachelor's degree in computer science and engineering from a good engineering college in Kolkata. Initially, she had worked at the company's Kolkata office, but had quickly realized that software engineering was not really her thing, though she was a very talented developer and trouble-shooter. So, she had enrolled in a part-time MBA program, majoring in marketing and minoring in human resources. Once she had obtained her master's degree, she had requested the management to switch her from software development to some other section. Her wish had been granted. She had been transferred to the marketing section. She had co-ordinated product launches, which she had enjoyed initially, but soon yearned for a change. Then she was re-assigned to human resources, which had been her minor in her MBA. She had at last felt quite at home. Then, she was transferred to Chennai, where she had reigned supreme for almost a year and a half. Then, without warning, it had all fallen apart.

Now, in her opinion, she was rotting away once again in software development, with next to no visibility, conferring with bespectacled nerds and having to listen to that conceited head of Encryption, Sreeja Ravishankar, prattle on about the importance of developing a secure application with the proper encryption codes. The only bright spot was Anup Sharma, whom she had had a thing for, but he had rejected her advances from the beginning, choosing instead to focus his attentions on the undeserving tease Riya Batra, who hardly gave him the time of day! And worst of all, she had to go back to working in shifts. Sometimes arriving and leaving office at ungodly hours! Bah! How unfair!

How she longed to be back in HR, where she once used to lord it over everyone! In those glory days, she had been literally walking on air. Writing interminable codes and developing software applications and packages had never really interested her, even though it came naturally to her. She had always held the opinion that people management was her real calling in life. Human resources fit her like a glove, or so she had thought. InfoSoft MicroTech seemed to be the perfect place to work, especially after altering her career path. The then HR head of the Chennai branch had been easy to work with and she was having a lovely time. Prakash Rawat had quit to take up a lucrative position with a U.S.-based cosmetics giant. Then

Shashi Kiran, who had just returned from the Middle East, where the company had opened its new office, was asked to take over the HR section in Chennai. In the Middle East, he'd been co-ordinating movement of suitable personnel from the company's existing pool and recruitment of local personnel. The company had given him a promotion and a significant raise in remuneration when he was called back to India. To Sanjana, this signaled the beginning of the end of her reign. Almost a year after he'd come to Bangalore, two young HR professionals, Riya Batra and Shalini Samuel, were recruited in a campus recruitment exercise. This, in Sanjana's opinion, had been a big mistake by the company, a "mistake" which had sent her career spiraling downhill.

Her "charm," which had worked like a miracle on Prakash Rawat, did not seem to have any effect on the wily Shashi Kiran, who had handled several overseas assignments and was quite an expert when it came to reading human nature, having dealt with various kinds of people from a myriad of socio-cultural and economic backgrounds. He had seen through her pretenses at once and her ingratiating manner only served to irritate him further, but she had obstinately refused to take the message and had tried to be arrogant and in many instances, had even tried to teach him how to do his job. This approach had worked well enough with Prakash Rawat, but Shashi Kiran had wanted no part of it. Though an extremely intelligent and meticulous executive, she had an inflated ego and a patronizing manner about her that grated on his nerves. He had tried to warn her several times, but she, out of sheer arrogance, had paid no heed to his warnings and had gone on her merry way, telling herself that once he realized how indispensable she was, he would come to respect her. But that had not happened. Instead, Shashi Kiran had gotten quite fed up of her manipulative ways and had sent her packing straight back to software development as soon as an opportunity had presented itself. And now she was paying the price for crossing the line too far with the boss. But as far as she was concerned, her perceived misfortunes were not her fault at all. It was due to the "favoritism" Shashi Kiran was showing towards Riya Batra and Shalini Samuel. Her considerably huge ego blinded her to the truth that the crux of the problem was her own refusal to adapt to changes as they happened, and as a result, she was now heading down a path of self-destruction that nobody seemed to be able to stop her from.

She scowled fiercely as she finished her conversation with Harish Kumar, the senior associate who looked after attendance and payroll. His ethics were questionable at best and he did not have a good reputation. But proof of wrongdoing never materialized, so the management couldn't find justifiable grounds to get rid of him, though several employees had complained bitterly about the man. He often skated on dangerously thin ice, but somehow managed to keep his nose clean and stay out of trouble.

Sanjana wanted to get Riya and Shalini into trouble and had asked Kumar if the log data could be tweaked. Though Kumar could play around with certain types of data at his end, he did not have authorization to access the HR database in which all personnel data, including daily In and Out times were maintained. Besides, if he was caught tampering with HR data, he was sure Mr. Kiran would haul him lock, stock and barrel before the Ethics Committee. The expression "taken to the cleaners and hung out to dry" would assume new meaning then. He could not talk his way around Mr. Kiran the way he used to do with Mr. Prakash Rawat, the previous HR head. Shashi Kiran was quick to spot a lie and pounce on it. If caught, Harish Kumar would stand no chance at all.

He was explaining all this to Sanjana, who was shaking her head in disgust. "I never figured you to be a coward," she whined, trying to goad him.

"I'm not!" Kumar was fuming. "What you're suggesting is madness, suicidal even. If Mr. Kiran catches even a whiff of what's going on, we'll both be out of the door before we know what hit us!"

"Well, Mr. Kiran is not always looking at the database, is he?"

"Sanjana, you know as well as I do that only Mr. Kiran, Ms. Batra, Ms. Samuel and under certain circumstances, Ms. Ravishankar and Mr. Patnaik have the authorization to access the HR database and modify personnel data. The rest of HR, Payroll and other departments have authorization to only view the data. We cannot manipulate or modify. Even if we somehow manage to hack into it, which is a near-impossible task, don't you think any anomalies would become apparent immediately? Besides, if we're caught tampering with the time logs of those two ladies, Shashi Kiran will not hesitate to bring any and all charges against us. By the time he's done with us, no company in any corner of the world would ever want to touch us. The term 'blacklisted' would not be enough to explain that phenomenon! It's too awful even to contemplate!"

"Arrgh!" Sanjana cried out in frustration. "Why are those idiots getting so much special attention? They don't deserve it, I tell you! They are just a pair of incompetent nincompoops! They don't know the ABCs of HR! I bet they are extending special favors to the boss to get all these special privileges! They conspired against me, got me out of the way and now are gloating about it! They only get by on their looks. Brainless bimbos! I'll not have it! I'll not!" Her face had turned red thanks to all this agitation, and the look in her eyes was so venomous that he took an involuntary step back.

Harish Kumar watched her quietly. He did not try to stop her tirade. He knew Riya and Shalini both had squeaky clean reputations. He also knew that Sanjana and Prakash Rawat had had some sort of special arrangement. Though unscrupulous himself, he wanted no part of her crazy ideas and schemes. He did not want to invite the wrath of Shashi Kiran, which could be swift and brutal, as he had witnessed on other occasions. And he knew Kiran's fury would be enhanced manifold if either of his golden girls was harmed, leave alone both. And if Kiran ever came to know about Sanjana's baseless but malicious accusations, only God knew what he'd do. The man was happily married and in his mind, philandering was an unforgivable sin. Kumar badly wanted to keep his job. He had a family to feed after all.

"Sanjana," he said as she stopped to take a breath. "Listen to me. Tampering with those girls' data is suicidal." She shot him an ugly look. "But," he continued in an attempt to placate her, "we'll come up with a foolproof plan to bring them to their knees. Okay? Just give me some time to think."

"Alright," she huffed. "But I want them out—fast!"

"I understand," Kumar sighed. "I better get back to work now," he said as he turned and left the glowering Sanjana to brood. As he walked away from her, his shoulders sagged with relief at successfully wiggling away from Sanjana and her insane plans at least for the time being.

Sanjana stared at his retreating back, shaking her head in barely contained frustration. Why oh why, she wondered in despair, did the management send Shashi Kiran to Chennai? Everything had been running smoothly, at least in her esteemed opinion, till he came and turned the HR section upside down. She glanced at her watch and sighed. It was time to get back to work and listen to more prattling from Sreeja Ravishankar.

CHAPTER 4

In the afternoon, Riya had to go down to the Development section to meet with the senior vice-president. As she walked along the foyer, she thought she caught Anup Sharma glancing at her furtively. He was standing just outside his cabin. Just as she turned around to verify, he had turned away and walked back inside. When she saw the door to the cabin closing, she shook her head doubtfully. Perhaps she had imagined the whole thing? At any rate, she didn't have the time or inclination to wonder and hurried on to meet the senior VP of development.

In the small outer office, the VP's secretary, a stocky, middle-aged woman, informed her that he was expecting her. Riya knocked lightly on the door and entered his cabin. His name was Satish Kumar, a tall, attractive man in his early forties whose chiseled, handsome face was dominated by a large, luxuriant mustache. He greeted Riya with a friendly smile and signaled her to take a seat. "Would you mind taking Sanjana off my hands?" was his opening remark.

Riya grinned cheekily from ear to ear and shook her head. "Thanks," she said. "But no thanks! Even though it's my boss who can take the final call on that, I know that's exactly what he'd say!"

"Smart chap, Shashi Kiran. Can't pull the wool over his eyes," Satish sighed dramatically. "Still, a man's gotta try!"

Riya laughed. She liked Satish Kumar and held him in the highest regard. "Nice try, but no can do!"

Then Satish's face turned serious and they got down to business. While she was conferring with him, Anup strolled casually into the cabin and took the seat beside her even though his presence was not really needed. But since he was overall manager of seven teams and just two notches below the VP in the company's pecking order, she simply held her tongue and did not say anything. His presence did not seem to bother his boss, so Riya decided to pretend he wasn't there and carried on with her discussion, bringing up spreadsheets with projected manpower requirements to support her argument.

Anup did not say much during the meeting, satisfying himself by making occasional remarks and expressed opinions only when Satish Kumar turned to him and specifically asked for his views. Riya caught him checking her out a couple of times, but on both occasions, he averted his gaze as soon as he realized she was onto him. She tried not to get flustered by this constant and intense scrutiny. Mercifully, the meeting ended in about forty-five minutes and she practically fled from the cabin, barely managing to squeak out a polite good-bye to Satish Kumar. By the time she got back to her own cabin, her nerves were a lot calmer and her breathing was almost back to normal. With a conscious effort, she put Anup Sharma firmly out of her mind and went about her job like the professional she was. The rest of the afternoon flew by.

It was almost six in the evening when Shalini turned off her PC, stuffed her tablet and mobile into her quite sizeable purse, cleared her desk and went to see if Riya was ready to leave. She was just winding up for the day and clearing her own desk when Shalini waltzed in, brandishing her brand-new GPS-enabled vibrating white cane in one hand as if it was a deadly weapon, which in her hands, it could very well turn out to be.

"Ready?" Shalini queried. Riya held up two fingers to indicate she would be ready in a couple of minutes. She nodded and took out her smartphone to ask her chauffeur to bring the car around to the main entrance. By the time she ended her call, Riya was ready. The two girls headed towards the elevators. Luckily, one was on their floor. They climbed in quickly and before the doors closed, somebody rushed in, out of breath. To their surprise, the girls found themselves looking at their boss, Shashi Kiran. He coolly set down his briefcase on the elevator floor and smiled at them.

Riya was openly gaping at him. She turned to Shalini. "What's the time, Shalu?"

"Six-oh-five," answered Shalini, consulting her talking wrist-watch. She too was giving him a perplexed look. "Are we dreaming sir, or are you seriously leaving office at this preposterously 'early' hour?" she queried with a mischievous twinkle in her eyes.

Shashi Kiran smiled. "Don't tell me the boss is not allowed to leave office at a decent time once in a while?" he teased.

"It's not that," answered Riya hurriedly before Shalini could come up with one of her wise-cracks.

Shashi smiled. "Are you girls free for dinner tonight?"

"Sure we are!" said Shalini happily, with nary a care whether Riya was actually free or not.

"You know, you could have extended me the courtesy of asking, Ms. Know-it-all," said an exasperated Riya.

"Oh, I'm sorry. Does Your Ladyship have plans for dinner tonight? A hot date perhaps?" asked Shalini sarcastically, though her tone was sweet as honey.

"No."

"So that makes the question irrelevant, doesn't it?" retorted Shalini.

"Yes, yes smarty. It does. But it wouldn't hurt to be polite," sighed Riya, knowing full well the futility of her argument.

Shalini gave her a hard stare. "With anyone else, yes. I know your schedule as well as I do mine, so why bother?"

Shashi Kiran was amused. "Girls," he said. "Although I'm enjoying this exchange immensely, I want to take you both out for dinner. We can discuss the plans for our venture then," he clarified.

"Discussion or no discussion, I'm always up for food," said Shalini, grinning broadly and licking her lips, as if she'd been starving the entire day. "But mind you boss. No cheapskates dinner. I want a sumptuous meal at a classy restaurant."

"Glut," muttered Riya.

"Excuse me? Does that mean you would be happy to nibble on crumbs?" demanded Shalini caustically.

"Calm down both of you," Shashi was getting flustered now. He had two teenage daughters and a young son who constantly argued with one another. He had never been good at mediating their fights and Riya and Shalini's behavior sometimes made him think he had five kids! "I'll pick you two up at eight. We're going to The Park. And Shalini, for the record, I don't think I have ever taken you two out for a cheapskates meal."

"Great! We shall be ready by eight sir. Will Shreya and Tina be joining us? And Abhishek too?" queried Riya, referring to Shashi's children, with whom the two got along splendidly.

"No, it's just the three of us. Can't get any business discussion going with the five of you in the same room, leave alone same table. Besides, they left straight from school to visit their grandparents."

"Oh! Okay then. We'll see you at eight sir. Bye!" the girls waved as they reached the entrance and found Shalini's chauffeur waiting beside her shiny new Volkswagen Vento.

"See you girls," he called out after them before he walked off towards his own car.

The two girls settled into the back of the car as the chauffeur drove swiftly and smoothly out of the office campus towards Alwarpet, where they lived in the same block of flats. The ride was made in a companionable silence as the girls were in a very reflective mood. They reached their apartment complex in twenty minutes and got out of the car. The chauffeur locked the car and handed over the keys to Shalini as he left for the day. Just as they turned around to leave, Riya ran smack into Derek, who had just finished parking his own car.

"Whoa! Careful," he said, catching his balance and managing to stay on his feet.

"What are you doing here?" she queried. Derek was a rising star in the advertising industry and Riya held him in immense regard, but she wasn't overawed by him, as many people tend to be. As a result, Derek found it easy and comfortable to talk to her. Shalini of course was a different matter altogether.

"I live here, remember?" though his words were addressed to Riya, his eyes were completely fastened on Shalini.

"I know that, genius. Sorry I almost knocked you over," she said, laughing at her ridiculous question. Derek waved off her apology with an easy smile.

"Hi," said Shalini, speaking for the first time. She was smiling shyly. His answering grin was threatening to split his rugged, handsome face in two.

"Hi," he responded cheerfully.

"Are you stalking me by any chance?" she asked, only half-joking. Her heart skipped a beat every time she saw him, but she always worked hard to try to hide the fact that she was attracted to him.

"Of course not," he said, looking amused. "Though it doesn't seem like a bad idea. There are worse ways to spend my time than stare at your pretty profile all day long!" As he said this, his fingers ever so gently caressed the back of her hand as it rested on the hood of the car.

Shalini blushed and immediately withdrew her hand as if a jolt of electricity had passed through her, but did not say anything and turned away feeling embarrassed. The usual witticism deserted her as the flirtatious remarks grew intimate. Harmless banter and flirting was all fine, but she did not know how Derek would react if she actually tried to act upon her attraction towards him. She did not want to risk having her heart stomped upon and her trust broken once again. She had mixed feelings about him living in the same upscale apartment building she and Riya were in.

"If the two of you are quite finished, we have to go now," Riya's words broke the tension.

"Sure," said Derek, not taking his eyes off Shalini. He badly wanted to claim those luscious lips of hers, but held himself in check. "See you around."

Shalini waved to him as Riya dragged her off firmly. If she had turned around, she might have caught the look of deep yearning on his face and the reverent way in which his hand rested on the same spot hers had rested not so long ago. He shook his head in frustration. If only she would let her guard down! He was slowly but surely getting under her skin. He could see that, but waiting for her to admit that was driving him insane. He needed to change his strategy. A full, frontal assault? He grinned to himself. She'd probably shoot him down on the spot, but he decided to think about the idea further.

Riya rode with Shalini upto the second floor, got down and saw her friend safely off to her flat before getting back into the elevator to ride up to the sixth floor where she lived.

Her apartment was a cozily furnished place with two bedrooms, a living room, kitchen, separate dining area and a balcony overlooking a beautifully landscaped park. It had a warm, welcoming air about it, a safe haven where she could relax. She prepared a tall mug of coffee and took it out to the balcony. She sat down in her favorite beanbag chair and thought of the day's events as she slowly sipped her coffee and looked out at the children playing far below in the complex's common play area. She sighed as she thought of Anup for what seemed like the bazillionth time in the last few years. He was a very nice guy and she REALLY liked him, but she couldn't bring herself to let him in. Since moving back to Chennai, Shashi and Shalini were the only ones who always stood by her, no matter what. The others... She shook her head. They did not deserve to be thought about. Should she take a chance with Anup and see how it goes with him? She wondered. She wasn't sure and she didn't want anyone to get hurt because of her, especially not a nice guy like Anup. She sighed once more. Would she ever be ready to commit to someone again? She honestly did not know if she ever would be. She finished her coffee and decided to take a shower before she changed for dinner. She got up and closed and locked the balcony door before heading towards the bathroom.

It was quarter past seven by the time Riya got out of the bathroom, wearing a fluffy pink bathrobe. She picked out a sleeveless sea green kurti over matching Patiala pants and dupatta from her quite sizeable and fashionable wardrobe and got dressed in a matter of minutes, then brushed her long curly hair until it gleamed and decided to leave it open for the evening. She then slipped into a pair of high-heeled sandals and grabbed her purse which contained her wallet, a tube of lip gloss, a compact mirror, her smartphone and a can of pepper spray. Glancing at her watch, she slung the purse over her shoulder. It was just after 7.30. Time to go see if Shalini was ready. Having locked the main door, she took the elevator down to the second floor.

Shalini opened the door as soon as she heard the doorbell ring, dressed in a sleeveless pink top over form-fitting black jeans. The top had a sash in the middle which helped show off her curves to their best advantage. Black high-heeled sandals completed her ensemble. Riya looked her over and gave an approving nod. "Good," she grinned. "At least you look presentable. Should take care not to scare the waiters off, you know."

"Riiiight," drawled Shalini. "You haven't cleaned up too badly yourself. Come on in. We still have twenty minutes to kill before the boss picks us up."

They sat down in two comfortable single-seater couches. Shalini's apartment was a replica of Riya's. They differed only in the décor. Riya had gone for a mixture of traditional and modern designs while Shalini had chosen an all-out contemporary style. "So what do you think this grand plan of the boss is?"

"Knowing the boss, it's sure to be swashbuckling and bold. But I can't for the life of me second-guess him. So I'm not even going to try."

"Yeah you're right," her friend nodded in agreement. "But the thought of a billion dollars is quite intoxicating. What I wouldn't do with my share!" sighed Shalini dreamily.

"Counting our chickens before they're hatched, are we honey?" asked Riya in a sing-song tone she knew would grate on her friend's nerves.

"Oh, don't be such a spoilsport!" she retorted, throwing a cushion at Riya who managed to catch the missile before it hit her head.

"I'm just being cautious," she said defensively.

"Yeah well. Don't tell me you haven't fantasized even a tiny bit about the money, Miss Goody Two Shoes," teased Shalini, knowing that the remark would infuriate Riya.

"Don't call me that!" Riya hurled the cushion back at the smaller girl, who had anticipated the move and managed to avoid the weapon by sliding down the couch. By this time, both the girls were roaring with laughter. "Alright, I admit I have thought about the money. But making a billion dollars is not going to be a piece of cake and I'm just wondering how much time and effort we have to invest in this before we see the results."

"Awww, big deal. As it is, we don't exactly have roaring social lives now, do we? So what if we have to spend a few hours in the evening on this? The money will more than make up for it."

"You're right," sighed Riya. Just then, they heard Riya's mobile ring. It was Shashi Kiran telling them he was downstairs. The girls got up, straightened themselves up and walked out the door. Before locking the door, Shalini nudged her friend and pointed her finger at the GPS-equipped white cane placed in a corner. "Do you think I should carry it?"

Riya shook her head. "We're going together. You've already been to the washroom. I don't forsee any instance where you have to move about on your own tonight. It would just be a nuisance. So come on."

"Alright Miss Clairvoyant," grinned Shalini. "I just hope I don't get the chance to say 'I told you so' this evening."

"Fear not. I'm always right," Riya's tone was boastful. "Besides, I don't want you poking anyone's backside at the restaurant with that contraption!"

"I won't dignify that with a comment," said Shalini with her nose in the air as they reached the ground floor lobby. They walked out of the building and immediately saw Shashi Kiran's dark blue Honda Amaze in the driveway with its engine running. Riya caught her boss's eye and he waved them over. The two girls walked quickly towards the car and Shalini climbed into the passenger's seat while Riya got into the back. Shashi quickly got out of the driveway and joined the traffic on the main road. "Shalini needs new clothes," he announced out of the blue.

"I do?" Shalini looked nonplussed.

"Yes, you do," he reiterated firmly.

"Whoa sir, hold on. Why exactly does she require new clothes? I think she has too many clothes already," said Riya, perplexed by her boss's sudden, unexpected remark.

"No honey," said Shalini sweetly. "I'm a girl. Therefore, I can never have too many clothes. But I'm also puzzled. Why exactly do I need new clothes sir?"

"Well, she needs some hotshot executive clothes," explained Shashi. The two girls looked at him, dumbfounded.

"And what exactly are those?" queried Riya, sounding clueless.

"Yeah, please clue me in," added Shalini, looking as enlightened as a baboon.

"Some smart trousers and jackets, full-sleeved shirts with cuff-links and formal skirts. Along with that, some formal evening gowns for black-tie events," he elaborated further.

"Right. And where am I going to wear all these evening gowns to? And I thought I already had shirts, trousers and jackets?" Shalini was looking as if she was about to lose her mind. Her boss wasn't making any sense at all. And what did her wardrobe have to do with anything anyway?

"Yes you do. But they are semi-formal. I want you to acquire a set of completely formal Western office wear and evening wear," answered Shashi mysteriously.

"And why only Shalini? What about me?" asked Riya, sounding indignant at being left out of whatever was going on in Shashi's mind.

"You already have what I need you to wear," replied Shashi, managing to confound the girls even further.

Shalini turned and looked at her boss's profile. "Would you please explain what our wardrobes have to do with anything?"

"Sure," he replied. "Shalini shall be accompanying me to certain functions where black-tie may be required. And she'll also be coming along with me to visit foreign dignitaries and business tycoons."

"And what the hell would I be doing, twiddling my thumbs?" Riya shot out, not caring what tone she used with her boss. At the same time, she was staring daggers at her friend, even though this sudden turn of events was not really her fault. But she did not care for logic and reasoning at that moment.

"Relax Ms. Riya," said Shashi with a wide grin, quite amused by her vehement reaction.

"Relax, my foot!" Riya stormed. This made him grin even wider. What a tigress!

"My, my, someone's on fire," said Shashi laughing.

Shalini had not uttered a single word since she had been informed of what was expected of her. She was staring open-mouthed at her boss. Was he trying to divide and conquer? She wondered. But, she reasoned, he wasn't the type to do that. Besides, he knew they worked best as a team. So what was he playing at?

Riya shot him a death glare. His smile grew broader still as he caught her expression in the rearview mirror. Thankfully, the young fireball was on his side. "I need you to accompany me while we meet up with important politicians and business moguls. I'm dividing the responsibilities so that the two of you would not be exhausted all the time. Also, when two of us are hobnobbing and lobbying, the third would be free to continue working on our project. It's a good way to optimize time and output."

"But why does she get to meet all foreign dignitaries?" complained Riya, slightly mollified by his explanation, but still not completely satisfied.

"Because Madame La Princesse can speak English with a delightful American accent whenever she chooses to," he said, with a sideways glance at Shalini, who was giving him a self-satisfied smirk. "Not to mention," he continued, "she's fluent in French and German. But when it comes to Indian languages besides Kannada and Tamil, well...," he shook his head sadly, "the less said the better. She can easily screw things up." Shalini's smirk had turned into a fierce scowl. "Can't risk that now, can we? And besides, Riya, you would be the first to admit that Ms. Shalini here can charm anyone without much effort."

"That's true," admitted Riya, smiling for the first time since the discussion started. "Now I get where you're coming from. And I'll happily drag her shopping the first chance I get."

"Gee, thanks," said Shalini acidly. "Discussing me as if I'm not here, planning my wardrobe with no concern for my preferences and completely dissecting my ability to converse in Indian languages. If you have bothered to notice, my Hindi and Telugu have improved dramatically now."

"I agree with the 'dramatically' part," mumbled Riya. "Especially where Telugu is concerned."

"And Mr. Kiran here is yet to reveal what this grandiose plan of his is and where we brainy beauties come in," added Shalini.

"All in good time, young ladies, all in good time," he said with a flourish. "Now for some food."

He turned into the driveway of The Park Hotel and drove up to the entrance. As they got out of the car, a valet came to take the keys from Shashi Kiran in order to park the car. The trio walked into the lobby.

CHAPTER 5

The trio walked into the coffee shop at The Park, one of their favorite restaurants. Shashi had reserved a table for three in the morning just before the girls had walked into his cabin. He had been sure of their acquiescence, since he knew very well how their minds worked. Neither young woman could resist an intriguing challenge. They were escorted to a corner table which afforded them some much-needed privacy.

"What do you want to eat?" Riya asked Shalini.

"Batter-fried prawns for starters followed by chicken carbonara," replied Shalini without pausing for breath.

"You sure you didn't memorize the menu?" muttered Riya. "How about chicken drumsticks along with the prawns for starters?"

"Is anyone going to ask what I'm going to have?" demanded Shashi, feigning indignation. "After all, I'm paying for the meal, ain't I?"

"But sir," said Shalini innocently, "you're the one who invited us. You should decide for yourself and then ask what we want to have. Isn't that the protocol Ri-Ri?"

"Yep," agreed Riya with a straight face. "Here sir. We've written down all that we want to have. Here comes the waiter. Please do order whatever you wish sir, seeing as you're paying for the meal!"

"Why, thank you Riya. How considerate of you," Shashi said sarcastically and smiled as he waved the waiter over and placed their orders. Once it was done, he turned to them. "Now for some serious business talk."

"Finally!" sighed Shalini. "I'm really eager to find out about my role as eye candy."

"Young lady, you'll stop referring to yourself as eye candy," said Shashi in a stern voice that immediately silenced Shalini. He held them both in the highest regard possible and he saw nothing wrong in chastising them as whenever one of them (mostly Shalini) tried to demean herself in his presence. In his eyes, self-debasement was quite different from humility and he would never allow either one of them to indulge in the former. And since the girls respected and admired and had great affection for him, he was the only one in the entire company who could address them in that tone and get away with it.

"I'm sorry sir," said Shalini in a small voice, suitably chastened. "I didn't mean it like that. Please do go on."

"We're going to design and develop an application for mapping competencies," he said in a measured tone. Shalini was looking pale and he needed to put her at ease once again. *She would make a good subject for a case study*, he thought in wry amusement. She was up one minute and down the next. An incredibly strong and courageous girl, she had one obvious flaw: her tongue had a somewhat unfortunate tendency to run away before her brain could catch up with it and this sometimes landed her in some really awkward situations. Ordinarily, Shashi never minded her smart-mouth. On the contrary, he enjoyed her sardonic wit, but when she put herself down like she had just done, he never hesitated to issue swift reprimands. He valued Shalini greatly as a person and admired her for her perseverance and strong will. He did not want her thinking of herself in such derogatory terms. She was a self-made young woman who had overcome nearly insurmountable odds to get to where she was today and he would not sit back and let her tear herself down like that, not even as a joke.

Riya's quite smart, he thought. She too suffered from much of the same insecurities which plagued Shalini, but she was never caught unawares and lost control of her tongue and would never make the mistake of putting herself down in front of him. He was proud of the person she had become and had come to rely on her sound, honest and unbiased judgement more and more in recent times. She had a great sense of fairplay, but could be quite ruthless when the situation demanded it. He smiled ruefully as he thought of Sanjana Agarwal and how efficiently and coolly Riya had dealt with the young woman's high-handedness a few years ago. Cold-blooded and ruthless, yes, but that was the only way to deal with someone like Sanjana.

He looked at Shalini, whose face wore a somber expression. "Relax, Ms. Shalini," he smiled. "I need you to flaunt your brain, not your pretty face. Got it?"

Shalini managed a slight smile while Riya shook her head resignedly. The girl's mood swings were quite legendary and she was thankful not to be the one to deal with the fallout this time. "Quite the drama queen, isn't she? We can deal with her shenanigans later sir," she said. "Getting back on track, aren't there a zillion models for competency mapping already?"

"Yes," conceded Shashi, "but none of them combine competency mapping, mentoring, leadership and human capital management. This is the way forward girls, and could become the ONLY way to bring down employee turnover rates. We need to take a futuristic view of things here."

"Let's say you're right," said Shalini, having recovered her composure and sounding like her usual self. "But other companies must have thought of this too, right? Such models must exist in other enterprises also," she insisted.

"They do," he confirmed with a nod. "But none of them hold a candle to what I have in mind."

"And how exactly are we going to make a billion dollars out of it?" queried Riya. "If we present our idea to the company board, they would want to copyright it in the name of the company."

"As I already said, the company is not involved in any way," replied Shashi. "This is wholly our personal project. Once we have programmed and designed the model, we'll sell it to the highest bidder."

Shalini's eyes had grown round as saucers. "Will it work?" her voice was doubtful. "I mean—" Riya gave a sharp kick to her amkle to stop her from saying anything else. Fortunately, her friend took the hint and covered her tracks as best she could. "I mean, would companies be willing to pay a billion dollars for our competency model? Even if it's out of the top drawer, as ours is sure to be?"

Shashi watched them both with amusement writ large on his face. "It's okay Riya," he said chuckling. "You didn't have to resort to physical violence to stop her from saying what she wanted to say."

"Oh well, I tried," said Riya in resignation. "Alright sir, so we develop a competency model which incorporates the concepts of leadership, HCM, mentoring and succession planning. What's the platform we're going to use? Which database will we be using for back-end support? What about the client program? And who shall be the end-users?"

"I'm counting on your brains for that Riya," he replied. "It's more your area of expertise than mine. As for the end-users, we're targeting HR visionaries."

"And what about me?" Shalini piped up. "Am I just supposed to sit around twiddling my thumbs without any purpose while she designs and develops it, then dress up in pretty clothes and turn on my irresistible charm in the evening?"

"That, among other things," said Shashi grinning wickedly.

"Like what?" demanded Shalini suspiciously.

"You, miss, will be responsible for conceptualizing the system while Riya designs it. Put that psychology degree of yours to good use. Get the books out, go online, whatever. See what concept best applies to our model and work on the design. Check out the available models and see how we can differentiate and distinguish our model from the rest. In short, find the *It* factor, the Unique Selling Proposition."

"You don't want much, do you?" she asked, her face smooth and completely devoid of any expression, but her eyes were glinting with growing excitement.

"Oh come on. Stop being such a drama queen. I can hear the wheels already turning in your head."

"Why us?" asked Riya abruptly.

Shashi looked at her thoughtfully, choosing his words with care. "Because you two are the best persons for the job. And I can trust you girls implicitly. And most important, I have boundless faith in your abilities. Besides," he grinned, "you two are the only ones I can actually contemplate splitting a billion dollars with!"

"Wonderful," cried Shalini. "So what sort of deadline are we looking at?"

"Three months," he said nonchalantly, with a deadpan expression, as if stating the obvious. "Six at the most."

"Right," drawled Shalini. "Will Santa Claus be paying us a visit then?"

Shashi laughed. "Now, why would I want him when I have my two equally magical elves to do my bidding?"

"If you don't watch out, you're gonna kill these elves of yours one day soon," Shalini's eyes crinkled with merriment as she uttered these dire predictions.

"Our friend really has a macabre sense of humor, doesn't she?" smiled Shashi. "For some reason, she seems bent on winning the Doomsayer of the Year award."

"She'll win with no contest," said Riya with a smile. "Jokes aside sir, Sanjana could prove to be a problem, a real thorn on our sides."

"Why?" queried Shashi. "I threw her out of HR because of her disruptive attitude. Why do you think she'd pose a problem to our plans? Far as I know, she doesn't even have the foggiest idea about this."

Briefly, she told him about the altercation outside his cabin that morning, leaving nothing out. Shashi's face grew redder and redder as the narrative came to a conclusion. His jaw was set in a firm line. "She wants to snoop around now, does she? Good. We'll throw her off the track. And how dare she insult the both of you like that? The whole organization knows about her dalliance with the former finance VP and now she has the guts, no, stupidity, to insinuate inappropriate conduct on your part! This will be dealt with appropriately!" he fumed. Not for one instant did he consider keeping the two girls at a distance to ensure that such malicious gossip did not hurt them. The thought never crossed the girls' minds either. All three were used to meeting troubles head-on, not running away from them.

"Don't trouble yourself with her sir," said Riya calmly. "She doesn't deserve the attention. We'll deal with her as we see fit. In any case, most of the time, her bark proves to be worse than her bite. If we simply ignore her, she'll lose interest I think."

"Just be on your guard always," he warned. "She's capable of stooping down really low when it suits her."

"So 'an eye for an eye,'" grinned Shalini.

"Shalini," he said in a warning tone.

Shalini sobered up immediately. "We'll stay out of her way as much as we can sir. But she has a knack of crossing our paths too often. We won't look for a fight, but if one comes along, we won't take things lying down."

"And I don't expect you to," Shashi's tone was even. "All I'm saying is, be careful whatever you do. She's a sneaky girl and I don't want her sniffing around either of you."

"Don't worry sir. When she gets a taste of the acid that can drip from Shalini's tongue, she'll walk away with her tail between her legs. Besides, she'll keep bugging us only so long as we pay her any heed. If we refuse to take her seriously and laugh off her comments, we shall be fine," said Riya in a reasonable tone.

"Fine then. All of us are clear about our roles in this project. Precision and caution are of utmost importance girls. Always remember that. Enthusiasm is good, but overenthusiasm might kill it before the project has a chance to take shape." The last proclamation was given with a sideways glance at Shalini, who did not seem to feel the weight of his stare.

The trio polished off their sumptuous dinner with relish. After paying the bill, he drove them back home and gave a thumbs up while saying goodbye. The girls grinned back at him and waved cheerily before turning around to go back into the building.

As they headed towards the elevator, the lights suddenly went out. They considered taking the stairs, but neither of them was too keen about the idea and decided to wait for the generators to start up and restore power instead. As they leaned against the wall, Shalini felt something—no, someone—groping her neck and let rip a bloodcurdling shriek, making Riya nearly jump out of her skin.

CHAPTER 6

"Wha–?" Riya started, as she struggled to get her bearings and wondered what had caused her normally self-contained, no-nonsense friend to scream bloody murder. The girl did have a penchant for high drama and Riya wondered suspiciously if this was her idea of a practical joke, or whether something really had startled her. She wouldn't put anything past her darling friend and the darkened hallway was the perfect setting if she was indeed playing a practical joke. If so, she was prepared to strangle her scrawny neck. However, the next second confirmed that it definitely was no prank on Shalini's part.

"Please calm down," said a familiar, cultured voice out of the darkness, which almost made Shalini scream once again.

"D-Derek Mathews?" stammered Shalini, in a shaky, uncertain voice which still held a bit of fear in it. The dark had never been her friend and it wasn't now. It always made her feel fidgety and unsure of herself and she never enjoyed being in a situation where she felt as if she was standing on shaky ground. To her, it was a sign of weakness and she hated feeling weak or vulnerable under any circumstance. She replaced the can of pepper spray which she had grabbed automatically as she screamed.

"Shalini?" he sounded surprised.

"Y-Yes," she tried to calm herself down.

"Yes, it's Derek. I'm sorry for startling you," his voice sounded sheepish now.

"As well you should be!" bristled Shalini, her heart still pounding from the sudden shock. "What are you doing, skulking around in the dark? I'm one hundred percent certain now that you're stalking me—us!" Yelling at him helped to settle her nerves a bit. The adrenaline was making her jumpy and extremely nervous.

For some reason, Derek found Shalini's angry outburst very amusing. He threw back his head and laughed. "That's a good one," he managed to choke out between guffaws. "But as I already made it quite clear, where you're concerned beautiful, I wouldn't rule it out! Anyway, I was waiting for the elevator, just like you. I live here too, as I frequently keep reminding you and the prospect of climbing ten floors in the pitch dark did not entice me at all. I don't particularly relish the idea of some jerk using this opportunity to jump me because I took leave of my senses and decided to take the stairs in the dark."

"Right," said Shalini, sounding contrite. She decided to ignore the part of his speech where he had called her beautiful and simply said, "I'm sorry for overreacting, but your uh, groping sort of startled me. If you hadn't spoken when you did, I might have temporarily blinded you."

He knew full well that she never went anywhere without her trusty can of pepper spray. He did not relish the idea of being on the receiving end of that. The thought made him grimace. "Good for me that I revealed myself," he said with a wry smile. "For the record, I wasn't groping. Sorry if it appeared that way. By the way, are you on your own or is Riya with you?" A note of concern had crept into his deep voice by then.

"Yes, I, the omnipresent one, am here," said Riya. "Didn't you hear my startled exclamation after her superb impersonation of a horror movie heroine?"

"Her scream must have drowned out your words," he said, laughing. "It indeed was superb. Realistic and bone-chilling. Can you do it again Shalini?" he was teasing now. "In fact, she could give any actress in a horror movie a run for her money!"

"Yeah, come on short stuff," Riya wheedled. "Good way to pass the time till they start the generators and besides, it would be fun to startle the other residents as well! Come on, let's play ghost!" Derek was laughing helplessly now and he was sure Shalini would have them for breakfast once the supply of electricity was restored. But he was enjoying himself too much to care about her wrath.

For the first time, Shalini was grateful for the darkness and did not respond to their relentless teasing. She knew it was Riya's way of lightening her mood, but this time, it wasn't helping at all. *Derek must think I'm such a baby*, she thought miserably. Her face was red with embarrassment and just as she was wishing that the floor would open up and swallow her, mercifully, the lights came on and the trio got into the elevator, Derek being chivalrous and letting the two girls get in ahead of him. During the ride upto Shalini's floor, she caught him blatantly staring at her.

"Is something wrong with me?" she blurted out.

"Nothing. Why?" he queried innocently, knowing perfectly well what she was referring to and completely unashamed of it.

"Then stop staring at me! You're creeping me out," she retorted grumpily, still smarting from the embarrassment of the screaming incident just a few minutes earlier. He did not respond, but just gave her an insolent look and smiled unapologetically instead. He could see that Shalini was wound as tightly as a guitar string and it wouldn't take much to make her snap, but he could also see that a part of her was enjoying the exchange and that was why she hadn't knocked him flat on his back yet.

Riya tried valiantly to hide her smile, but was not succeeding very well. Her dear friend, who was always so perceptive, had to be really dense if she couldn't see that the guy was quite into her. But then, this was Shalini they were talking about and when she chose to be ignorant of something on purpose, nobody could make her see otherwise. For such a smart girl, sometimes her self-esteem hit rock-bottom for whatever reason. She simply refused to believe that Derek, or any other man for that matter, would be genuinely attracted to her. But slowly and surely, unbeknownst to Shalini, Derek was causing chinks to appear in the barrier she had so carefully erected around herself over the years.

"Are you free for lunch tomorrow?" he asked Shalini just as the girls exited the elevator. She shook her head.

"Dinner perhaps?" he persisted.

Her only response was a noncommittal shrug and a wave as they walked off.

As Shalini went into her flat, Riya caught the front door before it slammed shut and grabbed her arm. "Why couldn't you be nice to him just now and give a proper answer to his questions?"

"I did," snapped Shalini irritably. "He asked if I was free for lunch and I said 'no.' I think that's a proper answer. Grammatically correct and all."

"Sure," snapped back Riya. "What about dinner? You don't have any plans to go out with anyone, not even me. Why don't you go out with him for ice cream or something? It might be fun," she cajoled.

"We have plenty of work to do," said Shalini, looking prim and proper. Her Miss Priss look, as Riya liked to call it. "No time for frivolities like that when there's important business at hand. A billion dollars is not a joke."

"You ain't fooling no one, sweetie pie," Riya sang out sarcastically, "If you believe that we're going to work throughout the day AND the evening into the night, I've got some news for you. Quit fooling yourself and those around you, 'my darlin' Prissy Pops! Time to wake up and smell the roses. Or rather, time to let Derek 'The Hunk' Mathews wine and dine you." She was deliberately being provocative, trying to get Shalini to do something about Derek.

Shalini shrugged as if the discussion held no interest for her. "There's no use talking about this now," she said with finality. "Good night."

"Whatever," snorted Riya, exasperated. "Good night." But the door had already slammed shut. Riya headed back towards the elevator, shaking her head. But she was smiling. Derek Mathews was slowly getting under Shalini's skin and Riya was sure that her friend would break soon and start dating him. Riya was sure he was the genuine article and that was why she had elected to champion his cause in this battle of wills. He was very persistent and obviously used to getting what he wanted. And now he wanted Shalini and it seemed quite clear that he was not taking no for an answer.

Way to go, Derek! She cheered silently. She fervently hoped her friend would get her head out of her backside soon, but she wasn't counting on it. Maybe it was time to take matters into her own hands. Her eyes glinted wickedly. Maybe she should play Cupid… She yawned and decided to think about it more in the morning. She changed her clothes, got into bed and closed her eyes with pleasant visions of her shooting arrows made out of flowers and chocolate straight at Shalini's heart.

CHAPTER 7

Riya woke up suddenly, heart racing and drenched in sweat. She took a few deep breaths and glanced over at the illuminated alarm clock on the bedside table. It was 03:16 A.M. She sat up in bed and tried to drink some water from the glass beside the alarm clock, but her hands were trembling too much. She clasped her hands together in an effort to stop the trembling and it helped to some extent. When her heart rate steadied, she slowly got to her feet and went to the window which of course, was locked. Quietly, she opened the balcony door and went out to lean against the railing, taking in deep, cleansing gulps of the cool night air. Gone was the jaunty, happy-go-lucky young woman who had fallen asleep with a smile on her lovely face. Her place had been taken by a trembling, nervous wreck who looked pale, wild-eyed and disheveled.

Will I ever truly be free of them? Will they ever let me move on with life? She wondered. A tear fell unbidden from her left eye and she wiped it away savagely. She had done enough crying for worthless fools and didn't want to shed any more tears on their account. These nightmares constantly plagued her and no amount of therapy was able to make them go away. This particular nightmare had been especially vivid and replayed scenes she never wanted to remember anymore, but her subconscious just wouldn't let her forget. The night air felt cool and soothing against her sweat-soaked skin and she finally felt calm enough to return inside. She got back into bed, but couldn't go back to sleep. After tossing and turning for quite a while, she looked at the time. It was 4:05 in the morning. She knew it was too early to call, but she didn't care, She dialed a number on her mobile which she could recite even in her sleep, and a sleepy voice answered on the third ring "'Lo?"

"Did I wake you?" she queried solicitiously, knowing how irrational the question must sound.

"No, you didn't. I have been up for hours pomdering the mysteries of the universe," said Shalini sarcastically. "Of course you woke me up, so why such a redundant question? What's up?"

"Couldn't sleep," Riya said simply.

"Come down to my place," Shalini responded and disconnected the call without waiting for her friend's response. Riya shook her head and rolled her eyes. Shalini was definitely not a morning person, especially considering the fact that it was the weekend. She quickly threw on a pair of sweatpants and a t-shirt over her camisole, left the apartment and took the elevator down to the second floor. Shalini opened the door before she could knock and beckoned her in. Her short, wavy hair was disheveled and she was trying to stifle a yawn. "A bad one, huh?" she queried, her eyes filled with understanding and sympathy.

"Yeah," replied Riya, slumping into the couch. "One of the worst ones yet."

"Do you want to talk about it? Shall I make some coffee? Or do you want to go to bed and try to sleep?"

Riya looked at her friend. There was no irritation or condescension in her expression or tone. She knew the other girl would do whatever she wanted, just to make sure Riya felt better. She decided to be unselfish for once and let Shalini rest. It wasn't as if all of Shalini's nights were filled with peace either. And maybe, just maybe, if she laid down beside her, she could get some sleep as well. She wanted to try it. "Let's hit the sack," she replied.

"Are you sure?" Shalini's concern was obvious. "I can make some coffee if you want to talk."

"We can talk at a more decent hour," she said firmly. "I want to see if I'm able to go to sleep if I share your bed."

"Be my guest," Shalini shrugged, leading the way into her bedroom. Riya followed her inside and both girls got under the covers. Shalini was asleep in a few minutes, but sleep eluded Riya for quite a while. As she lay in bed, she was comforted by Shalini's presence and the gentle, even rhythm of her breathing and finally drifted off to sleep just as dawn was breaking.

They eventually woke up at 9'o'clock in the morning. Shalini sat up and stretched like a graceful panther. She shook Riya awake. She too sat up and stretched with equal grace. "So what do you want to do today? Shall we start to work on our project right away or do you want to chill for a while?"

"I'd rather work just now and chill in the evening than the other way around," Riya said with a yawn.

"Then come on. Let's shower and eat something. Otherwise, I'm not going to be of much use."

"Yes, Ms. Glut," Riya grinned for the first time since she had come into her friend's home earlier that morning.

"Right," Shalini sighed. "So I'll make dosas for myself and you can help yourself to cold water since you don't believe in gluttony."

"Oh shut up," growled Riya. "I'm going to shower."

"And what exactly are you planning to wear?" Shalini called after her friend, who was heading to the bathroom in the guest room.

"That over-long red t-shirt of yours and my sweats," Riya hollered back.

"Fine, I'll see you in a bit," Shalini hollered back, heading towards her own bathroom. She showered and changed into a pair of Bermuda shorts and a comfortable sky-blue t-shirt and headed into the kitchen. She idly wondered what was taking Riya so long, then she concentrated on preparing breakfast. By the time Riya walked into the kitchen, the aroma of fresh, crisp dosas made her mouth water. Shalini was taking out steaming hot idlis from the microwave. All the ingredients needed for coconut chutney were chopped and neatly laid out on the chopping board. Riya put them in a mixer, added some water and switched it on for a couple of minutes. Once the chutney was nicely ground, she poured oil into a saucepan and fried mustard seeds and asafetida together before adding them to the chutney and mixing well.

A hot, delicious breakfast was ready and the girls sat down to enjoy the fruits of their labor. As they ate, Riya noticed that Shalini was in quite a contemplative mood. "What gives, Shalu?" she asked, startling her friend.

Shalini shook herself out of the reverie. "Nothing."

"Right, now tell me all about this 'nothing' that's distracting you from such a hot, delicious breakfast," Riya was insistent.

"It's Derek Mathews," Shalini sighed.

"What about him?" Riya asked calmly, wondering if perhaps her friend was finally seeing sense. "Is he bothering you? Did you have any further interaction with him after last night?"

"No," she replied.

"Then what?" She had an idea of what was coming, but she wanted to hear it from the horse's mouth itself.

"I do like him," admitted Shalini. "I mean, really like him. But...," Shalini's voice trailed off.

"Just afraid to come right out and tell him," Riya completed the other girl's sentence. "Yeah I know the drill. And yes, he likes you too. He made an obvious attempt to ask you out last night. A very persistent attempt, I might add."

"I mean, what if he rejects me outright? I'll look like a fool then," Shalini stated, acting as if Riya hadn't spoken at all. Her voice was barely audible.

Riya looked at her in disbelief. "Didn't you hear what I just said? He has been persistent in expressing his wish to get closer to you. Why in heaven's name would he reject you if you reciprocate the interest he's showing in you?"

"Well, what if it's all an act?" she demanded stubbornly.

"An act?" Riya was mystified. "And what purpose would that serve exactly?."

"Maybe he just wants me to be another one of his many conquests," shot back Shalini.

"And how do you, Ms. Prophetess, know he has had many conquests?" Riya was getting exasperated now.

"He's smart, young, handsome and rich. He's sure to have had several dozen conquests," replied Shalini, obstinately standing her ground.

"Right," said Riya, rolling her eyes. "Let's do the math, shall we? He's been living here for the last two years. How many ladies have we seen him with?" When Shalini did not meet her eyes, Riya smiled inwardly. "Answer me, dammit!"

"Well," Shalini started, "there was that young model—"

"Yes, and how long ago was that?" Riya pushed on, tightening the screws further.

"More than one and a half years," Shalini's voice was low.

"Well, I don't know how your crooked brain works, but in my opinion, if he just wants you to be another notch on his bed-post, I don't think he'd have patiently followed you around for close to two years now. It's just not worth his time and effort, you know."

"Well, maybe he thinks I'm a challenge and he's hatching some plan," Shalini was refusing to climb down from her high horse.

"Believe it or not, Shalini, you're not as important or impressive as you think," she exhaled in frustration. "And no playboy would be so polite and patient. He asked you out decently yesterday instead of simply grabbing you and—"

"Yeah, but—"

"And I might add that you put him off rather rudely," she went on.

"Yeah, but—" Shalini tried again.

"No ifs, no buts, no coconuts," Riya cut her off. "You like Derek Mathews. And I know for a fact that he's quite taken in with you. Once we finish our research today, I'll give him a call and ask him to meet us at Dhaba Express."

"Riya Batra!" Shalini gasped. "You'll do no such thing! For starters, you don't even have his contact number!"

"I can and I will. And I DO have his mobile number. He gave it to me a long time ago, hoping perhaps that I'd give it to you and you'd call him, but you've been too busy walloring in self-doubt and concocting your weird theories to pay any proper heed to his pursuit of you," said Riya calmly. "You've been a hermit long enough. It's time for you to be happy with a decent guy."

"What about you then?" The words slipped out before Shalini could stop them. She saw Riya's face fall and she mentally kicked herself for her thoughtlessness. "I'm sorry, Ri," she said in a contrite tone.

"It's alright," Riya smiled sadly. "I too have a confession to make. You see, I also like someone."

"Anup Sharma, I suppose," Shalini nodded, as if this wasn't really news to her.

"How did you know?" Riya could not mask the incredulity in her voice.

"Oh, come now! You cannot seriously ask me that!" she shook her head in exasperation. "I've known you for over three years and I don't need an advanced degree in psychology to know. It's written all over you every time you look at him. I've known this confession was coming for a long time now."

"It's that obvious then," she sighed.

"Yes, and that boy is more than willing to admit to anyone and everyone how he feels about you. So why don't you start dating him and see how it goes?" suggested Shalini. "He worships the ground you walk on, you know. And you have told me enough times yourself that you caught him staring surreptitiously at you."

"I know. It's just…" Riya's expression had darkened.

"You're not ready to let anyone in again and run the risk of getting your heart trampled upon," Shalini knew she had hit the nail on the head.

"Yes," admitted Riya. "He's a nice person and I know he'll not hurt me, but…"

"Ri," Shalini's tone was gentle. "Let go. Clinging on to old ghosts is preventing you from being happy in the present. Grab the moment girl."

"I know."

"Then what's blocking your way?"

Riya abruptly stood up and started clearing the table. "We've got work to do. Come on."

Shalini was frustrated, but she knew nothing could be gained by continuing the discussion. She cleared away her part of the table and carried the utensils to the sink, where she found Riya vigorously washing the plates and bowls she had cleared. "Easy there, honey," said Shalini. "You might break them if you're not careful."

Riya's shoulders relaxed slightly and she turned around and smiled at the smaller girl. "Sorry," she apologized. "Let's get to work."

"Sure Ri," replied Shalini agreeably.

The girls went into Shalini's bedroom and Riya looked around, searching for Shalini's tablet. "Where's the tab?" she asked when she couldn't find it.

"Oops!" Shalini slapped her forehead with the palm of her hand. "I must have left it in the car. I'll go and get it."

"Don't bother," said Riya. "I'll go upstairs and fetch mine."

"It's no problem," insisted Shalini, slipping into a pair of sandals. "It's bright and sunny and I can handle going down to the garage and back." She left, slamming the door behind her and took the stairs since it was only two floors.

She opened the car and got the tablet from the backseat where she had left it the previous evening. As she got back into the building, she almost ran smack into someone, who sidestepped nimbly at the last moment.

"Slow down beautiful, or you might knock someone out!" said a deep, husky voice.

Shalini couldn't believe it. Derek Mathews. Again.

"Do you have some sort of tracking device planted on me?" she blurted out before she could stop herself. "Something that alerts you every time I'm down here?"

"No," he shot back. "But it's not a bad idea at all, come to think of it."

Shalini wagged a finger at him. "Over my dead body!"

"And good morning to you too, pretty girl," he said sardonically. "Good manners seem to have deserted you this beautiful, sunny day."

"Whatever," she shrugged. Her heart was doing somersaults. His proximity was driving her senses wild and she didn't know what to do about it. In a pair of blue denim cutoffs and a polo shirt, he looked delicious, but she took a few paces to the other side, trying to put some distance between them.

Noticing her sideways movement, he sighed. "Shalini, I'm not a predator trying to attack you."

"One never knows," said Shalini noncommittally.

"Well, I'm not and you damn well know it!" he snapped, losing his cool for an instant.

"Yes," she let out a breath. "I've got some work to do. If you'll excuse me..."

"Are you free for dinner tonight?" he asked, stepping in front of her and blocking her path.

"No, I'm busy every night," she said smartly. "Now please let me pass."

"Fine," he moved, then caught her hand. "Why are you being so difficult?"

"I'm sure I don't know what you're talking about," she pretended to look ignorant.

"Yes you do," he said, a slight smile tugging at the corners of his mouth. "And soon, you'll admit how you feel about me."

"Well, don't hold your breath," she muttered. She wanted to pull her hand away from his firm grasp and she wanted him to hold on and never let go. She did not understand these conflicting emotions. They stared at each other, holding each other's gaze as if a magnetic pull was drawing them closer, neither wanting to break the spell. Derek could see in her eyes what she was refusing to acknowledge with words. She liked him, but something was making her hold back.

Finally, very reluctantly, he let go of her hand. "See you around," he said softly.

"Bye Derek," her voice was quiet.

She turned around and practically ran up the stairs to her flat. When she burst through the door, Riya took one look at her flushed face and demanded, "What's up, honey? You look like you've just been running a marathon!"

"It's him!" Shalini hissed. "I saw him!"

"Who?" Riya looked at her, waiting for an explanation.

"I ran into Derek in the hallway," she gasped out in one breath, still panting.

"Again?" Riya bit back a smile. "That guy seems to have an uncanny knack of knowing when he's likely to run into you."

"It's not a joke!" she burst out, then quickly told her friend about the incident. "And why is he living here anyway?"

Riya stared at her blankly. "Huh? What's that supposed to mean?"

"Why is he living here anyway?" Shalini repeated.

Riya stared at her. "Please tell me you didn't just ask me that! Have you lost your marbles? It's a free country and he can choose to live wherever he wants."

"I mean," Shalini hastened to explain. "Why is a rich guy like him living in an apartment and not in a proper bungalow or villa or something?"

"That rich dude," said Riya with a smile, "is also single. What's the use of having a fabulous mansion if you can't share it with someone? Besides, it's not as if he's living in a broom cupboard. His apartment is one of the largest and most luxurious in this complex and occupies the entire floor for God's sake."

"Whatever," Shalini was still flustered.

"Did you tell him you'd like to meet him for dinner tonight?" Riya looked at the shorter girl with her arms crossed.

"No," Shalini looked sheepish. "In fact, I told him I shall be busy every night."

"You really can be incredibly idiotic sometimes," sighed Riya, shaking her head. "Imagine how silly it's going to look when I call him and invite him to Dhaba Express when you've already told him in your incredibly dumb-ass way, that you're busy every night!"

"Crap!" sighed Shalini. "I didn't think of that! Maybe you shouldn't call after all," she said, hoping that her friend would take the hint and drop the idea altogether. "I don't want to look stupid." She opened her eyes as wide as they would go and tried to look beseechingly at her friend.

The look of guileless innocence, which usually worked wonderfully on most people, did nothing to fool or sway Riya, one of the few people who was totally immune to Shalini's charms. "No can do," Riya said firmly. "It's happening and it's happening tonight. No way for you to wiggle out of it now. If you end up looking like a fool, so be it. It's not my problem. You've brought it on yourself. Now deal with it as you see fit. Maybe this will teach you to watch what comes out of your mouth!"

"What a wonderful friend you are!" she said sarcastically. "I wonder how I got so lucky."

"Enough chit-chat," she said briskly. "Did you manage to bring back the tab in one piece or did you drop it somewhere during your rendezvous with Mr. Hot and Handsome?" She flashed a million-mega-watt smile on Shalini, which earned her an evil look from the other girl.

"Here," she threw the tablet at Riya, who fortunately managed to catch it before it fell to the ground.

CHAPTER 8

Riya switched on Shalini's tablet while her friend powered up her sleek, new laptop. Quickly, they went online and were soon engrossed in reading. Shalini searched for latest advances and updates to the concepts of mentoring, competency mapping, leadership and industrial psychology while Riya concentrated on evaluating the merits of different operating systems, database management systems and scripting languages and shortlisting the most feasible options. She also researched the possibility of cloud computing. The hours flew by and the girls had compiled quite impressive and detailed documents on concept and design by lunch-time.

Shalini's stomach growled, which made her glance at the digital clock on her laptop screen. It was one-fifteen in the afternoon. No wonder, she thought. "Shall we order something or do you want to make something at home?" she asked without looking up.

"I'll make parathas," replied Riya. "We ate out last night and would do so again this evening as well."

"I want your double-decker parathas," Shalini said.

"Ah! I of course, exist to oblige other people!" sighed Riya. "Fine. What about the stuffing? Anything in particular Mademoiselle would like?" she spoke in an atrocious French accent, which sent Shalini into a giggling fit.

"Anything will do, as long as it's delicious," Shalini drawled, after she had managed to sober up.

"Not demanding much, are we?" Sarcasm oozed from Riya's words.

"Stop talking and cook me some food, girly," Shalini's tome matched Riya's, who shook her head and walked into the kitchen muttering about creating a monster. But since Shalini had prepared breakfast, she didn't mind too much. The fridge was well-stocked and she quickly decided to make carrot parathas and mint chutney. Setting out all the ingredients on the kitchen counter-top, she quickly got to work. Within forty minutes, lunch was ready.

The appetizing aroma was too tempting for Shalini, who quickly saved her work and walked into the kitchen. "Something smells awesome," she declared.

"I hope the food pleases Mademoiselle as much as the smell does," grinned Riya.

"Can't answer that without tasting, can I, ma chere?," Shalini grinned back.

Riya unceremoniously plunked down a plate loaded with parathas in front of her. "Here. Bon appétit. Stuff yourself till you choke," she said sweetly.

"Thank you dear. Don't mind if I do," retorted Shalini, helping herself to the food. She placed one piece of paratha In her mouth and chewed thoughtfully. "Yummm!" she sighed contentedly.

"Glad it meets with Mademoiselle La Glut's approval," commented Riya dryly. "Now finish up fast. We have piles and piles of material to get through before our rendezvous with Derek in the evening."

"That's what you think," muttered Shalini to herself. "Prepared to be surprised my friend."

"What was that?" asked Riya sharply.

"Oh just telling myself how delicious these parathas are," replied Shalini innocently.

Riya gave her a suspicious look, but chose not to pursue the issue any further. She knew from past experience that it wouldn't be of any use. Instead, she changed the subject. "So heard from Anita and Shailaja recently?" she queried, referring to two of Shalini's oldest and closest friends.

Shalini chewed thoughtfully. "Talked to Anita yesterday," she said. "She and Manoj are planning to drop in the weekend after next with the baby in tow. She has started working part-time a few weeks ago, just taking on a few cases for the time being. She is thinking of sending the kid to day-care in a few months when she's ready to work full-time once again."

"I hope she finds a decent day-care near her place," said Riya.

"I hope so too. Good day care centers are too few and far between in India."

"Maybe we should start a chain of day-care facilities across the country," suggested Riya.

"Sure," agreed Shalini with a self-assured smirk. "When we get our share of a billion dollars, we can do all that and more."

"So nice to dream!" sighed Riya. "What about Shailaja?"

"Shailaja?" Shalini smiled. "Now that's interesting. She's knocked up."

"Huh?" Riya stared at her open-mouthed. "Since when?"

"She told me a couple of days ago. They had found out just then. Apparently, it was an accident. The girl was hysterical!" Shalini laughed, recalling the conversation.

"I have no doubts about that," said Riya, still looking stunned. "With twins, a boy and a girl no less, she may not have wanted a third child. It must have come as a complete shock."

"Tell me about it," agreed Shalini. "Anyway, since then, she and her husband have discussed it and have decided to go through with the pregnancy. And she's deathly afraid that it might turn out to be twins once again!"

"Now *there's* a thought! It would be so funny if that happens!"

"Sure. For us. And she'd probably dream up painful and exotic ways to kill us if we tell her that and if it comes true!" Tears of laughter were streaming down Shalini's cheeks.

"You're probably right!" Riya chuckled, visualizing the scene. "Can we hope to see her anytime soon?"

"Nope. Not for the next few months, probably not until after the baby is born. What about Preetam, Tanya and Shubhangi?" Shalini asked as both girls finished their meal and Riya cleared the table while Shalini washed the dishes. Their break over, they headed back to continue their research for their quest of making a billion dollars.

"Tanya's having marital issues," sighed Riya as she flopped down on the bed and grabbed the tablet.

"Who doesn't?" said Shalini rhetorically.

"True. It's all just the age-old, time-tested *saas-bahu* drama with little or no change in the plot. Shubhangi's still enjoying newly married bliss, just having a good time and taking things easy, and Preetam is just being Preetam, you know, a typical guy as usual," said Riya with a sigh, as if that statement explained it all.

"You mean difficult," said Shalini with a smile.

"Huh! Difficult indeed! Understatement of the century, but yeah," she smiled back. "He may be visiting us in a couple of months with his wife and little girl."

"Oh joy!" exclaimed Shalini. "Just what we need! Another hormonal dude sitting on our heads! Sometimes, it's easy to forget he's almost six years older than us! And how's his wife by the way?"

"Sweet, long-suffering Shikha is doing quite well. And she says fatherhood has brought about welcome changes in Preetam."

"Good. How's the little one?"

"She's fine, as far as I know. Cute as a button and rather the apple of daddy dearest's eyes! Anyway, come on. We need to concentrate on getting super-rich," grinned Riya. Shalini grinned back and nodded in agreement. Soon, the girls were engrossed in reading and making notes. The afternoon flew by and the sun was starting to go down. Riya poked Shalini in the ribs.

"Huh?" she looked quizzically at her friend. "What was that for?"

"That," announced Riya with a flourish, "is to commemorate the fact that you're about to become the second person to know how we're going to make a billion dollars." She looked pleased with herself, as if she had won the jackpot.

"How? By poking and prodding me?" she asked in a bored voice, used to her friend's theatrics. "For a minute there, I thought you were trying to molest my pretty self." A cheeky grin was plastered across her face.

"You wish," Riya snorted with derision, as if such a suggestion was sacrilegious. "Patience and all will be revealed my friend. Watch and learn."

CHAPTER 9 ·

Riya's tone was mischievous, but eyes were dancing with excitement, which sparked some interest and curiosity in Shalini despite herself, though she was still a little skeptical of her friend's tall claims.

"How?" she asked, only half-listening. But as Riya started to talk, waving her hands excitedly to emphasize her views and pointing to the tablet screen when she wanted to show Shalini something, the look on Shalini's face changed from indulgent interest to astonishment to incredulous amazement. She talked non-stop for fifteen minutes and when she finally stopped to catch her breath, Shalini was staring at her open-mouthed. The plan was bold, imaginative and highly risky, but if they could pull it off…

"That's genius Ri!" she said at last. "Now all we need is the perfect blend of concepts and we can present the plan to the boss."

"Yes, I think we can present the preliminary plans to him latest by Wednesday," Riya agreed, still flushed from her stroke of genius.

"I have narrowed down the leadership, succession planning and mentoring models we can use. All we need now is a proper competency model which can blend in with our plans. Throw in a bit of psycho-metrics and we'll be all set."

"You'll do it soon enough," said Riya confidently, knowing her friend was like a bloodhound with its nose to the ground when it came to sniffing something out.

"Thanks. Now shall we get ready? We have to be at Dhaba Express soon, right? Have you called Derek?"

"I texted him. He's out somewhere and will meet us there," said Riya. "I'll go home and get ready. Meet you back here in forty-five minutes."

"Fine," Shalini agreed with a deep sigh, shooing off her friend who apparently thought she was an aspiring match-maker. *Well,* she thought, *two can play that game, Ms. Batra. Just wait and see.* As soon as the other girl was out of the apartment and the door was locked and bolted, Shalini whipped out her voice-enabled smartphone and called Anup.

He picked up on the second ring and sounded surprised to hear from her. "Shalini? What's up?"

"Do you have plans for the evening?" asked Shalini without bothering with niceties.

"Not really," he replied, sounding puzzled. "I thought of catching a movie with friends later in the evening."

"Chuck the movie. How about meeting me and Riya at Dhaba Express around 7.30?"

"Really?" Anup was sounding excited now. "I'd love to!"

"Just as I thought," she grinned. "Now listen, I know you like her and have been walking on eggshells around her and I've had enough of that. I think it's high time you asked her out on a proper date."

"Sure, and what if she smacks me in public?"

"So what if she does? Are you going to keep your feelings bottled up for eternity and admire her from a distance all your life?" Shalini shot back at him. "Or perhaps wait till another guy comes and snaps her up?" her tone was dripping acid. She knew this arrow wouldn't miss its mark.

"What? No! Over my dead body!" Anup was screaming into the phone now and Shalini started to giggle.

"Easy there, big boy," she smirked. "I'm giving you an opportunity to prevent that catastrophe. It's up to you to grab it with both hands. And staring at her in office alone is not enough."

"I know. I shall meet you at Dhaba Express at 7.30. Whoa, hold on a second! Who told you I was staring at Riya? It's a lie!" he insisted.

"There, there," she said soothingly. "It's ok, Staring at a girl is not the biggest crime in the world. She noticed it and told me."

"Riya noticed?" he gasped.

"Yeah," said Shalini sardonically. "She's got eyes you know."

"Well no harm done I suppose," he mused. "By the way, which branch of the restaurant is the meeting-place?"

"The one on Greams Road."

"Fine," he replied. "And Shalini?" he asked in a soft voice.

"Yeah?"

"Thank you."

"Don't mention it. I shall probably be dead when she finds out, but if you can make her happy, it'll be worth it," she laughed and ended the call.

She walked into the bathroom and took a nice, hot shower, then dried herself and got into her bathrobe and walked into her closet. She rummaged through her clothes, rejecting several outfits before finally selecting a coppery red sleeveless cocktail dress with a belt around the waist. She chose matching footwear and quickly got dressed. Never one to wear much make-up, she applied just a touch of lipstick whose light brown shade complemented her attire perfectly. She then brushed her short hair till it gleamed in the twilight. She took a long, hard look at herself in the full-length mirror and was satisfied with what she saw: a pretty young woman looking natural and hot at the same time. Her eyes were her undoing, she decided. They were sad and wise, having seen more than they should. The pain she had undergone was reflected in her eyes, but there was also a hint of merriment which could make her eyes sparkle with mischief when she was in a good mood, which she was in now, though the merriment was clouded by a hint of apprehension.

She finally turned away from the mirror and sat on the bed to put on her pumps. Once she was done, she grabbed her clutch and walked into the living room to wait for Riya. Her friend was punctual as always and exactly forty-five minutes after she had left the apartment, the doorbell rang. Shalini smiled to herself as she got up to open the door for her close friend. Though she was sure it was Riya at the door, she still had the chain lock on when she opened the door to make certain it was Riya.

Her friend entered the flat, shaking her head in bemusement. "Your paranoia knows no bounds my dear," she commented wryly.

"Better to be safe than sorry," muttered Shalini. Riya rolled her eyes, but did not bother to comment, having heard this statement a zillion times from the smaller girl whose child-like appearance had gotten her into a lot of unwanted and uncalled-for trouble over the years.

Riya was dressed in a short black dress with a halter neck which clung to her and showed off her long, slender legs to their best advantage. Sleek black high-heeled shoes completed her attire. "The deadly woman in black," Shalini wisecracked.

"Yes dangerous lady in red, that would be me," retorted Riya. She took her friend's outstretched hand and they walked out of the flat together, locking the door behind them. They took the elevator down to the ground floor and headed towards the parking lot. Riya pressed her key fob to unlock her shiny Cappuccino beige Skoda Rapid and got into the driver's seat while Shalini got into the passenger seat. "Dhaba Express on Greams Road, right?" queried Shalini, as Riya revved up the engine.

"Right."

Shalini fiddled with the music system and decided to play a collection of English soft rock. "We listen to that crap all the time when we take your car and at your place," Riya whined. "Why not something more upbeat?"

Shalini did not bother to reply, instead fiddling around with the iPod she had connected to the music system before settling on a hip-hop number. "Upbeat enough for Your Highness?" she asked sweetly.

Riya sighed. "Play whatever the hell you want, but just tone down the volume. I need to concentrate."

"Yes your ladyship, your wish is my command."

After that, they rode in a companionable silence. "That's it!" Shalini exclaimed out of the blue, startling Riya, who hit the brakes so hard that they narrowly missed colliding with a motor-cyclist in front of them. She slowed down and brought the car to a stop near the pavement.

"What's wrong with you?" she screamed at her friend. "You almost caused a hit-and-run!"

"I know what conceptual combination would work best for our project," said Shalini triumphantly.

"Great. Congratulations. The next time you have an Eureka moment, try to be quieter about it and DO NOT have them while I'm driving," she said sternly.

"I'm sorry that I startled you, but a genius cannot be asked to think at particular times. If an Eureka moment happens, it happens, irrespective of time and place. I can't stop it. So stop yelling and try to be a better driver with zen-like concentration which nothing and no one can break," retorted Shalini in one breath.

Riya shot her a murderous look, but did not say anything. She quickly eased the car back into the traffic and drove towards Greams Road. To her credit, Shalini did not have any more Eureka moments and the drive was made in peace. When they reached the restaurant, Riya parked the car and slumped back in her seat, thankful to be alive and in one piece. "What are you waiting for? Get out," she snapped at her friend.

"My, my, the grapes are really sour today. Calm down and arrange your features in some semblance of normalcy, will you?"

Riya got out of the car in a huff and slammed the door angrily. "We almost rammed into an innocent motor-cyclist. If I hadn't swerved in time, we could be sitting in jail right now! And you dare to act like nothing has happened!"

"We didn't hit him, did we? And we're NOT in jail now, are we? Why are you so high-strung? You know I tend to have my 'moments' like a bolt from the blue sometimes. I'm sorry I shrieked, okay? Now can we please go in or do you want to stand here on the road and argue the entire evening about who did what? That would serve no purpose except to screw your mood even further, you know," Shalini was starting to get exasperated.

Riya took a deep breath and tried to relax her taut muscles. She knew what happened on the road wasn't really Shalini's fault, but she was shaken up by the experience and her friend was the closest punching bag available. She closed her eyes and took several deep breaths. After a few minutes, she opened her eyes and appeared relaxed. She smiled ruefully at Shalini. "Sorry," she mumbled. "It wasn't your fault and I shouldn't have gone off on you like that."

"No biggie," said Shalini generously. "Now can we *please* go inside for crying out loud?"

"Yes," agreed Riya. "Come on." The two girls linked hands and walked towards the entrance of the restaurant. Inside, they found Derek Mathews already waiting for them at a corner table. He rose as soon as he saw them approaching and greeted them both warmly and grinned from ear to ear as he pulled out Shalini's chair for her.

"Becoming a gentleman, are we?" Shalini smiled back at him. She looked like a kid on Christmas. "Sorry about last night and today morning," she said with an apologetic smile, blushing to the roots of her hair as she remembered how rudely she had turned down his dinner invitation.

"Don't be sorry. You're here and that's all that matters." Derek waved off her apology with a broad grin. "Ever considered auditioning for a part in a horror movie?" he asked mischievously. "That scream last night would land you the part quite easily!"

This made Shalini chuckle and immediately, the tension she hadn't known she was feeling lifted and she relaxed back in her chair. Derek was happy to see her relaxing slowly.

Riya shook her head and smiled to herself. If her thick-headed friend could only see the sparks flying between the two of them, her job would be a lot easier. Suddenly, she became aware of another presence at their table. She looked up and found herself staring into the twinkling blue eyes of Anup Sharma.

CHAPTER 10

She practically leapt out of her seat in shocked disbelief. "W-what are you doing here?" she managed to croak out.

"Joining you for dinner. Your little friend here was good enough to invite me to join you," he said, sounding calm and unruffled. Derek watched the scene quietly, giving Shalini a look of amused suspicion, which was wasted on the young woman.

"Did she now?" she snapped, turning to shoot Shalini a look with enough heat to scorch half the Amazon rainforest. But Shalini for her part, smiled and shrugged. The look of absolute innocence on her face was too much for Derek, who was trying hard to stifle a laugh.

"I did you a favor, honey. Now stop being such a whiny pain in the you-know-where and chillax! You will thank me later, trust me." Her angelic smile only served to rile up Riya even more.

"Don't hold your breath over it, you little witch!" Riya sighed and shook her head, annoyed, yet oddly pleased by the actions of her incorrigible friend. She arranged her face in a million giga-watt smile and turned it on Anup full blast, who grinned right back at her. Shalini was watching them feeling smug and self-satisfied. She was very pleased with her handiwork indeed.

"Why don't you guys take the table behind us?" she suggested. "You'll get more privacy that way."

"You wanna get us out of the way, Shalu?" Riya gave her a knowing look. Her tone had softened considerably.

"Maybe," drawled Shalini. "What do you say, Derek?"

"She's right," he piped up cheerfully.

Anup turned to Riya and took her hand in his. "Come on, we're obviously surplus to requirement. Let's get our own table."

Shalini smiled at them and turned to face Derek. "Shall we order?"

"Before that..." Derek took a deep breath. "I have something to ask you."

Shalini instantly became serious. "Yes?" she said, a hint of apprehension mingled with anticipation in her voice.

Derek was looking as nervous as she felt and she took solace from that. "Shalini I—" he swallowed, then tried again. "I really like you Shalini."

Shalini's heart was pounding so hard she thought it might leap out of her chest, but she did an amazing job of keeping a straight face. "Like me how?" she asked cautiously. "For the record, I like you too. You're smart, bright and nice and I think you'll be a lot of fun to hang out with—"

"I'm in love with you and want you to be my girlfriend," he blurted out in one breath, cutting her off in mid-sentence. "And get married to you when the time comes."

Her mouth was hanging open and she tried to process what Derek had just told her. It was evident that the last part had been totally unexpected. "Do you really mean that?" she managed to choke out past the dryness in her throat.

"Of course I do," he said earnestly. "I was smitten the very first time I met you. We met in the ground-floor lobby of the apartment building and we exchanged a few words, but it was your smile that took my breath away. A million LED lights cannot hold a candle to the powerful radiance of your smile," he said dreamily, thinking of that day two years ago when he had laid eyes on the petite, dainty-looking young lady for the first time.

"You're flattering me too much Derek," she smiled at him. "But it feels good. Doesn't it bother you that I'm, well, I'm the way I am?"

"If you mean does the fact that you are … specially-abled bother me, the answer is no. You're smart, independent, intelligent, warm, friendly, strong and beautiful both on the outside and inside and that's all that matters to me. You're the way you are because of a quirk of fate over which you had no control. How does that have any bearing on the wonderful person you are? Come on Shalini, why do you think a non-issue like that would be an issue to me? Do you think I'm that shallow?"

"A non-issue," Shalini repeated softly. "Not many people think that way, you know. I'm clinically and legally blind after all. And no, you're not shallow, but most men who cross my way…" She shrugged.

"Well, I'm not most men. In fact, I don't think I fit into any stereotype. I'm Derek Mathews, a humble human being who's insanely in love with a wonderful girl and hoping desperately that she'd give me a chance to prove that love. Call me a maverick if you want, Shalini, but please, just give me—us–a chance."

"But you hardly know me!" Shalini couldn't help herself. "How can you be so intensely in love with someone you know nothing about?"

Derek held up a hand. "Listen, I may not know what's your favorite food or favorite color and other such mundane stuff. But I know that you're a strong, warm, good-hearted person and that's all that matters to me. That and your indomitable spirit, which is reflected in your beautiful eyes."

"Derek I—" Shalini started.

"Shhh," Derek interrupted once again. "You don't have to say anything right now. Go home and think about it and then let me know at your own time."

Shalini smiled. "That's very sweet of you, but it won't be necessary for me to think."

"What do you mean?" he was the one feeling apprehensive now.

Shalini's smile was reassuring and shy at the same time and she was blushing to the roots of her hair. "It just means that I like you too and it would be an honor to be your girlfriend."

"Are you serious?" Derek's grin threatened to split his face. "You're not yanking my chain or something, are you?"

"Of course not!" Shalini feigned indignation, then she smiled broadly. "I came here meaning to tell you that I like you, but I was afraid that you might laugh at me for being presumptuous or worse yet, think I'm a freak and reject me outright," she confessed.

"You're NOT a freak," he said sternly. "You're a wonderful, strong and unique young woman and I'm very very proud of you. Get used to it, princess, because that's who you are."

"Thank you," she said softly. "You're a great guy Derek, and I'm lucky to have you."

"I'm the lucky one," he smiled. With that, he beckoned the waiter over and placed their orders. While they waited, he called up the well-known bakery Bakerman and asked them to pack two large slices of their famous death by red velvet pastry.

"You have another sweetheart I don't know about?" demanded Shalini. "Or a wicked sweet tooth?"

"Neither," he grinned. "It's for Madame Cupid in appreciation for somehow making you see sense and agree to meet me for dinner tonight."

"That devious minx, Riya?" Shalini asked huffily, wondering how her friend was faring with Anup.

"Minx she definitely is," Derek agreed with a hearty laugh. "Not sure about devious though."

"She's sneaky and devious," said Shalini. "She texted you though I told her not to." Shalini was enjoying the sound of Derek's mellow baritone and the way his eyes crinkled while he laughed.

"And look how well it has turned out," he reasoned. "I prefer to call her resourceful."

"Whatever," muttered Shalini petulantly, though she couldn't wipe the wide grin off her face. She hoped things were going as well for Riya as they were for her.

✳ ✳ ✳

A few tables behind the newly-formed couple, it was quite a different story indeed. Anup was staring at Riya, who was assiduously studying the menu as if it was the most interesting bestseller ever written, but in reality, not seeing anything. Finally, Anup sighed and gently removed the menu from her hands.

Riya glared at him. "What did you do that for?"

"Because I need to talk to you!" he snapped back.

"So talk," she retorted acidly. "No need to snatch things from my hand for that!"

Anup wondered what he could have possibly done that she was so antagonistic towards him. She had seemed happy to see him, hadn't she? To call her mercurial would be putting it mildly. Nevertheless, he ploughed on. "Well, what I have to say is pretty important and I'd prefer that we are looking at each other when I say it. You staring mindlessly at the menu, which by the way you were holding upside down, is not helping matters."

"So now that you've got my undivided attention," she snarled, not looking the least bit unrepentant, "go ahead and spit it out!" Beneath the bravado, she felt wary and uneasy, and looked around her, as if searching for a way to bolt should the need arise. Her eyes were darting all over the place and she was doing a stellar job of avoiding his intense gaze.

"Riya, please look at me," he implored. "I'm not going to eat you alive, for God's sake. Just please look at me."

"What do you want to say?" she asked, panic rising inside her. She wanted to bolt out of there before he uttered another word, but somehow managed to keep her bottom glued to the seat. She was wound up so tight she was surprised that a few nerves hadn't snapped and popped yet.

"Please relax," he said softly. "Riya, look. I have always admired you from a distance. But that's not enough anymore."

"And what exactly does that mean?" she asked, staring stonily at him. "Maybe it's better to continue to stare at me from a distance."

"Ahh! The staring business once again!" he let out a breath in an exaggerated manner. "No Riya. Staring at you from a distance makes me feel like a weird creep who's stalking you. I can't keep doing that anymore and quite frankly, that's just not enough for me."

"I think you'll have to be satisfied with that," she replied. "Maybe it's better for both of us to leave things as they are."

"I don't believe so," he was as obstinate as she was and this was getting on her already over-wrought nerves.

"So what do you want from me?" she demanded in a belligerent and hostile tone.

"Friendship," he said and sat back, waiting for the penny to drop.

"Friendship?" she repeated, sounding surprised. It was quite clear that she had not expected this. She felt intense relief wash over her along with a twinge of disappointment which she quickly tried to suppress.

"Yes, friendship," he reiterated firmly. "I want to hang out with you in or out of office, when the opportunity arises and get to know you better."

"That's it?" she asked, still unable to overcome her surprise at the turn of events. She had fully expected him to come on to her and hit on her, instead he wanted to be just friends. She was confused by his attitude and as a result, thrown off-balance. Had she read the signals wrong?

Anup smiled ruefully, as if reading her thoughts, his eyes gleaming with amusement. "For the moment, yes. That's all I want."

"For the moment?" Her guard went up again. The guy was seriously confounding.

"For the moment," he stated firmly, enjoying himself as he watched the myriad emotions flicker across her beautiful face.

Seeing that she was genuinely confused, he decided he had toyed with her enough.

"Riya," he said in a serious tone. "I won't lie or pretend. I have been very much attracted to you for quite some time now. But I know that for some reason, you're just not ready to let any man into your life yet. And yes, I came here this evening originally intending to ask you to be my girlfriend, but then realized that wasn't probably the smartest thing to do. So I decided to become your friend first," he saw her opening her mouth to protest and held up a hand, "with no strings attached," he finished, smiling reassuringly.

"But what do you stand to gain from such an arrangement?" she asked, curiosity getting the better of her.

"Your friendship," he said simply. "An insight into your life, I hope. In time, maybe you'll be ready to let your defenses down and let a guy into your life and when that happens, I hope that guy is me, but right now, I'm not thinking that far ahead. I just want to be friends with you and spend some time getting to know you. And most important, earn your trust."

"No pressure?" she asked disbelievingly. "No strings at all? There must be some catch," she insisted.

"Oh God!" he sighed. "Stop being so suspicious and paranoid for once! There's no catch, okay? Believe me when I say so. If you decide at some point that you want to be more than just friends, then we'll rethink. Right now, let's keep it simple."

"Are you for real?" she asked, still not able to believe her ears.

"Not what I wanted, believe me," he said honestly. "But then, pushing you into a romantic relationship would have been a disaster. I can see that now. I just want to be friends. Why is that so hard to believe?"

"Well, it's not every day that a hot guy professing intense attraction and great liking for a girl he hardly knows wants to be 'just friends' with her," she said by way of explanation.

"Riya...," he was becoming exasperated now. "I've been absolutely honest with you. I've told you I like you and am attracted to you and have been for a long time now and I've also made it abundantly clear that I won't push you and all I want from you at the moment is friendship. Why are you still being so skeptical? What do I have to do, climb a mountain strewn with broken glass to prove the truth of my words?" He kept his voice low, but there was no mistaking the frustration in his tone.

"I'm sorry," said Riya quietly. "But trust isn't something that's easy for me."

"I understand that," he replied, sounding calmer. "You don't have to trust me if you don't want to. Just be my friend. Give me the chance to know you better. Let me earn your trust. Come on Riya, I'm not asking for too much here!"

"No you're not," she let out a shaky breath. "Fine. We can be friends. But one wrong move and you'll be cut off without notice. Got it? There will be no second chances where I'm concerned."

He held his hands up defensively. "Yes ma'am. I got your point loud and clear. I'm right now feeling extremely sorry for my gender."

A smile came unbidden to Riya's face. "And why's that, Mr. Sharma?"

"There's no such thing as a win-win situation for us where it comes to women," he explained. "If we propose romance, we get cut off at the knees more often than not. And when we propose nothing but platonic friendship, we're looked upon with suspicion."

Riya's smile broadened. "I'm sorry," she said sincerely. "I didn't mean to come off as the cynical high-and-mighty Ice Queen. I just can't help it sometimes."

"It's alright," he said with an answering grin. "Shall we order?"

"Sure," she agreed. "We're splitting the bill, right?"

"If you wish," he shrugged. He was ready to take any approach that had even a remote chance of working. He liked her a lot and respected her and wanted her enough to try the friendship route first. But he was determined that sooner or later, he could break down the walls she had set up around herself. When that happened, he would push for a different kind of relationship. But now was not the time. He could see that clearly. She needed to trust him, understand that he was not a threat. She needed to come to him in her own time, on her own terms. He was prepared to wait. Besides, this friendship approach would help him to get to know her better. And it won't scare her off. It was a good move and he patted himself on the back for coming up with this strategy after Shalini's phone call.

During the meal, they talked about several things. Riya finally began to relax and unwind in his company. *Maybe he's being genuine*, she thought, but even if he wasn't, she didn't worry much, or at least, that was what she told herself. There were no strings attached. It was only friendship.

Once the meal was over, they said their goodbyes. Anup went in the direction of the men's room while she headed towards the exit. She became anxious once again as she thought of Shalini's inquisition which would surely come sooner or later. She would find the friendship part really hard to believe and would probably blame her for sending don't-come-too-close vibes. *Shalini's going to have me for breakfast,* she thought. Though she wasn't looking forward to the inquisition, she walked on doggedly to face the music.

CHAPTER 11

Riya found Shalini and Derek leaning against his car, talking intently. She took a few deep breaths, trying to gather her wits, which were scattered all over the map. When she finally got her breathing under control and got her best poker face on, she walked briskly towards Shalini and her companion. When she was a few paces away from them, she noticed they were holding hands. Unbidden, a smile came to her lips. *Looks like somebody had a lucky night*, she thought, feeling happy for her friend. She was glad that her attempt at playing Cupid had seemingly succeeded.

Derek noticed Riya out of the corner of his eye and turned to smile at her. "Hiya," he greeted her warmly. "I'm taking the little lady here for a ride," he announced. The little lady in question was grinning like a Cheshire cat.

"Oh cool!" Riya smiled. "Be careful though. If she takes a fancy to your wallet, she might decide to empty it! She has quite a taste for successful and handsome young men like you. Take care that she doesn't eat you alive!" She tried to keep her tone as light as possible to throw Shalini off the scent long enough to get her into Derek's car. She turned to face her friend. "Have a good time, Shalu!" she grinned.

Though Riya talked jauntily and looked cheerful, Shalini sensed something was off with her. "Where's Anup?" she asked suspiciously.

"In the men's room," Riya replied without missing a beat.

Though Riya was speaking the truth, Shalini somehow did not believe it, because the other girl's tone was too smooth and her attempts at light-hearted humor seemed forced. Her hackles were raised, but she couldn't pursue the issue now and decided to ask her once she was back home. Giving Riya a long, hard stare, she smiled sweetly and waved goodbye.

Damn Shalini and her sixth sense! Riya fumed inwardly. She knew Shalini suspected something and the bloodhound would not let go of it now she had a scent to follow. And she wasn't likely to forget either. Riya cursed under her breath as she headed towards her car. Her interfering little friend could be a pain in the wrong place sometimes. She vowed to have a serious talk with her and tell her in no uncertain terms to back off from her "love life." Though this time, she had to admit, Shalini's interference had resulted in a budding friendship. Still, she was determined to tell her that no more meddling would be tolerated, conveniently forgetting her own meddling in the other girl's affairs.

She reached home, undressed quickly and got into bed. She tossed and turned in her bed for a while, trying to go to sleep. She was still confused about Anup's intentions and her mind was refusing to switch off. Finally, she fell into a troubled sleep around midnight, thinking of Anup Sharma's twinkling blue eyes.

❀ ❀ ❀

Shalini got into the passenger seat of Derek's sleek black BMW and settled back comfortably in the plush leather seat. "Nice car," she sighed contentedly, leaning back.

"Glad you like it," he smiled.

"Where are we going, exactly?" she queried.

"I'm kidnapping you and taking you to my dungeon," he grinned devilishly.

"Really?" asked Shalini calmly. "In that case, I'm overdressed. Why don't you stop some place where I can pick up tight leather pants, ridiculously high high-heeled shoes, handcuffs, blindfolds and other props?"

Derek roared with laughter. "You're something!" he said at last. "Most girls would have run for their lives by now!"

"I can see through a man when he's bluffing. Years of experience with a bratty younger brother takes care of that aspect automatically. Now, are you going to tell me where we're going or not?"

"We'll go to Bakerman first to collect the pastry, then Gatsby 2000," he said promptly.

"Great! I 'don't get to go to pubs more than once a year." Shalini clapped her hands in glee.

"Tonight's your lucky night, my lady," he grinned at her child-like exuberance and enthusiasm. After all the high-handedness she had shown him in the past, this fun-loving, mischievous side of her was a pleasant and welcome surprise.

"Why thank you, kind sir," she said, matching his teasing tone.

Derek was happy to see that she was in good spirits and enjoying herself. He grinned back at her and asked, "So what do you usually do during the weekends?"

"Listen to music, listen to audio books, worship or just laze around," she said simply. "Or go out with Riya. Sometimes, Sreeja or Arvind might join us."

"You haven't been out on many dates?" he sounded puzzled.

"Not really. I haven't been interested in dating for a long time. Until now," she said without explaining further.

"May I ask why? I'm sure it's not due to lack of offers. You're a very charming, personable young woman."

Shalini laughed easily. "That's enough inquisition for one night. You can't expect a lady to reveal all her secrets on the very first date!" The deflection was subtle, but Derek noticed her reluctance and decided not to pursue the subject any further. He did not want to push his luck on their very first date.

"Fair enough," he conceded, though he was still reluctant to drop the subject.

"What about you? What do you generally do over the weekends?"

"I restore old bikes," he said, his eyes shining with obvious pride and excitement.

She smiled at the enthusiasm in his voice. "It's obvious you love it. What do you do with the vehicles once you have restored them? Do you sell them for a profit?"

"Yes," he answered proudly. "I do it for fun mostly. The money I make from it is not so important. I have always loved tinkering around with machinery trying to fix them since I was a kid. Now, it has turned into a passion. Quite a profitable one as well. I'm seriously thinking of turning it into a proper business venture at some point."

"Well, you seem to have the Midas touch," commented Shalini. "Mathews & Company is among the top ten advertising agencies in the country. It's an incredible accomplishment for someone your age." There was a hint of pride in her voice. Then she asked teasingly, "But that's all you do over the weekends?

Tinker around with old bikes? You don't wine and dine pretty ladies?"

"Oh, don't get me wrong. I'm no saint. Over the years, I have had my fair share of girlfriends, but none of them could come close to the girl I wanted most," he said, looking incredibly boyish. "And since the day I laid eyes on her, I haven't been interested in dating anyone else."

"If you mean me, I'm flattered but not fooled," laughed Shalini. "Do you feed that line to all the girls you take out?"

"No," he said quietly, growing serious. "Only to you. It's not a line, Shalini. I have never been able to commit to anyone because my heart was yearning for something. It was only when I met you, I realized what it was. A sense of belonging. After I laid eyes on you, I wanted to be with no one else but you and as a result, couldn't settle down with anyone else. It's been almost two years since my last romantic escapade. I've been wanting to ask you out, but you always seemed beyond any man's reach, so closed-off that I was hesitant to ask you out. You seemed to have too many invisible barriers around you."

"So why now?" she asked. "Don't get me wrong, I'm not complaining. I just want to understand how a commitment-phobe like you suddenly wants to commit to me full-time."

"Because you're the love of my life," he said simply. "I've never felt this way about anyone, ever. Every time I look at you, I feel a sense of contentment, as if I have come home at last. And I'm tired of waiting, hanging around for a glimpse of you. I want a real relationship, Shalini." He sighed wearily. "Look, I'm not expecting you to marry me tomorrow. But I want to be with you, spend as much time with you as you can stand and get to know you better. Shalini, I won't push you. Take your time and decide what you want out of this relationship. When you make up your mind, I'll be here, waiting. Meanwhile, let's go on dates, hang out with each other as much as possible and have fun." His tone was reasonable and conciliatory.

"Thank you," she said, touched by his words. "I like you a lot, Derek. It's just that I'm scared if I open up too much and let you in, I might get hurt very badly."

"I would never do that to you," he said vehemently, glancing at her out of the corner of his eye. "You hide your pain behind your vivacious nature. The rest of the world may be oblivious to that, but I'm not. Every time I look into your eyes, I can see right into your soul. You've been badly hurt in the past. How, when or by whom, I don't know. When you're ready to tell me, I shall be here. Trust me, Shalu. I'm not going anywhere."

Hearing him use her nickname felt strange, yet oddly familiar at the same time. "I know," she sighed. "Thank you. I'll tell you, I promise. Just give me sometime. Give us sometime." By then, they had collected the pastry from Bakerman and were nearly at Gatsby 2000, one of the popular pubs in the city.

"You got it, girl," he said smiling. "For now, let's go in and dance!" He parked the car in the first empty parking space he could find and quickly got out and ran around to open Shalini's door for her.

"I could get used to all this attention you know," she commented.

"That's the plan. I want you to get used to being treated like the princess you are," he replied, grinning as if he had broken a World record at the Olympics. "I want to spoil you, babe."

"Moving too fast, aren't we?" she teased.

"You'll be my babe soon enough," he said impishly. "Just wait and see. C'mon," he grabbed her hand and led her into the building.

They headed up the elevator to the famous pub and found the place packed with young men and women enjoying the weekend. The music was loud and pulsating and the couple started dancing with the others on the dance floor. Derek did not let loosen his grip around Shalini's waist for the entire time they were there. When they were finally exhausted and sweaty, they stopped to catch their breaths. They headed out into the balcony. The cool night breeze felt wonderful against their sweat-soaked skin. Cautiously, Shalini laid her head on Derek's shoulder, who held her loosely around the shoulders and waist. He wanted to hug her tighter, but didn't want to scare her away. She wanted to draw closer to him. It felt so wonderful to be held by strong, protective arms, but she held back, something in her refusing to let go of past wounds and deep-seated insecurities.

They stayed like that for a while, not saying anything, just listening to each other's rhythmic breathing. Shalini raised her head and looked at him. "What are you doing here, you gorgeous man? Wasting your time on me when you can have your pick of society beauties."

"For the last time princess, I'm not wasting my time. You're what I need, what I want. I have waited for you for a long time. And now that I finally have you, I'll be damned if I let you get away."

Shalini smiled, pleased to hear him say that. She wanted to prolong the moment, but she was tired to her bones and tomorrow, she had to continue her research. And there was also the chance that she might lose control, which could prove to be disastrous. Reluctantly, she asked him to take her home. He acquiesced, but he too, did not want to break the spell. Deciding to take a chance, he leaned forward and brushed his lips gently against hers. Her eyes flew open in surprise and shock, but to her own astonishment, she did not pull away and expletives did not stream out of her mouth. Emboldened, he deepened the kiss just a little, keeping it soft and gentle. Her lips felt warm and soft against his, and despite her initial hesitation, she tentatively returned the kiss. Finally, they broke apart and looked at each other.

"Shalu," he began.

"Shhh," she whispered. "Please don't say anything. I don't think I can take anything more tonight."

Though he wanted to say something, anything, to make sure she was alright, he held his counsel. "Let's go home," he said instead.

They took the elevator downstairs and headed outside to Derek's car. He opened the door for her and helped her inside, which earned him an amused smile. Climbing into the driver's seat, he headed off towards Alwarpet. They sat in a comfortable silence, listening to the mellow tones of Michael Learns to Rock, Shalini's favorite band.

When they reached their apartment complex, he accompanied her up to her flat, lingering at her door. She reached up and hugged him lightly. "I had a wonderful time tonight," she said honestly. "Thank you."

"So did I," he said in a soft voice. "For the first time in a long time. Good night Shalini. I'll call you tomorrow."

"I'd like that," she smiled. "Good night Derek."

CHAPTER 12

The next day, Shalini's blissful sleep was rudely interrupted by someone noisily and repeatedly banging on her front door. Cursing a blue streak under her breath, she angrily marched towards the door and flung it wide open, not bothering with the safety chain in her annoyance. To her surprise, Riya walked in, an anxious-looking Derek in tow. Shalini gave them a look which held a mixture of anger and puzzlement. "What's going on?" she demanded in a hoarse, sleep-filled voice which nevertheless held enough venom to paralyze both of them on the spot.

"Ask lover-boy here," Riya snapped back, sounding less than pleased herself.

She looked quizzically at Derek, who was looking sheepish. "What time is it, by the way?" she asked in a relatively calmer tone.

"Almost ten-thirty," Riya said laconically. She too was looking irritable and the knowledge that sometime soon, she would have to explain her previous night's actions to Shalini did not help to lighten her mood. Even though she had done nothing to put off Anup, she was sure Shalini would not see it that way.

"I called your mobile a few times, but you wouldn't answer," he said by way of explanation.

"So?" she asked, looking clueless and pissed. "It's Sunday," she said as if that explained everything. In her mind at least, it did.

He gulped. "I thought I had done something to piss you off and you've decided to cut me off," he explained, blushing slightly at how ridiculous and paranoid he was sounding.

Shalini gave him a strange look while Riya shook her head in exasperation. "Derek," Shalini began. "Let me put it like this for you. There's no need for you to walk on eggshells around me. If I don't like something you say or do, I'll say it straight to your face. I'm not a child to cut someone off without just cause. I had a wonderful time with you last night. It's very rare for me to be out till all hours like that and it wore me out completely and I decided to sleep with my mobile on silent mode. That's not really an outlandish or unusual thing to do, last time I checked. You didn't have to panic and come down all the way over here to check up on me. I appreciate the concern, I really do. But trust me, there's no need to worry. And a smart entrepreneur like you should know better than to panic at the drop of a hat," she finished in a gentle but firm tone. "And what's Riya's role in all this?" she asked, turning to face the taller girl, who was calmly sitting cross-legged on the couch, a silent spectator in the drama.

"Lover-boy called me since you weren't answering your phone," she explained acidly. "He wanted me to come down and check up on you. When I told him he was over-reacting and refused to do so, he came down to my place and dragged me along, or rather, sweet-talked me into coming along, for support in case you started hurling weapons at him."

Derek shot her a withering look to which she flipped him the bird. Shalini chuckled softly, imagining the scene that must have taken place in Riya's flat. "Chill both of you," she said. "Sorry you got dragged into this Ri," she said to the other girl in a conciliatory tone. "And Derek, please learn not to panic for anything and everything. With me being me, you have to relax. At this rate, you'll surely burst a blood vessel or two. And neither of us want that now, do we?"

"I guess not," he sighed. "I'm sorry I overreacted, Shalu. But I'm very protective. That's how I am. You'll have to learn to put up with that."

"I'll try," she promised. "I'm going to take a shower. Staying or leaving is upto the two of you." Saying this, she turned and walked back into her bedroom.

"She's not a morning person," Riya commented, seeing Derek's perplexed face.

"I can tell," he smiled wryly. "She seems to have quite a temper!"

"Oh, this is just a trailer," she retorted. "You should see her when she's absolutely riled up. Not a pretty sight."

"I have no such death wish," he said, putting his hands up as if to defend himself.

"So did you two hit it off last night?" Riya queried, curiosity getting the better of her.

"I think so," he said thoughtfully. "She likes me, but is hesitant to open up too quickly. She suffers from a lot of insecurities."

Riya snorted. "Who doesn't?"

"I don't know about others. I think she has been burned quite badly by someone or something in the past and that has resulted in her having a lot of issues, but she camouflages them really well."

"And how did you see past the front she puts up? It has proved to be quite effective with most people." Riya was curious about his insightfulness.

"As I told her last night, I'm not most people. I'm quite perceptive about a lot of things. That's why I'm so successful in the advertising business. Perceiving people's needs and desires is my core competency," he smiled ruefully. "Besides, let's face it, I have been obsessed with her for the last two years. I have had ample opportunity to observe and study her."

"She has not had it easy in life," Riya said reflectively. "You'll have to be extremely patient with her."

"I'm ready to do whatever it takes to make her trust me enough to open her heart to me," he said quietly. "She's the girl of my dreams, the love of my life and I'll do everything in my power to keep her at my side always and forever."

"Seriously, where did you come from? Who would have picked you to be such a romantic?" Riya was staring at him in fascination, unable to believe that such guys actually existed in real life.

He shrugged. "I'm no holy roller and have known my share of intelligent, accomplished, beautiful women in my life," he said. "But none of them could ever hope to come close to the wonder that is Shalini."

"Now I believe you're for real," she smiled at him. "Only someone who's insanely in love with her can describe Shalini as a wonder! Anyone who knows the little devil intimately can easily tell that your description is colored by love!"

"It's how I see her," he shrugged.

"Just treat her right," she warned. "She has been hurt enough. If you ever hurt her in any way, you'll have to reckon with me and my fist."

"I want to take care of her. Why the hell would I want to hurt her?" he was sounding annoyed. "I'm not a monster, you know."

She backed down. "Just saying. She's one of my closest friends. In fact, she's my soul-sister and I want to see her happy."

"So do I," he assured her. Just then, Shalini walked into the living room clad in a pair of capris and a neon green tank top which hugged her curves just so.

"Whoa! Who are you planning to blind, honeybunch?" Riya asked sarcastically.

Shalini had a wicked gleam in her eyes. "Neon helps me think clearly and creatively," she said sagely.

"Sure. After you have blinded and disoriented your audience, anything you say would seem clear," she shot back and stood up. "I need to get some work done. I'll leave you two alone now."

"I'm just leaving," said Derek hastily. "I came by only to make sure that she's alright," he gestured towards Shalini. "I'll call you and see if we can make plans to get together in the evening. Bye Shalini. Catch you later Riya." He waved to the girls and was out of the apartment before either of them could react.

Riya shot Shalini a quizzical look. "What's gotten into him?"

Shalini shrugged. "Beats me. I gave up trying to second-guess men and their actions a long time ago. Come on, let's get to work."

"Not so fast, Ms. Smartypants," Riya said firmly, grabbing Shalini by the hand and shoving her into the couch. "I want details of last night."

"I don't kiss and tell," Shalini said with a coy smile.

"Right Ms. Smartypants. I don't think you actually kissed, so start tellin', will ya?" she said impatiently.

"Shows how little you know," Shalini retorted.

Riya narrowed her eyes and looked at her suspiciously. "You *did?*" she couldn't quite keep the astonishment from her voice.

Shalini only smiled in response. Riya shook her lightly. "Come on. Spill. There's a lot to be done and I don't have all day to spare for this inquisition."

"Fine," Shalini gave an exaggerated sigh. "He's a great guy. Warm, understanding and affectionate. He took me to Gatsby 2000 and we danced for a while, then we just stood quietly outside, just the two of us."

"Then?" Riya pressed.

"Well," Shalini drawled. "He bent down and kissed me, lightly at first, then a little deeper."

"And you didn't pull away or push him away or hurl abuse at him?" Riya asked, still astonished at this unexpected twist.

"Surprisingly, no," Shalini answered, her tone very slightly tinged with surprise. "in fact, I um, returned the kiss."

Riya's mouth fell open. "Wow!"

"Yeah."

"You really must like him then."

"I think I do. He wants to know more about me. I'm not sure how much I can reveal without driving him away completely. He keeps asking me to trust him. I want to, but," she was looking pensively down at her hands.

"Just afraid that if you do, he might use that trust against you," Riya finished the thought for her. "You can't live forever in fear of what might or might not happen, honey. At some point, you have to let go and open up. Derek seems to be completely smitten with you. I think you can open up to him little by little, see how he reacts to each new revelation."

"Let's see," said Shalini noncommittally. "Right now, I'm having fun with him and would like to keep it that way for a while. Though I have to give him credit. He is one of the few who has bothered to see past my ... being different and view me as a human being and treat me like one. Oh and he bought you two huge slices of red velvet cake."

"For what?" she asked, arching an eyebrow.

"For being sneaky and bringing us together," said Shalini, grinning from ear to ear.

"See? What did I tell you? He's a smitten kitten!"

"Yeah and a cool dude too," said Shalini thoughtfully. "And a darn good kisser."

"He's a decent person," agreed Riya wisely. "I think the guy's a keeper."

"And what about you, Ms. Know-it-all?"

"What about me?" she asked innocently.

"Oh don't start with me! What happened with Anup last night? You seemed a bit off. Did he do or say anything wrong? If so, I'll wring his neck for you," she said helpfully. "Or crush his uh, family jewels if you'd like."

"Thanks, but no need." She took a deep breath and exhaled slowly. *Here goes.* "He said and did everything right. He admitted to feeling attracted to me and liking me, but did not propose a romantic relationship. He said he wanted to be just friends with me and hang out so we can get to know each other better."

"Seriously?" Shalini was incredulous. "Just friends?"

"For now," Riya was sounding relieved and disappointed at the same time.

"Friends with benefits?" she asked hopefully, only half-joking.

"Of course not!" Riya was outraged.

Shalini looked at her more keenly then. Her friend was twisting her hands into her hair, a sign that she was nervous and fidgety. "What did you tell him? Is that what you want? To be just friends?"

"Yes... No...," she sounded unsure. "I think I want more, but I couldn't come right out and say it. I just couldn't."

"Why couldn't you?" she demanded. "Are you going to let the past dictate your actions throughout your life? You have a right to be happy you know, just in case you've forgotten."

Riya shot her a glare, and Shalini glared back at her. "You know how it is," she tried to say by way of explanation.

"Yes I do. I also know that at some point, you simply have to let go and live in the moment. You just told me I have to start trusting Derek at some point. Well, I'm throwing those words right back at you, sweetheart. I want you to be happy. Start working towards it." Her tone was uncompromising. "If not now, then when? Don't let life pass you by. Just friends is fine enough, but if you feel at any point you want more, don't hesitate to tell him."

"Alright, I'll try," Riya gave in. "But I'm not ready to start dating him yet. We can hang out as friends for now. I'll see him outside office only in the company of others."

"Company of others?" Shalini repeated, trying to bite back a smile. "Are those his words or yours?"

"Mine."

"And does he know about that?"

"Not yet."

"Are you afraid of him or yourself?" Shalini asked, trying to provoke her friend to face the truth.

"Afraid of what might happen if I let him in," she said honestly. "I'm not ready for that yet."

"Fine, I won't force you. You can join me and Derek sometimes," she offered generously.

"Thanks. That would be great, if you don't mind us tagging along."

"Not at all. Now, let's get to work. We need to get rich!"

"I'm with you on that," Riya cracked a smile, just as Shalini had known she would. "Let's go to my place and I'll show you what I've done today."

"Sure," Shalini grabbed her laptop and the two girls left the apartment and headed to the sixth floor to Riya's flat.

She flung open the door and they stepped inside and headed straight to her bedroom, their movements totally in sync with each other. Riya's laptop and printer were lying on the bed and a sheaf of papers were spread around. Both the girls sat down and powered up their laptops. Riya logged into her e-mail account and quickly mailed a few attachments to Shalini. "Log in and download the attachments I have mailed you," she said briskly.

Shalini did so and soon found herself looking at a bunch of spreadsheets. She listened for a while as her screen-reading software read them aloud, uncomprehending at first, then realization dawned on her. She turned to Riya. "Explain," she said shortly.

"Glad to," she agreed and proceeded to explain how she had arrived at the most cost-efficient method to ensure success for their ambitious project. She also outlined the pros and cons of various software platforms and reasoned how she had finally decided it would be best to use a combination of Oracle and Dreamweaver.

"This is all very good," said Shalini. "But what about the trump card we discussed yesterday? How do we fit that in?"

"Patience. I'm getting to that," smiled Riya. Then she started to explain her master-plan to her friend. She asked her to open another document from the attachments she had mailed. This held a series of diagrams and graphs. As Riya explained each step, Shalini's excitement was growing by the second. She started to believe that they could really pull it off. Her friend's answers to all her queries were quite plausible and convincing. An hour later, Riya slumped back in bed, her explanation complete.

"When you first told me yesterday, I had my doubts as to whether we could pull it off," began Shalini in an awed tone. "But now, I'm doubly confident we can."

"Thanks for the vote of confidence," Riya smiled. "These are just preliminary plans though. I still have to refine the diagrams before presenting them to the boss. Now, let's hear your brainwave which almost caused a hit-and-run yesterday," she poked Shalini in the ribs.

Shalini quickly mailed a few documents to Riya, her screen-reading software reading out every step in the background. "Open the one titled Leadership, Charisma and Strategic Advantage," she urged.

Riya opened the said document and one look at it and she knew what was running through Shalini's mind, but she wanted to hear it from the horse's mouth itself and so turned expectantly towards her. "Go on. I'm all ears."

Shalini grinned diabolically. "Yes my friend. You're right in your surmise. We shall start with the managerial grid and…" she outlined her idea as succinctly as possible. Then she asked Riya to open another document and continued the explanation. Forty-five minutes later, she was done.

"It's really ingenious," Riya said wonderingly. "And the genius lies in its simplicity. Now we have to find a way to integrate the concepts into the software module. That's going to be real hard work."

"I know."

"A good job, smartypants."

"Thank you. And likewise to you too."

"I'm starved."

Shalini rose. "I'll order pizza. Domino's or Pizza Hut?"

"Pizza Hut. Let's order two personal pizzas, garlic bread and dessert."

"Good idea," she agreed. The order was placed and the girls decided to watch television till the food arrived. Reruns of one of their favorite sitcoms were running on a satellite channel and they settled down comfortably on Riya's plush couch to share a few laughs. When the food arrived, they ate it straight out of the boxes and then headed back into the bedroom to continue working.

CHAPTER 13

It was almost six in the evening when the girls finally decided to stop working for the day. As Riya powered off her laptop, she heard her mobile ring. It was an incoming call from Anup. She was staring at the screen as if it was playing the most fascinating movie she had ever seen when Shalini piped up from behind her, "You going to answer it or do you intend to stare at it forever?"

"Y-yes," she managed to stammer out, but, she was still staring transfixed at the screen. Shalini had had enough by then and decided to take matters into her own hands. So she took the phone out of Riya's nerveless fingers and attended the call.

"Hi Anup, this is Shalini," she said in a cheerful voice. She listened for a moment, then said, "She was in the washroom. I'll give the phone to her. She's here now." She shoved the phone into Riya's hand, who gave her a bemused look. "Relax. Just friends," Shalini mouthed, which seemed to have some effect on her friend.

She quickly snapped out of her trance and cleared her throat before saying a hearty "Hello!" into the phone. *We are just friends. Friends don't panic when they talk to each other*, she reminded herself.

"Hi, I just wanted to say hello," he said shyly.

"Hello to you too," said Riya with an arrogant confidence she was far from feeling.

"Do you have plans tonight?" he queried.

"Not really," she responded before she could stop herself. She wondered where he was going with this.

"Will you join me for dinner?"

She was flustered for an instant, but recovered quickly. "Sure. Can Shalini come with us?"

Anup let out an exasperated sigh. "Fine. I'm not an ogre who wants to eat you alive, you know. And the last time I checked, two friends can hang out with each other without a chaperone."

"I am aware of that," she responded evenly. "I just thought it'd be nice if she could join us. You can get to know her better too. She's quite an interesting character." Riya was feeling quite pleased with herself for what she obviously thought was a smart recovery on her part. The look of derision Shalini shot her way suggested otherwise.

"I know," he sounded amused. "I have interacted with her often enough. We all work for the same company, remember?"

"Yeah, I know," she said sheepishly. "So can she join us?"

"Alright, alright," he said in a resigned tone.

Riya muted the phone while she asked Shalini if she could join them for dinner. Shalini gave her an Arctic glare which could have frozen the Thar Desert, but nodded her consent. She took the phone off mute and told Anup they'd be happy to join him for dinner.

"Be ready by eight," he said. "I'll pick you up. Text me your address." He disconnected the call.

As soon as Riya ended the call, Shalini rounded on her. "What's with you?" she demanded. "Why can't you go out with him on your own just once? You're just *friends*, remember?"

"I'm not ready for that yet," said Riya calmly.

"Riiiiight," Shalini rolled her eyes. "I'll bail you out this once. After tonight, you handle this *friend* of yours as you see fit."

"Thanks," Riya smiled, completely unapologetic about dragging her friend into her dinner plans. "I seem to remember someone generously saying Anup and I can hang out with her whenever we wanted. And here I was under the illusion that Shalini Samuel was a woman of her word!"

"Whatever," Shalini waved her off just as her mobile rang, the voice alert signaling a call from Derek. She decided to deal with Riya later and answered with a smile in her voice, "Hello?"

"Hey Shalini," he greeted her in a deep, husky voice.

"Hi yourself," she smiled into the phone. "What's up?"

"You up for a drive around nine-thirty?" he asked.

"Sure," she replied. "I'm going out with Riya for dinner. Anup's joining us. You can pick me up directly from the restaurant. I'll text you as soon as I know where we're headed."

"That's cool, but one question. Why are you tagging along? Being a third wheel is no fun, trust me," he said teasingly.

"It's not actually a date," she sighed. "Just three friends hanging out."

"Yeah right," he snorted with disbelief.

"Tell me about it," she said with feeling.

"Anyway, text me where I should pick you up," he said, laughing at her tone.

"Will do. Bye Derek."

She found Riya standing in the balcony, clutching the rails tightly, her breathing ragged. She touched her gently on the shoulder. "Something's eating away at you. Spill."

Riya spun around to face her. "You must think I'm acting like a silly child," she said softly.

"No I don't," Shalini replied. "Look, what happened to you was terrible. Nobody deserves to go through that. Not even Sanjana," she smiled. "After that, it's extremely difficult to trust someone enough to have a relationship with him. I understand your reticence. But you have a choice here, sweetie. You can let the past haunt you and rule your life forever or you can beat the demons back and give yourself a chance at a happy life. It's upto you. I'm not saying you hand over your heart to Anup straight away, but at least give him a chance and see how it goes."

"I will, when I'm ready. Right now, I don't want to be alone with him. He sees right through my barriers and that ... unsettles me," she finished. "That's why I asked you to accompany me."

"It's not a problem with me," said Shalini, empathizing with her friend's pain. "You know I'll always be here for you, though I may give you a difficult time about it sometimes."

"Thank you," she said. "And I mean it. Don't make any smart-ass comments, please."

Shalini laughed. "I'll head downstairs now and get ready."

"Alright," Riya walked with Shalini up to the elevator and was relieved to see others inside the car. She waved and walked back into her flat to get ready.

Half an hour later, Shalini heard the doorbell ring and guessed it was probably Riya. She opened the door with the chain lock on and then flung the door open for Riya to enter and wrinkled her nose in distaste at the taller girl's attire, a severely conservative dark blue salwar-kameez with a dupatta thick enough to be a small blanket. Her hair was pulled back tightly into a bun and she had chosen to wear her spectacles instead of her normal contacts. The whole ensemble made her look ten years older than her age. Shalini herself was dressed in a fitted aquamarine blue top with cap sleeves over black jeans which fitted her snugly and her wavy hair was bobbing and bouncing prettily every time she moved her head. "Who are you and what have you done with Riya Batra?" she asked by way of greeting. She was met with silence as Riya pushed past her into the living room. Shalini followed her in, but did not let the subject drop. She knew that her dear friend had many such disgustingly horrible pieces and avatars in her kitty for occasions which any other normal self-respecting, red-blooded young lady would have used as an excuse for shopping at the most exclusive designer boutiques.

"Whose funeral are we attending?" she asked sarcastically.

"Don't be a jerk," Riya snapped. "I don't want to give Anup any wrong ideas."

"And what would this wrong idea be, exactly?" she stood with her hands on her hips, refusing to let the matter drop. "Enlighten me, please."

"I don't want him to think I'm stringing him along," she said dryly.

"And dressing up like a widow is going to convey that?" Shalini shook her head in frustration. "That approach would work if all he wanted was a quick roll in the sack, but he's in love with who you are, Ri. I'm hundred percent sure of that. And no matter how you dress, that's not going to change," she said sensibly. Her normally smart friend seemed to have lost a few vital brain cells and was acting like a complete loon. "Besides, you have been beating me over the head with the fact that he wants to be just friends so often that I'm sick of it. So there really isn't any need to look like you're in perpetual mourning. Not to mention that any self-respecting young man would rather NOT be seen with any lady friend who goes around dressed like that!"

"I guess you're right," she conceded reluctantly.

"Of course I'm right. So why don't you change into something which doesn't resemble sackcloth and ashes?"

"There's no time," she said stubbornly.

"The hell there isn't," Shalini snapped. "Your cream tights are here. You can wear that with the black top Anita gave me," she dragged her reluctant friend into her bedroom and shoved the clothes she described into her hands. "Change quickly. I don't want to be looking at the Walking Dead all evening. And while you're at it, be kind enough to take down that ridiculous-looking hairdo and try to look young and alive, not like an eighty-nine-year-old with one foot in the grave, will you?"

Riya did not bother to reply to the sardonic words, knowing full well that her friend was right. She shooed Shalini out of the room and shut the door and started to change. Once she was dressed, she took out the pins holding her hair in place and let the silky curls hang in cascading waves down her back. She couldn't do much about the spectacles, but when Riya glanced at the mirror, she felt she looked a lot better than she had done fifteen minutes ago. She left the bedroom and joined her friend in the living room who gave an appraising look and finally nodded in satisfaction.

"Much better," Shalini said approvingly. "You look stylish and elegant."

"Thank you for your approval," Riya said snidely.

"Anytime," her friend shrugged nonchalantly, apparently not noticing Riya's unpleasant tone. "For a very smart girl, you can be incredibly dumb at times."

Riya flipped her the bird. At that moment, her mobile rang. It was Anup, telling her he was waiting in the driveway. The girls quickly locked up and headed downstairs, where they found him sitting behind the wheel of his black Renault Duster. Shalini tried to push Riya into the passenger seat, but she successfully repelled the attempt and Shalini had to get in beside Anup to avoid a scene. She rolled her eyes heavenward, but did not make any comment. The look of disappointment on Anup's face was priceless.

"Where are we going?" asked Riya pleasantly.

"It's a surprise," said Anup, smiling.

"Oh, please tell us. I have to text Derek so he can pick me up after dinner," chimed in Shalini.

"Planets and Stars, the newly opened pub cum restaurant," he said, giving in with a wry smile.

"What a coincidence. Derek took me to Gatsby 2000 last night and you're taking us to another pub tonight. What's it with you foreign-educated guys and hip places?" she teased.

"We're going only to the restaurant tonight," he said, smiling at Riya's reflection in the rearview mirror. "But yes, we foreign-returns like to pamper our lady friends."

"So how do you usually spend your weekends?" Riya asked, determined to be pleasant and sociable and not show her nervousness. *Just friends*, she told herself through gritted teeth.

"Talk to my family occasionally, ride my bike around and paint," he replied warmly.

"You're an artist?" Riya could not hide the surprise in her voice.

He laughed self-deprecatingly. "I wouldn't call myself that. I dabble in art as a hobby."

"What sort of paintings do you usually do?" she was genuinely interested now. Shalini sighed inwardly with relief. She had been afraid she would have to do most of the talking to fill awkward silences. While that wouldn't have posed a problem, she much preferred for Riya to do the talking. Quickly, she texted Derek where they were headed and sat back and listened to the car radio.

"Landscapes and seascapes mostly, but sometimes I do portraits and still-lifes too," he said, warming up to the topic.

"Can I see them?" Art was one of Riya's passions.

"Sure, I'll take you to my place one day," he offered.

"Let's see," she answered vaguely.

Anup knew she was retreating back into her shell and he tried to stop her from doing that. "What about you?" he asked. "Are you interested in art?"

"Oh yes! I paint landscapes and sometimes, portraits. I'm also quite good at handicrafts and glass painting."

"Great!" said Anup enthusiastically, quickly recovering his good mood. "Then maybe you can accompany me to art shows sometime."

"Maybe," she smiled. She did not see any harm in that. Besides, it might be fun. They continued their artsy conversation till they reached the restaurant. Meanwhile, Shalini fiddled around with the music system for a while and finding nothing to her taste, started listening to her iPod, effectively tuning out the animated discussion taking place right next to her. She was incapable of drawing anything that looked like it's supposed to even if her life depended on it!

When they reached the restaurant, Riya grabbed Shalini's hand as they went inside. "Having a good time?" Shalini queried.

"So far so good," Riya answered noncommittally. "If he doesn't cross the boundaries of friendship, we'll be good."

Shalini wanted to say something, but wisely kept her opinions to herself. The restaurant was nearly dark, illuminated only by soft blue lights, which gave the impression of being in a twilight zone. It was quite a romantic setting. They were shown to a table in a secluded corner, which afforded them a measure of privacy. "Drinks anyone?" Anup asked.

"A glass of white wine for me," said Riya promptly.

"And I shall have a cocktail. Let's see. Along Island iced tea I think," said Shalini after hesitating for a moment. Riya squeezed her hand beneath the table.

Anup ordered the drinks, which was brought over promptly by a smartly dressed waiter. Riya and Anup studied their menus for a while before placing their order. Just as their starters arrived, Shalini's phone rang. It was Derek. "Hey," she greeted him.

"I'm picking you up in fifteen minutes," he said without a greeting.

"But we just arrived," Shalini protested, though she was happy to hear from him. "I thought you were picking me up later on."

"Change of plans," he said mysteriously.

"At least let me finish dinner," she whined.

"I'll join you guys for a drink, then I'm dragging you out of there whether you've finished eating or not," he was insistent.

"Alright," she caved. "Then get your backside here."

"On my way, princess," he grinned and ended the call.

Riya looked at the bemused expression on her friend's face. "What's up?" she asked.

"Derek's picking me up in fifteen minutes," she responded.

"What?" Riya was stunned. "But you can't leave! We just got here!"

"Tell my brand spanking-new boyfriend that," Shalini shot back.

"Of course Shalini can leave," Anup joined the conversation. "I brought you here and I'll take you home. Don't worry, I'll get you back home before midnight so that you don't turn into a pumpkin!"

His attempt at humor earned him a withering look from Shalini, but he was rewarded with a gorgeous smile from Riya who found the remark very amusing. They finished the starters by then and the waiter served their main course. Just as they were halfway through the meal, Derek arrived and joined them at their table, taking the vacant seat next to Anup. He waved the waiter over and ordered coffee.

Shalini gave him a quizzical look. "Coffee?" she queried. "You don't want to have a glass of wine?"

"I don't drink and drive," he explained. "Even if it's a single glass of wine. Especially with you in the car, it's a risk I'm not willing to take."

"Ahh," nodded Shalini as if Derek had just explained the meaning of life to her. "I'm precious cargo, of course." This earned her a "yeah, right" look from Riya, who was used to Shalini's overly dramatic ways, and an amused smile from Derek, who was learning something new about Shalini every time they interacted. Anup just shrugged. This conversation obviously did not concern him.

Unbeknownst to the two girls, Derek had decided to pick Shalini up earlier than he had planned to give Riya and Anup a chance to be alone with each other. Also, he had wanted Shalini to himself for a while before she started another work week the next day.

Riya looked at her in amusement. The girl had forgotten her table manners and was shoveling the food into her mouth as fast as she could. She was done in a matter of minutes and decided to skip dessert. "Let's go," she pushed back her chair and stood up.

"Alright," Derek agreed. They waved good-bye to Riya and Anup and walked off hand-in-hand.

CHAPTER 14

Once they were in Derek's car, Shalini turned to him and smiled. "Thank you for getting me out of there," she said. "Riya's my friend and I couldn't say no to her when she asked me to join them for dinner. This way, they get some time alone with each other and I don't get killed. Win-win situation!" She clapped her hands with glee. "Well, for me anyway," she added with a wicked smile.

"You're the most crooked person I know!" Derek shook his head in amusement. "But I love you anyway!"

"I take that as a compliment," she grinned.

"Anyway, I'll be happy to rescue you anytime, princess," he smiled. "Now where to?"

"How would I know?" retorted Shalini. "You pulled me out of there before I could have dessert, so now take me someplace where we can get delicious ice-cream."

She was pouting and looked incredibly cute. It took all of Derek's self-possession not to kiss her right there and then. "As you wish, my dear," he acquiesced instead and drove to Svenzen's on utthamar Gandhi Road, an ice-cream parlor known for its delightful flavors.

"Have you had dinner?" she asked, remembering she wasn't the only one with a stomach.

"Yes," he said. "I got together with a few friends and we decided to have an early dinner. Do you want to catch a movie after we're done with the ice-cream?"

"I don't know," she hesitated, looking uncertain and nervous.

"Don't worry," he said reassuringly. "Trust me."

"I do," she said quietly. "Believe me, I really do."

"Good," he smiled. "So ice-cream and a movie it is then."

As they drove along, she asked, "Which church do you go to?"

"All To Jesus in Anna Nagar. What about you?"

"All Saints," she answered. "But these past few months, I have switched over to a small, independent church. It's called Christ In Us."

"I used to go to Christ Church, but not to worry. The Almighty will understand," he smiled at her. "After all, independent churches are also part of the body of Christ."

"That's true. Therefore, He better understand," she grinned back at him. "My parents keep on giving me crap about the preachings in my church. They are old-fashioned and don't really like it that I have left the organized fold."

"Lecturing is their job," he replied as they drove on.

❋ ❋ ❋

Riya was fiddling with the cutlery, pushing the food around with her fork and spoon, rearranging the contents of her plate quite artlessly for an artistic person. Anup was staring at her, concern evident in his brilliant blue eyes.

"What's wrong?" he asked finally.

"Nothing," she mumbled.

"Riya," he sighed. "Perhaps this wasn't such a great idea. If being alone with me is making you so uncomfortable, I'll take you home. Finish your food." He sounded disappointed and slightly irritated. He was a decent, well-behaved young man, but Ms. Batra behaving as if he was the world's biggest rogue and womanizer was starting to annoy him a little bit, but not enough to give up on her and walk away.

Riya looked up from her plate, which had held her undivided attention since Shalini's premature departure. "No," she said at last. "I'm sorry. I know I'm probably not being good company just now. Let's finish dinner and go for a walk."

"Really?" Anup asked cautiously, not wanting to get his hopes up just yet.

"Yes," she smiled. "Really. Friends take walks together, don't they?"

"Sure they do," he smiled back, unable to hide the note of relief in his voice. "Now will you please stop pushing the food around and actually start eating it? And what would you like for dessert?"

"Chocolate soufflé," she said promptly and made a sincere attempt to finish the food on her plate.

Once they finished dinner, Anup paid the bill despite Riya's protests and they exited the restaurant together. "You can pay next time we go out," he said in an attempt to appease her. She nodded grumpily, which made him laugh. Riya was one independent chick and quite proud of it too, but that was one of the things he loved about her.

He drove towards Alwarpet, intending to park the car in the visitor's parking area of Riya's apartment complex and then take her for a walk. They reached her place in less than half an hour and got out of the car.

"You can go home if you want," he said magnanimously. "No pressure to take a walk with me."

"Don't give me a chance to change my mind," Riya smiled ruefully. "Let's go for a walk. Let it not be said that Riya Batra reneged on her promise."

"Well, when you put it that way..." his eyes twinkled. "Nobody should be allowed to say that about my good friend! She, after all, is a woman of her word. Come on."

They walked side by side inside the compound, talking in a low murmur. Anup wanted to hold her hand, but restrained himself. He did not want to scare her off just as she was starting to show signs of thawing a little around him. "Where does your family live?" he asked.

"My dad's currently posted in Assam and my mom's with him. He's a colonel in the Indian Army," she explained.

"That sounds interesting and quite exciting. You must have traveled a lot while growing up," he observed.

"Oh yeah," she said, her eyes dancing with excitement. "Sometimes, he was posted in really remote places, but my siblings and I enjoyed it a lot."

"So what do they do now? Your siblings I mean."

"My brother is a mechanical engineer currently working in Germany and my sister is a speech therapist in Mumbai."

"Sounds like an interesting family," he commented. "They're younger to you?"

"No," she smiled. "I'm the youngest. And the brattiest I should say."

He laughed heartily at that. "I have no two way doubts about it! Do you like living in Chennai?"

"Yes," she answered. "I have always liked Chennai. It's a big city, but not so big that getting from one place to another takes hours, like it does in Mumbai. The weather proves to be a bit too much at times, but nothing that I can't handle. In recent times, the social scene has also undergone revolutionary changes. My dad was posted here for a year when I was a kid and I fell in love with the place. I have always wanted to settle down in Chennai or Bangalore, and when I got admission to the MBA program at Indian Institute of Management, Bangalore, I jumped at it. Then InfoSoft MicroTech offered me a great job and lucrative package and posted me in Chennai and well, the rest, as they say, is history," she smiled. "I'm happy that I got the opportunity to live and work here. This place is home now."

"The city does have its own unique character," Anup agreed. "What about your mother?"

"Well, she teaches school off and on. With the sort of nomadic life she has led all through her married life, her career has kind of taken a backseat. But these days, she's quite busy freelancing as an interior decorator."

"That's very good."

"What about you? Isn't Jaipur your hometown?"

"Native, yes," he responded. "But I was born and brought up in Bangalore for a while, then we moved to Chennai when I was about twelve, so this is my hometown now."

"You've got a younger sister I believe?" queried Riya. By virtue of being in Human Resources, she could access any employee's personal records. And for obvious reasons, she had studied Anup's file quite thoroughly indeed.

"Yes. She's completing school this year and wants to study fashion designing."

"Cool!" exclaimed Riya. "I always wanted to do that, but well, circumstances made me an HR professional. So all of you are artistic in your family?"

"Not really," he smiled. "My dad cannot write or paint or do anything creative even if his life depended on it. He's a mathematician, so everything in life is about numbers and equations for him."

"He's a professor?" she asked.

"Yes, and he does his own research as well."

"And your mother?"

"She's a doctor."

"Your family sounds interesting, not to mention highly qualified and accomplished."

"Well, yeah, but it was quite lonely growing up there. My parents were always busy and it was just me and my sister most of the time. While I was in my teens, she was still a kid. And then I went to the US to study at MIT and we sort of drifted apart."

"Oh," she said. "You're living with them now I suppose?"

"No, when I returned to India, I got my own place. My sister and I have reconnected, but things are still awkward between me and my parents," he said, a faraway look in his eyes.

"Bridge the gap," Riya said quietly. "None of us are going to live forever. Talk to them, mend whatever fences need mending and let everybody be happy."

"Sure," he snorted. "Clapping with one hand is impossible, as you probably know. As for mending fences, they have to be around long enough to help."

"You can always start the process and they'll soon follow," argued Riya, not caring if she was stepping into sensitive territory.

"If they even notice," he huffed.

"Don't be such a stubborn, cynical jerk!" she shot back at him.

He suddenly smiled. "You look quite lovely when you're riled up like that! Like a beautiful tigress with her claws out."

"You ain't seen nothing yet," she grinned. "You should see me when I'm *really* telling somebody off! Ask Shalini. She'll tell you that I'm a certified dragon who breathes fire! But seriously, try to patch things up with your parents."

"I'll try," he said. They had stopped walking and now stood facing each other. "We should do this again sometime," he said quietly. "Talking to you is... reinvigorating."

"Yes," she agreed. "I feel the same talking to you. And I'm sorry about freezing you out earlier."

"It's alright," he waved off her apology. "Are you free sometime next week?"

"Not during the week," she hedged. "I'm free Friday evening."

"Good, I'll take you to my place then. Bring Shalini along if you wish," he said with a quirky smile.

"Thanks. I'll do so, provided she doesn't have prior plans," she said cautiously. "If she does, can we postpone it to Saturday?"

"Sure," he said agreeably. He was willing to put up with Shalini for as long as it took to get Riya to feel comfortable around him. He didn't want to push her too far too soon and risk triggering her flight instincts. No sir-ee. He had told her they were just friends and that's how it would stay for now.

"I had a good time," she said, her head cocked to one side and a half-smile on her lips. "Thank you."

"I should be thanking you," he retorted.

"I better get back home now," she said.

"Okay," he agreed reluctantly, disappointed that their time together was drawing to a close. "I'll walk you up to your apartment."

"That won't be necessary," she said hurriedly. "Good night Anup."

And she waved goodbye to him and walked inside the building and disappeared from view in a few seconds. He waved back and headed to his car, shaking his head at her mercurial moods. She had been so friendly and then suddenly, she had become closed off for some unfathomable reason. He shook his head slowly. All he had suggested was that he walk her up to her flat. It wasn't as if he had made any inappropriate suggestions. He let out a deep sigh, then got behind the wheel and drove off. Figuring out a woman was not something that could be accomplished in one night after all. Greater minds had been bamboozled by them throughout history. And the woman he had chosen was more complicated than the problems of many countries. She was a complete conundrum, an enigma. He wondered if he would ever be able to figure her out.

CHAPTER 15

The next day, Riya woke up at seven, feeling like she had been run over by a freight train, which was not an unusual occurrence, but last night, she had gone to bed in good spirits and had therefore, expected a peaceful night. This however, had not been the case. Her nightmares had been haunting her again, but she hadn't wanted to disturb Shalini last night. For one thing, she wasn't sure at what time her friend had gotten back from her date with Derek and for another, she hadn't been in the mood to answer any more questions. Her weekend, which was supposed to be a period of rest and relaxation, had turned out to be anything but. Her emotions were all over the place. Her past haunting her in her sleep and her present conflicting emotions about Anup had caused a very restless night. Instead of feeling refreshed and ready to tackle the challenges of the coming week, she was feeling tired and irritable. But she pushed the exhaustion aside as she got out of bed, trying to get her game face on to tackle the challenges of the day ahead. She wished she could call in sick, but knew that several fires had to be put out and she couldn't afford the luxury of sleeping in. Besides, they had to update Shashi Kiran about the progress they had made on the competency project and he would be worried if he heard that she was sick and if he could, send in a fleet of doctors to keep an eye on her. She quickly took a shower and got dressed in a pair of brown trousers and cream shirt which fit snugly around her willowy frame, then went into the kitchen, made some coffee and placed two pieces of whole wheat bread in the pop-out toaster. She had neither the time nor the inclination to prepare an elaborate breakfast, so she waited until the pieces of toast popped out, then placed them in a plate and grabbed her coffee mug and went into the living room where she finished her breakfast as quickly as possible, then texted Shalini, asking her if she was ready to leave. Once she received an affirmative reply, she quickly rinsed her coffee mug and plate, grabbed her purse and car keys, locked the apartment and left.

She met up with Shalini, impeccably clad in a pair of black trousers and white full-sleeved shirt, on the second floor. They went downstairs and out into the parking garage and got into Riya's Skoda and drove off to office, trying to beat the morning rush-hour.

"So how was last night?" she asked Shalini.

"Great!" Shalini grinned. "He took me out for ice-cream and then we watched 'Conjuring 2.' He was a perfect gentleman the whole time."

"Meaning he didn't try to put the moves on you. Good. I think the guy's in for the long haul, but it's better to be cautious. I'm happy for you, short stuff," Riya smiled to see her friend looking so happy and radiant. "So how do you feel in his company?"

"Safe," said Shalini promptly. That one small word speaking volumes. "Well taken care of, protected, loved. And dreamy when he kisses me."

"Great," she hadn't labeled him a nerd, weirdo, psychopath or a moron yet. This was a good sign and Riya was pleased to hear her sounding positive about a man for once. She decided to question her later about the kissing part.

"What about you?" asked Shalini. "Did you run screaming for the hills as soon as I left the restaurant?"

"Not quite," said Riya with a cheeky grin.

"Let me guess," said Shalini in a theatrical manner. "You pushed the food around and around in your plate until he lost patience and hurled his cutlery at you. Or better yet, perhaps he beat you over the head with his plate." She looked hopeful. "All the things I wanna do to you, but cannot!"

"Wrong again," Riya was still grinning. "But you're right about the pushing the food around part. He asked me what was wrong, then offered to take me home if I was feeling uncomfortable."

"And you jumped at the chance of course," sighed Shalini, knowing her friend and her likely reactions quite well.

"Well, wrong again, Wisey. He brought me home, then instead of shaking hands with him and heading straight upstairs as you probably expect, we took a walk inside our apartment complex."

"A walk?" Shalini could not hide the surprise from her voice. "Let me get this straight. By walk, do you mean a proper walk or are you referring to you running away and him trying to catch you?"

"Oh, ye of little faith," Riya smiled sardonically. "Prepare to be surprised. We went for a proper walk."

Shalini was looking at her with evident disbelief. "You managed not to freak out, freak him out or cause bodily harm to the poor sucker and actually took a walk with the guy?"

"Yes," said Riya, looking pleased with herself. "See? I'm not a complete evil ogress after all!"

"Not so fast," retorted Shalini. "What did you do during this walk of yours?"

"We talked."

"About?"

"His family and mine. It seems he rarely talks to his parents. I told him he should patch things up with them and—"

"In other words," interrupted Shalini unceremoniously, "you gave him grand-motherly advice."

"*Friendly* advice," she corrected.

"Whatever. It all translates as lecturing," shrugged Shalini. "Then?"

"Well, he invited me to his place on Friday and said I could bring you too if I wanted."

"Now we're getting somewhere," muttered Shalini.

"I told him I'd like that and if you're not free on Friday, we'll shift it to Saturday. He agreed."

"Fantastic!" cried Shalini sarcastically. "Why exactly would *I* want to visit his place when I might have better use for my time?"

"Because you're my friend and I said so," said Riya, looking smug and self-satisfied.

"Riiiiiiiight," she drawled. "What happened then?"

"He offered to walk me upstairs and I said no, bade goodbye and went on my way."

"Of course you did," Shalini snorted. "He doesn't seem like the type who jumps a woman in her flat, or anywhere else for that matter, you know. He doesn't have 'sex criminal' written all over him."

"Yeah I know that," said Riya patiently. "But we're just friends, remember? I don't want him to think I'm sending him mixed signals."

Riya and her obsession with mixed signals! Hopeless! Shalini shook her head and was about to ask what 'mixed signals' could possibly be sent by letting Anup walk her up to her flat, but just then, they reached the sprawling complex which held the offices of InfoSoft MicroTech, having managed to beat the rush-hour traffic.

Muthu, the friendly security guard who was on day-shift waved them through. The office building was an imposing seven-storey structure housing various departments of the company and a cafeteria whose standards rivaled those of any modern high-end restaurant. The complex also had a large landscaped garden with a well-maintained fountain, a large parking lot with designated parking spaces and an indoor sports complex with a well-maintained indoor swimming pool, state-of-the art gym, indoor facilities to play basketball, tennis, squash and badminton and a room with tables for playing pool, snooker and billiards. The sports and fitness center had been constructed as a means to counter stress and thereby avoid employee burnout. People could be seen in the center when they come off shifts or before they begin their workday. All in all, the entire office complex was impressive and the two girls were immensely proud to be a part of all of it.

Riya parked the car in her designated spot and they entered the main building, whose sleek, modern exterior complemented the plush, cool interior perfectly. A thickly carpeted lobby, where a receptionist was seated behind a large desk, led to gleaming chrome-and-glass doors which would open to admit one person at a time only after their InfoSoft MicroTech ID was flashed. The chairman and board of directors of the company had thought of switching over to a retina scan as a means to ensure that only authorized personnel were permitted to enter in all the company's offices around the world a few years back, but had finally concluded that it would be security overkill, and the idea was put on the back-burner for now. Visitors could enter into the building only after they had been cleared by security.

The girls entered one after another. They had arrived quite early and found only a few people milling around or at their cubicles. They got into an elevator and pressed the button for the fifth floor, which housed the HR and Domestic Projects sections. When the elevator doors opened, they walked into a lobby furnished with plush, comfortable couches and a coffee table. Just as in the main lobby, a receptionist was seated behind a desk. The attractive young woman in her early twenties waved at them and they waved back at her and smiled. They pushed open another set of chrome-and-glass doors and walked through a well-lit corridor to their respective cabins.

"We have to assemble our ideas to present to Mr. Kiran," said Shalini in a hushed voice. "Right now, it's a jumbled mess."

"I know. Let's iron out the details of the upcoming campus recruitment drive as soon as we can so that we can focus on the other stuff."

"Won't he be angry if he finds out we were working on that in the office when we're not supposed to?" queried Shalini anxiously.

"Oh, stop being such a dummy! I won't tell him and neither will you," she snapped, fixing her with a look hot enough to make icebergs evaporate.

The effort was wasted on Shalini, who shrugged, unimpressed by her friend's display of irritation. She went into her cabin and powered on her PC and then brought up a spreadsheet containing a list of colleges where they were planning to conduct campus recruitment drives in the next few months. Names and contact numbers of placement cell co-ordinators were listed against each college and Shalini started calling them one by one, confirming the dates on which the company would be visiting their campuses to conduct recruitment exercises.

Meanwhile, Riya was haranguing with the psychometric institute to which the company outsourced the task of preparing the questions which would be used for the written tests. They should have been in her mailbox as well as on her desk before she had arrived, but so far, there was no sign and the person on the other end of the phone was either super-idiotic or trying to be over-smart. She had time for neither and gave him a piece of her mind. In fifteen minutes, the attachment arrived in her mailbox.

After putting out this fire, she created a spreadsheet containing the names of various departmental representatives who would be accompanying HR representatives to each college. This required a lot of patient bargaining on her part and the promise of added incentives for being part of the recruitment process before she could convince them to come on board.

By the time both the girls finished, it was twelve-thirty. Shalini's desk phone rang and it was Riya telling her to get the tablet and meet her in the ladies' room. Shalini was sick of talking on the phone by then and did not need to be asked twice. She quickly grabbed the tablet and the GPS-enabled cane and went to the ladies' room, where she found Riya waiting. The two girls did not speak, instead sitting side by side as they got down to business. It would soon be their lunch hour and they hoped their documentation would be complete before the break ended. Neither of them particularly relished the idea of skipping lunch.

Some of the women stared at them quizzically as they came and went, but no questions were asked and the girls did not volunteer any information. To their immense relief, Sanjana did not visit the ladies' room on their floor. An encounter with her was not something either of them particularly wanted, especially not then.

They quickly brought up the spreadsheets and documents they had worked over the weekend and prepared a preliminary project proposal using the data at their disposal.

It was one-thirty by the time they finished. They knew the document was very rough and would look completely different by the time Shashi Kiran was done with it. Riya thought of mailing it to him, but decided it would keep till the evening. Then, both of them stood up and headed down to the cafeteria, where they found Sreeja and Samyukta just finishing their lunch.

"Some people are late," Sreeja remarked. "And I thought you were never late where food is concerned."

"Work comes first," retorted Riya with a straight face.

"Yeah right," Sreeja snorted mockingly.

The girls did not bother to respond and concentrated on filling their plates. They got back to the table just as the other two women were about to leave.

"Why don't you sit with us till we finish?" Shalini invited.

"Sure thing," said Sreeja, sitting right back down.

"I have to get back," said Samyukta regretfully. "The boss is being bossy today."

"Happens," said Riya sympathetically. "See you later."

Sreeja looked at Shalini keenly, whose face was glowing and eyes were shining despite the exertions of the morning. "Who's the guy?" she asked with a knowing smile.

"What guy?" Shalini responded, the epitome of sweetness and innocence.

"Oh c'mon!" Sreeja exclaimed. "It's written all over you! If it's not a guy, then you hit the jackpot and got your hands on a few crores over the weekend. Which is it?"

Riya was grinning wickedly at her friend's discomfort, who was squirming in her seat. "Oh I'd say she got both this weekend. A hot guy who's also stinking rich." If looks could kill, Riya would have instantly dropped dead in her chair by the death glare Shalini was shooting her.

Sreeja's eyes widened. "Details!" she demanded. "Who's this guy?"

"Derek Mathews," Shalini mumbled, wilting under Sreeja's intense scrutiny. "We went out a couple of times. That's all."

"Derek Mathews, Chairman and Managing Director of Mathews & Company? The hunk who keeps dropping in here from time to time?" Sreeja queried.

"The one and only," chimed in Riya helpfully.

Sreeja looked at Shalini thoughtfully. "He was here last Friday, wasn't he?"

"Yes, on business," said Shalini somewhat defensively.

"Believe what you want, sweetheart. Any one of his higher-level minions could have handled the negotiations. I believe he keeps coming here to see you."

"I'm sure I don't know what you're talking about," she said, trying to sound noncommittal.

"Continue to be blissfully ignorant if you choose," Sreeja waved her off. "Tall, dark, handsome and rich," sang out Sreeja. "When you hook 'em, you *really* hook 'em, don't you madam?"

"I didn't hook him!" Shalini spluttered. "He lives in the same building as us and he asked me out, not the other way around!"

"Same difference," Sreeja shrugged. "I have spoken to him once or twice. He's quite smart."

"Yes he is," said Shalini in a softer tone. "And while we're on the topic of manhunting, Riya here got asked out too." This time, it was Riya who went on the offensive, pointing her fork at Shalini with murderous intent.

"By Anup Sharma no doubt," said Sreeja matter-of-factly.

"Yep," confirmed Shalini. Riya was looking elsewhere, trying to pretend she wasn't there.

"And did you put him out of his misery finally and say yes?" asked Sreeja with an impish grin. Anup's attraction towards Riya was well-known all over the office.

"We're just friends!" Riya shot out, annoyed.

"Right," said Sreeja, rolling her eyes. "Whatever you say, love."

"It's the truth!" Riya said hotly.

"Sure," said Sreeja, laughing. "No need to get wound up, my dear. And for the record, I didn't fall off the pumpkin wagon yesterday! Come on girls. Let's get back to work. We'll continue this discussion later."

"Fine by me," said Riya with obvious relief.

CHAPTER 16

Riya caught up with Shalini as they reached their cabins. "Why did you have to open your big fat mouth and tell the whole world about my personal life?" she demanded. She was looking like an angry pit bull, ready to tear down everything in her path.

"Relax," said Shalini calmly, unfazed by her irate friend. "Anup would have trumpeted it to the entire office by now anyway, and besides, I only told Sreeja, not the whole world. Because sweetie, believe it or not, the whole world doesn't really care one way or another who you see or don't see. So don't flatter yourself. And anyway, you've made it perfectly and *sickeningly* clear that the two of you are just friends. So what's the big deal?"

"Let's get back to work," Riya snapped, not bothering to answer the question. She knew that Shalini was right and that was irritating her even more.

"Gladly," muttered Shalini.

Fifteen minutes after they returned from their lunch break, Riya's desk phone rang. "Riya Batra," she said in a clipped, formal tone.

"Get hold of Shalini and come to my office," said Shashi Kiran in his usual laconic way.

"Yes, sir."

She called Shalini. "Boss is calling."

"Coming," Shalini responded, locked her computer screen and joined her friend. "Sorry about earlier," she murmured.

"It's alright. And I'm sorry for snapping at you," said Riya generously.

"Water under the bridge," Shalini waved off the apology. "Let's see what the boss has to say."

They entered Shashi Kiran's cabin together. His expression was unreadable. "Sit," he gestured towards the chairs in front of his desk. They sat down and stared expectantly at him.

"How's the campus recruitment drive shaping up?" he asked.

It took a moment for the girls to switch gears and it was Riya who answered first. "The questions are ready, all neatly packaged and in place," she said and for the next ten minutes, the girls took turns to explain the preparations made for the upcoming campus recruitment exercise covering top colleges in the major southern cities of Bangalore, Chennai, Kochi and Hyderabad.

"Why aren't we covering colleges in tier two cities?" queried Shalini.

"That's phase two," Shashi told her. "We'll be doing that next month."

"Alright," she said and leaned back in her seat. "When are you going to discuss the contents of the e-mails we sent yesterday?" she demanded. "They are quite rough, but—"

"We agreed not to discuss that in office," he cut her off coldly.

Shalini hadn't expected him to get angry over her question and shrank back. "Sorry sir," she mumbled.

Shashi smiled. "Relax," he said. "I'll say this much. I'm impressed by what I have seen so far. Keep working on those lines. What Riya is suggesting is incredible, but I want a feasibility report on that. I'll mark the revisions and changes I expect and mail it back to both of you. It's up to you to decide whether all that is possible. Now run along and make sure everything is ready for the recruitment exercise. It starts on Wednesday and I don't want any issues or glitches cropping up at the last moment."

"Yes sir," said Riya with a smile. "It'll be perfect to a fault. You can count on us."

"I always do," he smiled.

The girls walked out of his cabin to their own seats and carried on with their tasks throughout the afternoon. Finally, at four-thirty Riya stretched back in her seat and closed her eyes for a moment. Everything was ready from her end. She called Shalini's desk phone. "How's it going?" she asked.

"All set and ready to roll," she responded. "I have tied up all the loose ends I can think of. I expect we shouldn't have any problems."

"Let's hope nothing crops up at the last moment," said Riya.

"Yeah, me too," replied Shalini. Her mobile started to chirp a lively tune. "I have to go. Derek's calling."

She dropped the receiver back in its cradle and answered the call on her mobile. "Hey," she greeted him.

"Hey yourself," she could hear the smile in his voice. "What are you up to?"

"Just boring office stuff. What about you?"

"We just landed a pretty big account," he said cheerfully. "Good money, not to mention a very reputable client."

"Good for you!" she whooped.

"Thank you, pretty girl," he said.

"You're most welcome," she grinned.

"What are you doing in the evening?" he asked.

"I have some work to do, but I should be done by eight. Why?"

"I want to go out and celebrate with you," he said, sounding happy.

"Umm," said Shalini. "I have been eating out for three nights in a row now. Why don't you come down to my place and I'll make a simple dinner for us and we can hang out?"

"You serious?" he asked. "I'm game for anything as long as you're part of the deal."

"I am," she confirmed, her grin growing wider. "Meet me at my place at eight then."

"Yes ma'am," his tone was playful now.

"Good. Now go back to minting crores while we salaried people trudge along."

"You'll be the death of me, princess!" Laughing, he said goodbye and ended the call. Shalini couldn't wipe the goofy grin off her face for the rest of the day. She was still grinning when Riya came into her cabin at a quarter to six.

"Ready to leave?" she asked, then noticed the smile. "What's that big cheesy thing plastered across your face?"

"I'm ready," said Shalini with a smirk. "And I'm sure I don't know what you're talking about."

"Of course you don't!" snorted Riya. "Tell me what's up."

"Derek called. He's meeting me at home around eight to celebrate."

"Celebrate what?" Riya asked, staring at her blankly.

"His company just landed a big account."

"Wonderful. That means we have to finish work on the project before he comes over at eight," said Riya thoughtfully.

"No. It means *I* have to finish work before then. You can continue working into the night," said Shalini as if clarifying something important. "Unless of course, your 'friend' Anup has something planned for the both of you."

Riya stared at her, but did not say anything. Sarcasm would be wasted on the other girl and any angry retort would be met with an irritating, all-knowing smile. So she decided not to spoil her mood and let it go. Shalini quickly powered off her PC, grabbed her purse and joined her friend as they left the office.

They stopped for groceries on the way home and both of them were lugging heavy bags as they entered the apartment building. "What I wouldn't give to have a fleet of servants at my beck and call!" sighed Shalini.

Riya did not respond, having heard this often enough in the past. "Your place or mine?" she asked instead.

"Mine," she replied.

They got off on the second floor and walked into Shalini's flat. Riya dumped her grocery bags in a corner of the living room while Shalini put away her supplies in the kitchen and refrigerator. By seven-fifteen, they were in Shalini's bedroom, hunched over their laptops.

"What are you working on?" asked Shalini.

"I'm doing a feasibility analysis of what we discussed," said Riya. "I want to complete it by Wednesday or Thursday. If he gives us the go-ahead after seeing that, we can start putting the package together. What about you?"

"I'm developing detailed data flow diagrams depicting the conceptual part," she explained.

"You can do that?" asked Riya, not hiding her surprise.

"Recently learnt how to. The latest version of my screen-reading software is a dream come true," Shalini said without further explanation.

"Quite impressive," muttered Riya.

"Yeah, thanks to advances in technology," agreed Shalini.

After that, they worked in silence for the next forty-five minutes. Then Riya said, "I'm mailing you what I have done so far. Then I'm going home to continue."

"Fine," said Shalini, looking up and rubbing her eyes. "I'll go wash my face, freshen up a bit before he shows up."

"Prettying up? Good idea," Riya nodded seriously. "You don't want to scare him off too soon." She nimbly moved out of the way to dodge the pillow hurled at her, left the room and showed herself out of the apartment.

CHAPTER 17

Derek came to Shalini's apartment at eight-fifteen, casually dressed in a pair of Bermuda shorts and a V-neck t-shirt, which showed off his well-toned, athletic frame to its best advantage. He looked young and carefree, not at all like the rising advertising mogul he was. Shalini too had changed into a comfortable pair of capris and an open-necked t-shirt and although she didn't know it, looked like a cute teenager.

"You look beautiful as always," he commented.

Shalini laughed. "I look like a vagabond and you know it!"

"No," he insisted. "You look natural and cute."

"Thank you," she smiled. "Even though I know that you're saying that out of the kindness of your heart!"

"Learn to accept a compliment, pretty girl," he said in exasperation. "There's no need to be overly humble and self-deprecating, you know."

"Sure," she nodded and let it go at that, thinking to herself how amused Riya would be to hear Derek describing her as humble. "What would you like to eat?"

"Whatever you're making," he shrugged. "I'm not fussy about food."

"I'm making brown rice *puttu*," she said. "It's a South Indian delicacy."

"Yeah I know," he said. "I've had it once while I was visiting Kerala. I'll help you make it."

"You'll help me eat it," she smiled. "I don't want you messing up my sparkling clean kitchen."

"C'mon," he coaxed. "You can do the mixing. I'll do the cooking."

"Alright," she gave in with a slight grin. "Since the cooking part involves putting it in and taking it out of the microwave, you can help."

"I'm a good cook you know," he complained.

"I'm sure you are," she said in an attempt to placate him. "But I really don't want you to mess up the kitchen tonight. Sometime next week, you can cook me something exotic."

"Deal," he agreed.

They prepared the *puttu* and ate it with ripe bananas. After dinner, they lounged in the couch, leaning against each other and watching television. "I like being with you like this," he murmured into her hair. "Lounging around with you in this casual manner without having to dress up and go to fancy restaurants and pubs feels like the most natural thing in the world. It feels like I've come home at last."

"it feels the same for me too," she admitted softly. "I *really* like you Derek."

"I'm glad you do," he said. "I want you to be able to say 'I love you' to me real soon. Don't worry, I'm not pressurizing you, but I'm crazy about you."

"I know you are," she answered carefully. "But there are things about me you don't know. I'm not sure you'll feel the same way about me once you know them."

"Shalini," he said firmly. "I know you sometimes have self-esteem issues. And something or someone in your past has hurt you pretty badly. It's written all over you. Not to everyone perhaps, but I can see right through the walls you've put up around yourself. I don't know what was done to you or who did it, but your non-existent dating history tells its own story. You're only twenty-five and very smart and beautiful. Your previously single status must have been self-imposed, I'm sure. Something is blocking you emotionally. Forget about it, please. The past is history. I don't care how good or bad you were back then. All I care about is the person you're now. That's the girl I fell in love with two years ago. And that's all that matters. It wasn't your looks which caught my eye first princess. It was your smile. And then it was your caring, helping nature. So stop torturing yourself and learn to enjoy living in the moment."

"That's quite a speech," Shalini said grinning, trying to lighten the mood.

"I'm serious!" he snapped.

"Relax," she said turning serious. "I like what I'm hearing. And I like you—a lot. So yes, I have decided to take a chance and leave the past behind and move forward with you. But I have to warn you of one thing. My insecurities may sometimes make me clingy and possessive and sometimes, I may just withdraw into myself. Are you ready for all that?."

"Not a problem," he grinned. "I would quite enjoy you clinging to me as much as you want! And as for withdrawing into yourself, that ain't gonna happen because I won't give you the chance. Simple."

Shalini laughed. "You don't know what you're getting yourself into, mister."

"No," he agreed. "But I'm excited by the unknown, not scared by it."

"Great," sighed Shalini, leaning against his chest, which was rock-solid. "Mmmmmm. This feels nice."

"It sure does," he agreed, tightening his arm around her waist. He turned her face around and kissed her softly. "How does that feel?"

"Mmmmm," was all she could manage before he claimed her mouth again, this time exploring with his tongue. Though Shalini's initial response was tentative, she allowed herself to be pulled along by the Derek Wave and her response became more enthusiastic. When they finally came up for air, he looked at her and said, "God, you taste wonderful, princess."

She smiled shyly, a blush creeping across her lovely features.

"You make me want to keep kissing you," he went on, leaning forward and doing just that, taking a firm hold on the back of her neck. When they finally pulled apart, he grinned at her. "If we keep this up, neither of us would have a chance to stop what comes next."

"I guess you are right," she agreed, her face turning serious. "Derek I—"

"Don't worry," he said reassuringly. "I know it's too soon and I don't think either of us are ready for it."

She nodded in agreement. "Is it okay if we just hang out and talk for a while?" her voice was hesitant.

"Sure." Since he didn't want to scare her off, ever, he mentally took a step back from the passion that was building up between them. "What did you study prior to obtaining your MBA? Engineering?"

"Good God, no!" she laughed, glad that he had changed the subject. Kissing him had made her feel as though her heart had somersaulted into her stomach. With the change of subject, the mood turned light once again.

"What's wrong with engineering?" Derek asked, clearly not understanding the reason for her sudden outburst of mirth.

"Nothing," she smiled. "It's just not my cup of tea."

"So what *did* you study?" he persisted.

"Psychology."

"Interesting," he commented.

"It is," she agreed with a firm nod.

"Psychology these days comes in very handy in business," he went on. "Especially during negotiations. Getting a measure of the other party sure helps a helluva lot."

"It sure does," she smiled. "It comes in mighty handy while dealing with a culturally diverse workforce such as what we have at my company."

He nodded, then changed the subject. "What about your family? I have caught glimpses of them once or twice with you during some of their visits here. Where do they live?"

"They live in Coimbatore. My dad's a psychiatrist, quite well-known over there, and my mom's an English language professor. I have a younger brother who's studying to be a lawyer. He'll graduate this year."

"You visit each other often?" he queried, curious to know everything about the fascinating young lady in his arms.

"Once every two months," she answered, wrinkling her nose. "*If* they don't piss me off!"

"So visits are subject to conditions?" he teased.

"Of course," she smiled back at him. "What about you? Where does your family live?"

"My parents are in Mumbai. My dad's a chartered accountant and my mother's a fashion designer. So you can see where I get my creative genes from," he smiled fondly. "I have two younger sisters, identical twins actually."

"Identical twins!" Shalini exclaimed. "That's so cool! It must have been fun growing up with two girls who looked exactly like each other."

"Fun and quite confusing at times," he grinned at the memory. "Sarah works with my mom in her chain of boutiques and Andrea is a sports journalist."

"Hold on a minute," said Shalini, sitting bolt upright. "*The* Andrea Mathews is your sister?"

"Yes she is," he was looking puzzled at her reaction.

She hastened to explain. "I'm a sports nut. And I'm a big fan of Andrea's broadcasts and columns. She's very knowledgeable and her writing sometimes makes me feel like I'm reading elegant lines of poetry."

He grinned in amusement. "My sister's fan. Well, if you behave yourself, maybe one of these days, I'll introduce you to her."

"Yeah, sure," she rolled her eyes. "So a chartered accountant, a couple of fashion designers, an acclaimed sports journalist and an advertising tycoon. Quite an accomplished bunch."

"Yes we are," he smiled with evident pride. "We all are. Now, if we could just add a brilliant HR professional with a background in psychology, it would be wonderful."

"And you the most accomplished of them all," said Shalini teasingly, ignoring his comment which alluded to her.

"I don't know about that," he said humbly, switching gears. "I still have a long way to go." *Don't push too soon*, he told himself.

"That maybe so," said Shalini, "but look at how far you have come already. Your company is already ranked among the top ten ad agencies in the country. And it's been only a few years since you established it."

"I want to go global Shalu," he said passionately. "There are so many new vistas out there just waiting to be explored and conquered."

"You'll conquer them all," she said in an encouraging tone, looking up at him. "When the opportunity presents itself and the timing is right, you'll be ready to conquer the world, my dear Alexander."

"Yeah, and I hope to have you at my side when I do so, my lady," he said, leaning down to place a gentle kiss on her forehead. This made her blush furiously, but she couldn't hide her smile. "What good is a conquering hero without his girl beside him?"

"You do say the sweetest things," she purred contentedly. "I just hope you're real and I'm not dreaming you."

"I'm real enough," he murmured against her hair. "I'm not going anywhere. One day soon, you'll realize that." She smiled and yawned, which made him laugh. "Am I that boring?"

"No," she mumbled. "You're very romantic. I'm just so sleepy."

"Then off you go to bed," he said, but reluctant to let her go. "I'll take you out for lunch tomorrow."

"But my lunch break is for only one hour!" she protested.

"We'll go somewhere close to your office. I'll get you back to work on time," he promised. "Can we hang out in the evening too?"

"I'm sorry," said Shalini regretfully. "I have to complete some important tasks and I already sort of partially canceled on Riya tonight. It would be quite unfair to her if I do it two nights in a row."

"I understand," he said, trying to hide his disappointment. "At least I'll get to see you at lunch tomorrow."

"Yes," she agreed. "And Wednesday's sure to be a busy day. Our campus recruitment drive starts that day."

"I wish you were working for me," he said wistfully. "That way, I can play with your schedule anytime I want!"

"Keep wishing," she said wagging her finger at him. "But that's one wish which is not going to come true anytime soon."

"We'll discuss this again sometime in the future," he said. "Now, you catch some sleep." He let her get up from the couch and walk him to the door. He leaned down and placed a chaste kiss on her lips before walking out of her flat. "Good night," she said softly as she closed the door behind him.

CHAPTER 18

Tuesday morning flew by relatively uneventfully. The girls were busy taking care of last-minute details for the campus recruitment exercise starting the next day. Shashi Kiran had had a talk with Riya the previous night, telling her of the changes he wanted them to make to the project proposal and making a few suggestions, all of which she had noted down in a document and mailed to Shalini.

Before they knew it, lunchtime was upon them. "Coming?" queried Riya.

"Derek's taking me out to lunch," she said with a wide smile that threatened to split her face in two.

"Things getting serious between the two of you?" she asked.

"Maybe, I don't know," said Shalini honestly. "He's intelligent, smart, warm and caring. An overall nice guy."

"And he's completely smitten with you," Riya pointed out.

"Yeah, that too," said Shalini reflectively. "But what if it's all too good to be true? I don't want to end up as just another notch on his bedpost, you know."

"Well, if that's the case," said Riya sensibly, "he need not go to all the trouble of wining, dining and sweet-talking a stubborn jackass like you. It's too much trouble. There are enough women out there who'd be more than willing to do his bidding. He's one of the country's most eligible bachelors and definitely one of the wealthiest young men in the city. He really likes you, short stuff. Though for the life of me, I can't figure out why!"

"You're impossible!" Shalini giggled. "Now keep quiet. He'll be here any moment now and I don't want to be verbally abused in his presence!"

Just as she finished speaking, Derek appeared in the corridor and walked towards the two of them, giving a friendly wave to both the girls. "Ready?" he smiled at Shalini.

"Sure," she said, grabbing her purse. She quickly waved goodbye to Riya and held out her hand for Derek to hold.

He took her out to lunch at a nearby Chinese restaurant. "So how is your day shaping up?" he asked.

"Busy," she answered. "Last-minute glitches have to be straightened out and the nitty-gritties taken care of. I have to fly to Bangalore this week-end."

"Why?" he queried.

"We're visiting two colleges in Bangalore on Saturday and since I'm kind of familiar with the place and speak the local language fairly fluently, my boss thought it would be a good way to liaison with the college authorities if I went along."

"Are you going alone?" he asked, concerned.

"No," she sighed. "Sanjay from Projects and Deepak from Encryption are coming with me. You don't know them. I'd much rather it be Riya and Sreeja."

"Fear not," he smiled. "I'll fly down with you to keep you company."

"But it'd be such a waste of time for you," she protested. "I'm sure you have better things to do."

"Time spent with you is never wasted, princess," he gave her a winning smile. "I'll pay a surprise visit to my Bangalore office. Keeps the staff focused and alert and on their toes."

"You're a mean boss," she commented dryly.

"Sometimes," he agreed. "When it's called for."

"You just made the trip sound a lot more bearable," she confessed.

"Happy to help," he sang out. They finished their meal and he dropped her back at work and headed on his way.

Just as she sat down, Sanjana stormed into her cabin. "Who were you out with?" she demanded.

"Why is it any of your business?" Shalini shot back. She was not in the mood for Sanjana's nonsense right now.

"You met with Derek Mathews, CMD of Mathews & Company!" she threw at her, looking as if she had made a monumental discovery.

"So what if I did?" Shalini challenged.

"Are you thinking of quitting and moving over to his organization?" she was insistent.

"Sanjana—" Shalini was lost for words. Her good mood from lunch vanished. "Don't you have anything better to do than pry into other people's personal lives?"

"When your 'personal life' happens during office hours, I make it my business!" Now she was sounding like she had lost her mind, which Shalini suspected she might very well have.

"What are you, the Lone Ranger?" Shalini was losing her patience. The other girl was getting on her nerves and she didn't want to get into a shouting match with her. "I do what I please during my lunch break," she said evenly. "I can go out with whoever I want."

"Don't dodge the question!" Sanjana snapped. "Are you jumping ship?"

"And how would it affect you if I did indeed jump ship?" Shalini asked, her tone still controlled. "Why are you so curious?"

"Because then you'd be committing treason!" she exclaimed triumphantly, as if she had suddenly stumbled upon a gospel truth. "Then Mr. Shashi Kiran would know your true colors!"

"Treason?" Shalini bit back a smile. "Honey, if you're high on something, I suggest you take the rest of the afternoon off and get it out of your system. If you're not, please leave. I have got plenty of work to do and time is a luxury I can't afford to waste listening to your crazy theories."

"I—" Sanjana spluttered. "Don't you dare brush me off like that! I know you, Riya and Mr. Kiran are planning something and now you're hobnobbing with a bigshot CEO. I want to know what's going on!"

"Please leave, Sanjana," she said wearily, wishing the cabin had a door which could be shut on her face. "Just go," she said dismissively, turning to the PC and completely ignoring the other girl, who was sputtering furiously.

Not knowing what else to do, Sanjana walked out of the cabin. Harish Kumar was nowhere close to figuring out a way to make life hell for Shalini and Riya and Sanjana was getting more and more frustrated and bitter with every passing day, and as a result, acting crazier by the minute.

A few minutes later, her desk phone rang. It was Riya. "Good job with Dragon Lady," she said. "I heard everything. I think her brain's unhinged, but we'll keep it to ourselves for now."

Shalini laughed. "You're right. By the way, Derek's flying down to Bangalore with me."

"Good for you!" Riya cheered. "At least you have something to look forward to. I shall be bored senseless in Hyderabad this week-end."

"I know," she replied, a plan forming in her mind.

They went on with their respective tasks throughout the afternoon and into the evening as well. It was seven by the time they were ready to leave. Shalini's chauffeur brought the car around to the main entrance and the two girls tumbled into the backseat without exchanging a single word. They were completely exhausted, but their day was not over yet and somehow they had to find a second wind to work on their project.

Riya received a text from Anup asking her if she was free for dinner that night. Since she had neither the time nor the inclination to deal with him just then, she texted him back saying she was busy and was looking forward to visiting his place on Friday. They reached home and decided to freshen up before starting work again. Riya saw Shalini to her door and headed upstairs.

Both the girls showered and changed in their respective homes, ate whatever was left over in their refrigerators and booted up their laptops. They had decided to video-conference with Mr. Kiran.

Riya started the program and Shalini quickly came on screen. They gave a request to Shashi Kiran, who too came on screen immediately. For an hour, they discussed the latest changes to their plans before Shashi finally smiled in satisfaction.

"It's a good plan, girls," he said. "Once we have Riya's feasibility report, we can commence work."

"Good to hear that, sir," said Shalini in obvious relief. "When do we have to start visiting all those dignitaries you told us about?"

"Once the prototype is ready," he answered. "I think that should be a couple of months from commencement."

"A couple of months?" squeaked Riya. "That's cutting it a bit too close. Make it three sir. We can't—"

"Fine, I'll give you three months to come up with the prototype, but I shouldn't hear 'can't' from either of you ever again!" he cut in.

"Alright, alright," said Shalini in a placating tone.

"Good," he smiled. "Both of you have had a long day and it's going to be another tomorrow. Go get some sleep. Good night girls and well done so far."

"Thank you sir," Riya said. "Good night to you too."

"Yeah, good night sir," Shalini piped up before all of them signed off.

CHAPTER 19

The next two days saw Riya and Shalini running around like chickens with their heads cut off. Written tests had to be conducted, answers evaluated and results declared within a matter of hours, which was then followed by group discussions and personal interviews. It was almost midnight by the time the girls reached home and tumbled into bed on both the days. Added to this, Sanjana's irritating nagging had them on edge. Rajesh had accosted Shalini just as she was leaving from her office to one of the colleges and had been especially rude. She had not bothered to exercise her usual self-control and had ripped him apart. He had walked off, muttering dire threats under his breath. He too thought something was up after a talk with Sanjana and tried to irritate Shalini enough to make her blurt out whatever it was, but to no avail. As a result, he was beyond frustrated and resorted to verbal assaults. Shalini had given back as good as she had gotten this time and had not relented until he had walked away.

No interviews were scheduled for Friday morning, so the girls got ready unhurriedly and arrived in office a few minutes later than usual. The list of selected candidates had to be finalized today. Since that was a job for Shashi Kiran and other higher-ups, they had no reason to rush.

Shalini would be heading to Bangalore and Riya to Hyderabad the next day. The day was spent liaisoning with the colleges they were supposed to visit the next day and taking care of all the necessary arrangements. The morning flew by before either of them realized it. Derek had called Shalini quite a few times the past couple of days, just to say a quick hello and reminding her to eat on time and not run herself ragged. She had enjoyed these little distractions. They made her feel wanted and cherished. Now, he was calling her again. "Free for dinner tonight, princess?" he asked hopefully.

"Sure," she said with a smile. "The first proper meal in two days. I'm looking forward to it."

"Good," he said. "I'll pick you up at eight."

"Riya and Anup might join us," she told him. "They have plans to go to his place afterward. She invited me along, but after dinner, you and I can go somewhere by ourselves."

"No problem," he said easily. "As long as you are part of the picture, I'll tolerate anything."

"Thanks," she grinned. "And you better not use the word 'tolerate' while talking about my dear friend!"

"Sorry," he laughed. "See you tonight."

Meanwhile, Riya was talking to Anup on her desk phone. "Sure," she said. "Shalini will be joining us." She looked up to see Shalini standing in front of her. "Hold on," she said into the phone, then turned to Shalini and mouthed "what?"

"Slight change of plans," she said apologetically. When Riya frowned at her, she continued, "Derek and I'll be joining you for dinner. Then we'll head out while you go to Anup's place."

"That wasn't the deal!" Riya hissed. "Why don't you and Derek come with us to Anup's place?"

"Riya—" Shalini began.

Riya realized how desperate her voice must have sounded and checked herself in time and passed a hand over her eyes wearily. "It's okay," she said quietly.

"He won't make any moves on you," Shalini said reassuringly. "If he so much as looks at you cross-eyed, give me a call and I'll come and chew him up and spit him out!" she finished with a wicked smirk.

Riya smiled weakly. "Thanks, but I don't think that will be necessary. Next time, don't you dare bail on me!"

"I won't," she promised solemnly.

They went home from office as usual and quickly showered and got dressed for dinner, then decided to work till they were picked up. Both of them were sitting and working in Riya's couch and were going through the first draft of the feasibility report Riya had managed to prepare that morning and during lunch. Shalini made some additions to the report and Riya edited the contents a little. They had just saved the document when Riya's doorbell rang.

"That'd be your date," Shalini grinned.

"In the name of all that's good and holy, we're just friends!" Riya exploded. Shalini's constant ribbing was getting on her nerves.

"Whatever," she shrugged nonchalantly. "Open the door for your *friend*."

Riya marched up to the front door, grabbed the handle much tighter than necessary and flung it open to find Derek standing outside with a single red rose in his hand. He looked nonplussed seeing the angry young woman.

"It's for you," she snarled at Shalini. "Lover-boy looks dashing and romantic with a red rose and all."

"You don't have to bite my head off for that!" Smiling softly, Shalini rose up to greet Derek, who hugged her lightly and kissed her on the forehead. "Hello beautiful." She was wearing a sleeveless light green frilly top over black tights. "You look adorable tonight," he handed the rose to her.

"Thank you. You don't look so bad yourself," she said. He was dressed in a pair of dark blue jeans and a casual white shirt with two top buttons undone.

"You two are enough to give me diabetes!" muttered Riya sullenly.

"At least we're the real deal!" Shalini shot back. "It's not sterilized artificial sweetners we're feeding each other!"

"I give up," she said in a resigned tone. "Do I have to be subjected to this lovey-dovey performance all evening?"

"It's up to you," shrugged Shalini as if she didn't care one way or another. "We can always go elsewhere if we make you so sick."

"I'll suffer through it," said Riya hastily, knowing full well that her dear friend would make good on her promise at the slightest hint. Derek stayed out of what looked to him as a full-blown quarrel, preferring to watch from the sidelines in case he got caught in the crossfire.

Fortunately, before the argument got any further, the doorbell rang again and this time, it was Anup looking suave and elegant in a light blue shirt and black slacks. He shook hands with Derek and said hello to both the girls.

"Shall we leave?" queried Derek.

"Sure," they chorused.

"We'll take my car," said Derek.

"Fine by me," said Anup. "I came by cab and my place is close to the restaurant we're going to. Riya and I can walk down there."

"How will Riya get back?" asked Shalini.

"I'm big enough to take a cab, grandma," said Riya.

"No need," said Anup assertively. "I'll drop you back. It would be my pleasure."

"Thanks," smiled Riya.

They piled into Derek's BMW and sped off towards the intimate little multi-cuisine restaurant in which they had made reservations. Once at the restaurant, they were shown to a corner table, which gave them some much needed privacy. The lighting was muted, giving the place a very romantic feel.

"Drinks anyone?" asked Anup. "This place serves amazing cocktails."

"A margarita for me," said Riya promptly. "Are you trying anything, short stuff?"

"A grasshopper I think," said Shalini.

Riya gave her a look. "Are you sure? Won't that be too strong for you? Your threshold for alcohol is not exactly high after all."

"Not to worry," Derek piped up. "I can sling her across my shoulder and carry her home if she passes out!"

"That's a cheery thought," said Shalini wryly. "I just hope I don't have to take you up on that offer!"

Since Derek and Anup would be driving, they did not order alcohol, sticking to virgin mojitos instead while the girls ordered cocktails. Their drinks came and they continued talking in low murmurs while taking small sips. The waiter then took their orders for starters.

Suddenly, Shalini's phone rang, its shrill ringtone shattering the quiet ambience of the restaurant.

CHAPTER 20

She stared down at the phone. The voice alert read out an unfamiliar number. Frowning, Shalini answered with a quick hello, thinking it was probably a wrong number. But after a few seconds of listening to the person on the other end, the blood drained from her face. "No way," was all she said, gripping the fork near her plate by the wrong end so tightly that the ends tore into the skin of her palm, making four distinctive holes and drawing blood. Riya was watching her, a worried look on her face. By the time she disconnected the call, she looked sick. Derek was looking worried too. She looked nothing like her usual jaunty self. "Shalu?" he said softly. She sat rigid, like a statue, and did not respond. Derek doubted she even heard him.

"Shalu?" Riya said with more urgency in her tone than Derek's. "What's wrong?"

Shalini took a few deep breaths. "I have to go," she finally whispered, her voice hoarse and raw.

Anup looked between the two girls, searching for answers and finding none. "Do you want to head back home?" he asked in a concerned tone.

"No," she said quickly. She turned to Derek, "Can you take me somewhere? I—I need to get some air. You guys carry on with dinner," she said generously.

Riya gave her a hard stare. "Shalini Samuel," she said in a quiet, determined voice. "Tell me what's wrong." She picked up a few tissues and pressed them to her friend's bleeding palm. The other girl didn't seem to notice the blood. She looked shell-shocked, her eyes glazed and unfocussed.

"Shalini Grace Samuel!" she snapped. "Look at me, dammit!"

"What?" she nearly jumped out of her seat at the sharp note in her friend's voice. Derek was growing more and more worried by the second, but he did not interfere with Riya's interrogation, who obviously had some idea of what had upset the other girl so much while he was completely clueless.

"Tell me what's wrong!" Riya bit out savagely as she continued to try to stem the bleeding, which had thankfully nearly stopped.

"Later," she said, trying to focus her gaze. "At home, not here."

In the meantime, the waiter brought their starters and served them around, but none of them paid any attention to the appetizing food in front of them, their attention completely focused on the stupefied young woman at their table.

Riya had had enough by then. Not a patient person to begin with, she couldn't bear not knowing, so she pushed back her chair and stood up, dragging Shalini up with her. She turned to the guys. "We're going to the ladies' room," she informed them matter-of-factly. "We'll be back in a few minutes." They nodded, bemused at the sudden turn of events. Derek wanted to take Shalini in his arms and tell her that everything would be alright, but he held back, silently allowing Riya to take the lead.

The ladies' room was nearly empty except for a tall young woman touching up her lipstick. The two girls headed to a sink in the corner, Shalini walking as if in a trance. Riya helped her wash off the blood from her palm, then wiped it dry using a tissue. She then tied a makeshift bandage around the wound using more tissues. Finally, she straightened up and admired her handiwork. "It'll do for now," she said soothingly. They were alone in the ladies' room now. "Breathe," she ordered.

Shalini gulped and took a few deep breaths. Some color was returning to her cheeks. "Who was it on the phone?" Riya asked in a soft, soothing voice, as if talking to a wounded animal.

"Sudarshan," she said in a barely audible whisper.

Riya rocked back on her heels, stunned. That one word had knocked the wind out of her. She looked at Shalini, understanding dawning on her. "Why?" she asked, not knowing what else to say. It was clear that this wasn't what she had expected to hear.

"He drunk-dialed," she said, her eyes filling up with tears. "And said ... some shocking things."

"After all these years," Riya whispered in a shocked voice. "What does he want?"

"He says he has photos," Shalini looked at her miserably. "I have to tell Derek. I'm sure he'll call things off between us once he comes to know of this. It will be over between us just as I was starting to grow closer to him."

"I think you're wrong about that," said Riya softly. "Anyway, he's the least of our worries right now. I'll come home with you and we can discuss it and see what can be done."

"No," said Shalini, a firm note in her voice for the first time in the last fifteen minutes. "You stay here and finish dinner. I'll go with Derek, explain this aspect of my life and if he wants to end it, then it's better to do it sooner than later."

"As you wish," Riya sighed. "Just remember, I'm only one phone call away. And for what it's worth, I think you're wrong about Derek. He doesn't seem like the kind of guy who would assign any iota of importance to an issue that's been dead and buried for a long time now."

"You're probably right. Let's see," The girls returned back to their table to find Derek and Anup talking intently. Anup saw them approaching and stood up. Derek quickly followed suit. He took one look at Shalini and immediately put a comforting arm around her. "Hey," he murmured softly. "Feeling better?"

"Get me out of here," she muttered by way of answer, relaxing slightly at his soothing touch, silently wondering if it was the last time she would be able to enjoy it.

"Happy to oblige," he smiled gently down at her, unable to hide the concern and worry in his soft brown eyes. They bade goodbye to Anup and Riya and headed out of the restaurant.

"What happened to her?" asked Anup curiously. "Who called?"

"Someone she knew a long time ago," answered Riya, refusing to say anything further. Besides, it wasn't her secret to divulge.

They started their dinner, Riya barely picking at her food, her mind preoccupied with the little information Shalini had shared with her. Though only a few words had been exchanged between them, it had been enough to tell her all she needed to know. She snapped out of her reverie when Anup asked her what she would like for dessert.

"Um," she thought for a moment. "A hot fudge sundae," she said.

Anup beckoned the waiter over and placed their orders for dessert, a hot fudge sundae for Riya and a molten lava cake for himself.

They ate in silence, Anup frequently stealing glances at Riya, whose face was bathed in the soft glow of the muted lighting. Pale yellow shadows danced across her lovely features and made her look ethereal. She absently swept back an errant lock of hair behind her ears as she ate her dessert. Even that simple, unconscious movement was elegant and graceful. He could see the concern writ large on her face.

"Do you want to go straight home?" he asked solicitiously.

"No," she replied. "She won't be home for a while and me sitting around waiting for her to get back would only make me more anxious and fidgety."

"What do you want to do now?" he asked as he signaled for the check.

"I want to do something physical, expend some energy," she said. "Let's jog to your place."

He looked at her as if she had landed from outer space. "Are you high? Have you been snorting weed or something?"

"Of course not," she snapped. "Why do you ask?"

"You want to jog for three kilometers right after a heavy meal," he said slowly. "Not exactly what anyone in their right senses would do."

"I have done it before," she answered calmly. "The worst that can happen is vomiting. Besides, I haven't really eaten that much. Come with me if you want. I'm going." She stood up and grabbed her purse. Anup too stood up.

"Fine," he conceded. "Let's jog down to my place. I have a punching bag there you can pummel if you want," he offered with a lopsided smile.

"Good. Just what I need," she smiled. "Thanks."

They quickly paid the bill and left the restaurant. Once outside, Riya took off at a breakneck pace, causing Anup to call after her. "You'll break something in those shoes," he said between breaths. "Slow down!"

"I have done it before," she panted. "Don't worry!"

"Women!" he sighed, then got into step beside her, easily matching her loose, graceful strides as the two of them headed towards his apartment. As they jogged side by side, he couldn't help wondering if they would ever spend a normal evening with each other like other people. Right now, it looked like a very remote possibility. But he was not at all deterred by that thought.

CHAPTER 21

Derek had his arm around Shalini's waist as he steered her firmly towards his car and ushered her into the passenger seat. He got in behind the wheel and turned the key in the ignition. The engine came to life with a throaty roar. He looked at her. "Where to?"

"Somewhere outdoors," she replied mechanically. "Somewhere quiet. I don't want to be in an enclosed space right now. I feel all kinds of queasy." Her voice sounded strange and hollow, even to her own ears.

"Somewhere quiet and outdoors," he repeated wryly. "Quite a tall order, Ms. Shalu."

A ghost of a smile appeared on her face. "Yeah," she said, sounding almost human. "Since you're trying to woo me, this is your chance to show your prowess."

Derek grinned. "That's my girl. Always challenging. I was starting to worry if she had disappeared! Alright, I know just the place."

He quickly reversed the car and drove for a few minutes, coming to a stop in front of a small park. "Come on," he jumped out and rushed to open her door.

He held her hand and squeezed reassuringly as they walked into the park. They came to a deserted park bench and sat down. Neither of them spoke for a while. Then Shalini finally said, "Derek, I have got something to tell you. After hearing it, you may not want to see me anymore. If so, I shall accept your decision without protest."

"Look," Derek began patiently. "Before you go all melodramatic on me, please understand this. *I'm in love with you.* I have been for a very long time. Nothing you say can possibly make me leave you. I'm not a nincompoop to throw away the girl of my dreams with both hands when I have just managed to latch on to her with my fingertips." He held up a hand to ward off her protests. "And I have seen a lot more of the world than you have, so I don't think whatever you're going to say will shock me. And whatever it is, it's alright," he said in a softer tone.

"Derek, I know you're not a moron like most men," she began. Then she smiled sadly. "But this is something ugly and I needed to warn you before I told you."

He opened his arms wide. "Lay it on me, princess. Let's hear how bad you've been."

She took a deep breath and gathered her thoughts. "While I was in college," she began slowly. "I was seeing someone."

Derek looked at her strangely, wondering for a moment if she had lost her mind. "Really? *That's* your deep, dark secret? In case you haven't noticed, this is the twenty-first century and most people who are single date other single people." Shalini was smiling at him, amused despite herself. It seemed to Derek that she was making much ado about nothing.

"Ah Derek," she said shaking her head at him. "I didn't fall straight out of medieval times into the modern era. Listen without interrupting, please. Just for a few minutes till I explain everything."

He sat back and waited. "It was when I was pursuing my master's degree. I studied in one of Tamil Nadu's top business schools in Trichy. He was a good friend, or at least I thought he was. One fine day, he proclaimed undying love for me. I too had feelings for him, or thought I did. So we started dating. I guess I was drawn to him mostly out of loneliness. My dearest friend had gone to another city to pursue her higher studies and due to circumstances, I had to join the MBA program at BiM, one of the top business schools in the state, despite getting admission in Melbourne University's master's program in psychology. He was the only one whom I could talk to without feeling as if I'm struggling to get my point across," she continued. "It seemed as if all the others in my class were tuned to a different frequency than me."

"So a friendship blossomed into love," said Derek, trying to hide the jealousy from his voice. "So what happened after that? I'm assuming you guys broke up for some reason."

"Yes," Shalini said softly. "I thought he really loved me. Please understand that my self-esteem was at an all-time low in those days. But nobody would have believed it if they took a look at my academic records, which were always impeccable. I graduated number one in my class, despite the inner turmoil I was going through and despite my...condition. I was often thought of as a freak by several people who crossed paths with me."

"You're an amazing young woman, Shalini," he said quietly. "Don't let anyone tell you otherwise."

Shalini gave him a grateful smile. "Thank you. Anyway, our relationship lasted for one year. It ended on the day of our final examination. I'm a Christian and he was from an a different family background who refused to consent to the match." She took a deep, shuddering breath. What she had to say next was quite awkward. "He said he couldn't marry me against the wishes of his family, but was quite happy to—" She swallowed and looked down at her feet, not able to meet his intent gaze. "—to have me as the 'other woman,'" she finished, unable to say the word "mistress."

"Sounds like a prince of a guy," he said sardonically. "So what was your response to this amazing offer?" he asked, already guessing her answer. He spoke in a barely contained voice, though he was burning with fury. He had had dalliances with several ladies in his wild days, but he'd never lowered himself to treat them like dirt. He had always respected the women he was involved with and never deliberately humiliated anyone. And all his relationships were with no strings attached. Both parties knew where they stood, so there was no room for misunderstandings and humiliations later on. Besides, he had never promised marriage to any of the women he'd dated. Until he met Shalini, that thought had never crossed his mind.

"I told him to stick it where the sun doesn't shine," she said with a wan smile, recalling the memory.

"And?"

"He was enraged and shouted that I'm being unreasonable and foolish, then raised his arm, attempting to hit me. Reflexively, I moved away and then punched him below the belt with everything I had. This infuriated him further, but thankfully, we were standing in the campus quadrangle and the scene was attracting a crowd. So he backed off."

"And you called things off after that?" he asked, hoping she had. The guy seemed like a real sleazeball.

"Yes."

Something in her tone of voice made Derek look at her keenly. "What is it, Shalu?"

Her head snapped up, eyes filled with such raw pain that it almost tore Derek apart. "What is it, Shalu?" he repeated in a more urgent tone, holding her hand gently, not taking his eyes off her.

Shalini took a deep, steadying breath. What came next was not pleasant, but it had to be said. "He—" she gulped, then tried again. "He paid me a visit that evening."

The way she looked when she said it made Derek's blood run cold. With an effort, he kept his tone level. "Where were you staying in those days?"

"I was sharing a house with two other girls," she answered softly.

"So what happened that evening?" he asked, his gaze warm on her lovely face, which had gone pale again.

"I was alone that evening," she stopped to quickly gulp in some air. God, she hoped she could get through this ordeal and come out the other side in one piece. "My room-mates had plans. He came."

"And?"

"I refused to open the door at first, then he started making a scene in front of the house, so I let him in," she smiled wryly. "Looking back, I realize it wasn't probably the smartest thing to do, but at that moment..." her voice trailed off.

"You were embarrassed," Derek guessed. When she nodded, he went on, "You don't have to beat yourself up for having a normal, human reaction sweetie."

"I don't know," she sighed. "Anyway, to cut a long story short, he attempted to rape me."

Derek went completely still. For a long moment, there was absolute silence. Derek took several deep breaths to control the rage within him that was threatening to boil over. It wouldn't help Shalini if he lost his cool now. He got up from the bench and walked a few paces away, then came back. Shalini felt him get up and could hear him walking back and forth, but since she couldn't see much, she didn't know what he was up to beyond that. Since she didn't hear a car start, she at least knew he hadn't abandoned her here. Not yet anyway.

She felt him sitting back down. In a voice totally devoid of emotion, he asked, "So what happened?"

Shalini prayed for strength to get through the next part. When she finally spoke, it was in a flat monotone. "I opened the door for him, but stood in the doorway so that the door could be kept open. I didn't trust his intentions at all. Then—" her voice faltered. Derek took her hand and squeezed reassuringly. She took comfort from the simple gesture and found the strength to continue. "It all happened so fast, I couldn't react. He shoved me inside with such force, I fell to the floor halfway across the hall. Before I could catch my breath and get up, he had shut the door and was upon me. I fought, screamed, kicked and scratched, but to no avail. My efforts earned me a few hard slaps and some well-aimed punches." Her voice was coming out in sobbing breaths now as she remembered the absolute terror she had felt that long-ago evening. Tears fell and she wiped them away savagely, but they kept coming. "He ripped my clothes off." It took a tremendous act of will to utter the words.

Derek was not able to stand it, any of it. Her heaving sobs, the shattered look in her expressive brown eyes, her face which had completely drained of color and her small body trembling and shaking like a leaf. Without a word, he scooted over to her and enfolded the petite young woman in his arms, her head cradled against his hard, strong chest. "It's alright now," he whispered gently as he kissed her hair. "You don't have to do this, Shalu.

You don't have to tell me any of this. It doesn't matter one bit, sweetheart. It doesn't change anything." He badly wanted to pound something until his hands bled, preferably the face of the scum who had caused Shalini, his strong, beautiful, happy-go-lucky Shalini to look so broken, so lost.

The steady way his hands stroked her back calmed her a little and she drew back, but not away. "What probably saved me from getting raped was his ego," the ghost of a smile tugged at the corners of her mouth. "He got off me and clicked pictures of me in that sorry state. It gave me a little time to recoup and regroup. I forced myself to think. When he tried to get on top of me, I was ready. I got on my knees as if to…" she blushed to the roots of her hair. "Anyway, he thought he had won or something and was laughing like a loon. I caught hold of his balls and squeezed for all I was worth. He howled and howled," A smile, a real one, bloomed as she remembered Sudharshan's high-pitched howls. "I heard someone pounding on the door and managed to somehow go and open it. In walked one of my room-mates and in an instant, sized up the situation."

"Hold on a moment," said Derek, reeling from what Shalini had just told him. "Back up a little. You squeezed his balls and made him howl?" He looked at her in wonder.

"Yes."

"Wow!" He bent down and kissed her gently on the lips. "You're one dangerous little lady, aren't you?"

"I guess I am," smiled Shalini, looking hopeful. Perhaps everything would be alright after all.

"Go on," he encouraged. "Did you turn him in?"

"No," she sighed. "I—I chickened out," she admitted, looking sheepish.

"Why?" Derek was genuinely surprised. He knew Shalini wasn't a coward."You had a good case."

"Yes," she nodded. "But I just wanted it over and done with. Besides I didn't want my family to be dragged through the ordeal of a full-blown court trial."

"Your family doesn't know?" he was shocked now.

"No," she shook her head. "It felt unnecessary to drag them into the mess I had created."

"Shalu, they are your parents, your brother! Surely they would have understood!"

"Derek," she said quietly, "I didn't want them to know because they, meaning my parents, could get really judgemental and sanctimonious. 'Oh poor little Shalini! All that big talk and look what it got her. She should have listened to us when we told such and such, blah, blah, blah.' I didn't want to hear it then and sure as hell don't want to do so now."

Derek decided to drop the subject. Obviously he didn't understand her family dynamics. There appeared to be a lot of tension and undercurrents he wasn't privy to. Not yet anyway. "So what happened then?" he asked instead.

"My room-mate and I sort of threatened him."

"Sort of?",

"We told him if he'd leave quietly and stay out of my life, we would forget the whole mess. But if he tried to create trouble again, there would be consequences," she replied, remembering.

"So he left?"

"Yes, but not before vowing to get back at me and ruin my life when I least expect it or some such," she said. "It took all of my remaining mental strength to stay upright and deal with him. Only when he was safely out the door and it was locked and bolted behind him I allowed myself to collapse to the floor in a heap." She touched Derek's cheek lightly. "If all this is making you re-think—"

"Princess," he said gently, "you don't want to piss me off. If you know what's good for both of us, do not dare complete that sentence."

"Derek—" she began again.

"Shalini, if you think that my feelings for you are governed by what some scum did or did not do to you a hell of a long time back, then I guess I'm wasting my time. Apparently, you don't seem to be the person I thought you were," he ground out, frustrated. He could see his words had hurt her, but what was he to do? She was behaving like a typical soap opera heroine, trying to martyr herself.

Tears welled up in her eyes once again, but she blinked them back and let out a breath she hadn't realized she had been holding. "Okay Derek," she said quietly. "You have made your point. I won't insult either of us by insinuating that my past might influence your feelings for me. The reason I'm telling you all this is because that scumbag called while we were at the restaurant and told me he was going to send those photographs to my office in addition to posting them online and making sure they go viral. He would, of course, graciously reconsider if I agree to sleep with him." She sat back and waited for him to react.

When Derek spoke, it was in a cold, hard tone his business associates and competitors would have recognized and steered clear from. "Right. So he has put his cards on the table. Why in God's name are *you* so torn up about it?"

Shalini stared at him as if he had gone insane. "Didn't you hear any of what I just said? Derek, in those photographs I'm practically... Well, those photos are indecent, okay? They could ruin me!" This conversation was not at all going in any of the ways she had envisioned.

"Wrong," he bit out fiercely. "That can only happen if you allow it to."

"Excuse me?" she was becoming furious now.

"You heard me," his tone was hard and uncompromising.

"What the hell are you talking about?" she glared up at him.

"Those photos do not have the power to ruin you. Nor does that asshole. The only thing that could ruin you is you."

Shalini shot him a dirty look. "Okay Mr. Philosopher. Are you suggesting that I sleep with him to get hold of those photographs? Use my feminine viles to seduce him so that he would succumb to my charms and hand them over like a lamb?" she was too angry and frustrated to care what she was saying.

Derek was watching her, fascinated. Though her words were acting as kindling to the hot rage already burning within him, she was still managing to take his breath away. With her eyes flashing and mouth set in a grim line, she looked like a warrior queen and it called to him on a deep, primeval level. So instead of snapping out the angry retort that was on the tip of his tongue, he leaned down and kissed her. Not softly, not gently. No sir-ee. It was an act of all-out possession. He simply devoured her mouth. She gasped out in surprise and anger, but as he deepened the kiss, her arms went around his neck and pulled him closer as he ravaged her mouth. When they finally pulled apart, both of them looked dazed.

"Shalini," he said quietly. "I love you. Nothing's ever going to change that. Now you have to tell me what you intend to do about the current situation. How do you propose to handle it?" He held up a hand as if to hold off any possible protest. "And no, I have no intention of watching from the sidelines while you deploy your feminine wiles to charm any and all copies of the photographs, hard or soft, away from the moron. I credit you with more intelligence than that. Tell me what you want to do and I'll help in any way I can."

For a long moment, she was quiet. "Do you mean that?" she asked at last.

"More than I have ever meant anything in my life," he declared fervently.

During the course of the exchange, her posture had subtly changed. She was no longer slouching in a dejected manner, but was sitting bolt upright and there was a dangerous gleam in her normally warm brown eyes. "Then he's going down," she said with finality. "Hard."

"Tell me sweetie," he said. "What's going on in that devious mind of yours?"

Her lips quirked up in a smile. "Why, blackmail him of course," she said matter-of-factly.

"Huh?" he was confused. "How?"

"A sleazeball like him is sure to have trampled on a few innocents on the way in the last few years. We just need to track his movements till we find the dirt we are looking for."

"And if we don't?"

"Oh we will find dirt alright," she said confidently. "Bullies like him prey on the gullible and the innocent. If we dig deep enough, we'll come up with something. Then with you beside me, we can threaten him," she was positively glowing with glee at the prospect.

"You seem to be a dangerous young lady," he said with a relieved smile, happy to see her looking like herself again. "Thank God you're on my side!"

She smiled wryly. "I don't know about being dangerous Derek. I'm fighting for the life I have built and my dignity. When dealing with scum, one has to play dirty."

"True," he agreed. "What's the loser's full name? I'll get the ball rolling on the dirt-digging project."

"Sudarshan Lakshmipathi," she replied, the words tasting bitter on her tongue.

"Where's he currently working?"

"KVG Technologies," she said In a monotone. "A small IT concern in Whitefield, Bangalore."

"The sicko didn't get picked up by any of the major companies?" Derek's tone was clipped and businesslike. He was not a violent person by nature, but at that moment, he could and would have broken Sudarshan Lakshmipathi's neck without any remorse.

"He was," she answered with a nod. "But he wouldn't settle down anywhere for long and kept bouncing from one company to another. Ultimately, that sort of mindless job-hopping is not viewed favorably by HR, so he's paying the price now. Plus, I came to know that he was asked to resign by his previous employer."

"Seems to be a real charming guy," he said dryly. "How in God's name did you, a sensible, intelligent girl, manage to get mixed up with this unsavory character?"

"I wish I knew," she answered with a humorless smile. "It's a question I have been asking myself countless times."

"Alright," he said briskly. "Let's discuss what needs to be done and then get around to doing it. We're in this together Shalini. I don't want to hear any protests about this from you."

"Don't worry," she said, a genuine smile blooming on her face for the first time since the phone call had interrupted their dinner hours ago. "I pick my battles carefully and this is not one of them. I want to take him down and I want to do it with you."

"Hallelujah!" he smiled fondly at her. "You are flying down to Bangalore this weekend, aren't you?"

"Yes," she confirmed with a nod.

"Good. I'm accompanying you. We'll deal with this issue once your interviews are over."

"Sounds like a plan," she said with a decisive nod. "But won't it be a waste of time for you?"

"I have already told you I shall pay a surprise visit to my office there," he reminded her.

"Oops! So you did," she smiled. "It totally slipped my mind with all this hungama. The hard taskmaster routine of course."

"I've got to be if I wish to rise to the top of the industry by the time I turn thirty-five," he countered. "Anyway, what's going on in your mind?"

"I'm thinking we'll pay him a surprise visit," she declared.

"Sudharshan?" he queried.

"No, the Prime Minister," she retorted with a straight face. "Of course I meant Sudharshan."

"And do what, exactly?" he asked, though he had an inkling of what was coming.

"Hopefully, by the time we get to him, we should have enough dirt to bury the jerk. We'll blackmail him and get the photographs from him," she replied matter-of-factly.

"Seems like a plan. Where was he working prior to KVG Technologies?" he asked. "If he had been asked to leave for whatever reason, it would be as good a place as any to start."

"I–I don't remember," she stammered, faltering for a moment.

"Think!" he snapped.

She pinched the bridge of her nose and tried to focus. Suddenly, it came to her. "Mitra Software," she answered. "Owned by—"

"Rakesh Mitra," he finished. "I know the guy and his company. We handle their advertising account."

"That's such a great piece of luck!" she exclaimed. "Can you talk to him and find out the reason behind Sudarshan's resignation?"

"We're flying out to Bangalore first thing tomorrow as planned," he said, a slight smile playing on his lips. "I'll use the trip to sort things out."

"Just get me the details," she said quietly. "And let me handle him. He needs to be taught NEVER to tangle with me again. And I'll be the one teaching him that lesson."

"Yes you will," he smiled. "But please let me help you. I don't want you to go through this alone."

"This could get ugly and messy, Derek," she said cautiously. "I don't want your name and reputation getting sullied because of your involvement in this."

"There's no room for argument," he said in a hard, determined voice. "I've waited for you all my life. Now that I've found you, I wish to stand by you in good times and in bad. And besides," he grinned. "I have to earn your love. And this just might be the chance to do it!"

"Fine," she gave in, smiling. "It means a lot to me. What do you plan to do?"

"Ah!" he sighed, his eyes gleaming wickedly. "I'll get the ball rolling on the dirt-digging project and Mitra Software is as good a place as any to start. And when I uncover the reason, and trust me I will, I shall march directly to KVG Technologies and negotiate something with the slimeball."

"No," Shalini shook her head firmly. "You'll dig up all the dirt on him you can find at Mitra Software and hand it over to me. *I* shall march to KVG Technologies and confront him face-to-face."

"Fine," he agreed, not debating the issue any further for the time being. "At least let me tag along to watch the fun."

"Alright," she acquiesced. "We may have to extend our stay in Bangalore by a day."

"That won't be an issue for me," he said confidently.

"Aren't you worried about getting into trouble?" she asked, concern evident in her voice. "I mean, it's my mess. So I really don't care how much trouble I get into while cleaning it up. But you really don't have to be inviting trouble by getting mixed up in all this."

"Oh yeah?" he challenged. "Please take a good, hard look at me and tell me if you think I care about getting into trouble!"

"But why?" she asked, bewildered. "You can simply break things off with me and walk off unscathed."

"Do you want me to?" he asked, the lid he had kept on his temper threatening to burst open.

"No," she said hastily. "Of course not. I'm just saying you could. No scandal, clean slate and all that."

"You want to know why I'm not taking the easy way out," he said in a controlled tone. "Because I hate men who wish to use a lady's past to blackmail her!" he snarled. "And because," his tone softened, "I don't take kindly to people who cause distress to the love of my life."

Shalini's eyes stung as finally, her composure began to crumble and the tears started to flow as they hadn't three years ago. "But we only started dating less than a week ago!" she said between sobs. "Why would you take such a risk for a girl you just started seeing?"

"You don't understand, do you?" he shook his head impatiently. "Yes, we have just started to date. And I don't know how many more times I have to repeat myself before it gets into your head, but here goes. I fell in love with you a long time ago. Not for your pretty face, mind you. For your lovely smile, helpful, vivacious nature and the look in your eyes which says you have seen more than you should have. And for that love, I shall do anything. But don't feel pressured to feel the same way about me because I'm helping you out. When you start to love me—and you'll do so pretty soon—it should happen naturally, not out of gratitude or anything else," he finished softly.

Shalini managed to crack a smile. "That might happen sooner than you think," she said, wiping away her tears. "I have liked you for a long time too, but I didn't do anything about it because I didn't want to be hurt again," she confessed.

Derek smiled and got to his feet, pulling her up along with him. He hugged her gently for a few moments, then pulled back and smoothed her hair into place. She was looking a lot better now and he could feel her fighting spirit taking over. He held her at arm's length and looked at the determination on her face. "What're you thinking?" he asked gently.

"He's going down," she said in a much stronger voice. "By the time I'm done with him, he'd wish he had never laid eyes—or hands–on me ever!"

"Attagirl!" he cried exultantly. "You had me worried there for a while with all your weeping and sniveling," his eyes twinkled mischievously.

She punched his shoulder playfully. "I don't snivel!"

"Riiiight," he drawled and then chuckled when he caught the death glare she was shooting him. He raised his hands in front of him defensively. "Alright, alright, my Jhansi ki Rani!" he grinned. "Let me find a place to feed you and then take you home. Our flight leaves very early in the morning, so we need to get some sleep if we want to go in with all guns blazing tomorrow."

"My appetite has returned," she announced. "Why don't we go get some hot tandoori chicken?"

"Sure," he readily acquiesced. "Only chicken? You haven't had any dinner and I somehow don't like the idea of you nibbling on just a few pieces of chicken."

"No, something along with it."

"Then come on. Let's go and feast on tandoori chicken and whatever else we can get our hands on. I'm famished."

"Alright," she said, linking hands with him. "Can't have the rising star of the advertising world starving to death!"

Derek grinned and shook his head, all the while wondering how he had gotten so lucky. Despite the googly she had just been dealt with, Shalini hadn't lost her sense of humor and her smile was as radiant as it had ever been. She was a keeper and he was determined to hold on to her for dear life, no matter what.

CHAPTER 22

By the time Derek dropped Shalini home, it was almost eleven. She found Riya anxiously pacing her living room like a caged wild animal. As soon as Shalini bid goodbye to Derek and closed the door after him, Riya pounced on her. "Tell me!" she demanded. "I want all the details. Don't leave anything out."

Shalini slumped on her couch, totally exhausted by the emotional highs and lows she had experienced in the past few hours, but she knew that her friend would not rest easy till she received a complete explanation. She tried to change the subject. "I will, but first tell me how things went with Anup," she said.

"Don't change the subject!" Riya snapped. "Tell me what that low-life said! What did he want?"

"Derek's not a low-life," she tried to hedge.

Riya was sputtering now, not comprehending why Shalini would even attempt to throw her off track. "Don't play dumb with me!" she snarled. "You know what I mean. Out with it, or I'll beat it out of you!"

Shalini took a deep breath. "He threatened to send those ... photos I told you about to the company and post them on any and every social media outlet he can manage."

"Oh really now!" Riya's face turned red with, anger. "What does he hope to accomplish by doing that? And more important, what exactly does he want from you in return for *not* releasing them?"

"To keep him warm at night," she answered diplomatically. "What else? As for what he hopes to accomplish, apart from an attempt to humiliate me, I can't think of anything."

"Doesn't he have a wife for doing just that? Keeping him warm I nean," Riya's voice had reached fever pitch. "And as for humiliating you, he can forget it. Not gonna happen."

"Ri...," Shalini started.

The other girl closed her eyes and took a deep breath for a moment. Then she asked in a much calmer voice, "Why now?"

"Remember I heard from some of my old classmates that his marriage was breaking down? My guess is, it has happened sooner than we thought and he's lashing out at the one person who used to take all his shit and still put up with him—a.k.a, me. But he doesn't realize I'm not the same shy, naïve young girl anymore."

"I think deep down, he realizes that," said Riya wisely. "That's why he has resorted to blackmail."

Her eyes were filled with cold fury. "Maybe so," conceded Shalini. "Whatever his twisted reasons are, I don't care anymore. I have decided to stop running and start fighting. I'm tired of living in fear of a scumball like him and I'll be damned if I give him that satisfaction!" She looked grimly determined. "My past is just that—past! I can't change it now even if I wanted to, but I don't have to run from it either."

Riya slapped her on the back. "Well said, my dear. A commendable decision and of course, I'll be right beside you."

"I know," Shalini smiled gratefully. "And now, so is Derek."

"Yeah, let's come to that," said Riya, sitting next to her friend. "What did he say?"

"He was furious when I told him the whole story. He's plenty mad at Sudarshan just now and will be flying out to Bangalore with me first thing tomorrow morning. Together, we'll try to find a way to screw him where it hurts most." She smiled diabolically, "I wouldn't want to be Sudarshan right now, but I'd give an arm and a leg to be a fly in the wall of Mitra Software, his previous employer, tomorrow."

"How?" she queried, sounding very interested. "How exactly are you planning to accomplish that? I don't want you inviting trouble through hot-headed recklessness. The guy's not going to back off easily, you know. People like him rarely take a hint even if it's staring at them right in the face."

"I'm well-aware of that. Derek knows the guy who owns and runs Mitra Software. The company asked him to leave for some reason and I've asked Derek to find out what it is. Once he's done digging, I'm planning to use any dirt he comes up with to our advantage and screw Sudarshan over royally."

"Derek agreed?"

"He was eager to do more damage, but I told him it's my mess to clean up," said Shalini firmly.

"I'm liking this dude of yours more and more," her friend was grinning evilly. "It's about time Sudarshan finds out what goes around must come around. Meanwhile, for our part, we have work to do. As they say, offense is the best form of defense. Let's see what attack strategy we can come up with before you land in Bangalore to diffuse this bomb before it has a chance to ignite," her face wore a cold, calculative look.

Shalini looked at her thoughtfully. "I can hear the wheels turning in your head. What are you thinking?"

Riya did not respond immediately. Instead, she got up and went to open the French windows. The cool night air blew gently into the cozy living room. She stood by the railing for a few minutes, then abruptly turned back and closed the doors and took her seat back on the couch. Shalini was staring at her, nonplussed.

"What was that all about?" she asked, looking perplexed.

Riya's smile was cold and mirthless. "Your call log has a record of the number he called you from or did he block it?"

"It has the number," Shalini confirmed. "He must have figured I would be too terrified to do anything except give in to his demands."

"Yes, he does not know that you and I met and became friends and well, petite, innocent Shalini just does not exist anymore. But what he doesn't know won't hurt him. We are going to turn the tables on him."

"Do you want me to call the police and report an obscene phone call?" asked Shalini.

Riya shook her head dramatically. "Nothing so simple or elementary like that, my dear."

"Oh?" Shalini's interest was piqued. Riya's retaliations were always ruthless, imaginative and diabolical.

"Here's what we're going to do..." Riya outlined her plan and after a moment or two, Shalini nodded along enthusiastically.

"And after that, tomorrow, you're placing a call to Anita," continued Riya. "She's an expert on cyber laws and we might need her help. And since you're going to be in Bangalore anyway, see if you can squeeze in a visit."

Shalini nodded. "I'm on board," she said. "When do we launch the attack?"

"Tonight on all the social networking sites and apps we have accounts in. First thing tomorrow in office. His credibility has to be nullified first. Once that's done, the threat is as good as neutralized."

"Neutralized?" Shalini looked at her, bemused. "You're talking like a professional assassin or a spy. If there's a course on catastrophe management, you'd pass with flying colors," she concluded, only half-joking. "And don't you have to leave for Hyderabad tomorrow?"

"My trip has been postponed to Sunday evening. We have rescheduled the recruitment exercise for Monday. Mr. Kiran did not offer any explanation and I didn't ask. And for the last time, this is not a catastrophe," said Riya sternly. "We have a mini-crisis situation here and we're coming up with the most effective way to deal with it. And just for the record, if there's a course on catastrophe management, I'll be the faculty, not a participant! Now, we need every electronic gadget we own which can connect to the internet."

"My laptop, tablet and mobile," said Shalini immediately, going to retrieve those items.

"Same here. Let me get my gear," Riya said, leaving the flat and returning in a few minutes with her backpack. "Let's finish up fast and try to grab a few hours' sleep. I have to go into office tomorrow for a while and meet with the boss and I don't want to be fuzzy-headed and half-witted around him."

"Point taken," agreed Shalini, her laptop and tablet already powered up and raring to go. She logged into the internet from her mobile as well. Next to her, Riya was also doing the same. The bed looked like the command center of a space station.

The girls worked feverishly for forty-five minutes without taking a break, switching from one device to another, logging into various social networking websites and apps to post the same message to all the groups they were a part of. This included their office group and Shalini's school, college and church groups as well. The message, written beneath the mobile number from which Shalini had received the call earlier, was simple, stark and to the point without mincing any words. It read:

BEWARE OF CALLS OR SMS/MMS FROM THIS MOBILE NUMBER, ANY OTHER UNKNOWN NUMBER OR ANYONE CLAIMING TO KNOW ME, MS. SHALINI SAMUEL. THE CALLER IS AN IMPOSTOR AND A CYBER CRIMINAL WHO PREYS ON YOUNG WOMEN AND TRIES TO VICTIMISE THEM. HE ALSO HACKS INTO SOCIAL NETWORKING ACCOUNTS AND MANIPULATES THE PICTURES TO CREATE INDECENT IMAGES. IF YOU RECEIVE CALLS FROM THIS NUMBER OR ANY UNKNOWN NUMBER, PLEASE BE ON YOUR GUARD. AND IF YOU FIND POSTS OF INAPPROPRIATE PICTURES ON YOUR PAGE, REPORT THE ABUSE IMMEDIATELY. THANK YOU.

Once the first phase of their operation was complete, they began to send e-mails marked :URGENT STRICTLY CONFIDENTIAL to the respective administrators of each social networking site. Their e-mails were clear and succinct, first quoting the mobile number and telling the administrators about the threat received from that mobile number to release compromising photographs publicly using social networks. Each e-mail included a digitally water-marked photo of Shalini, who was the account holder being threatened. They were urged to be on the look-out and ensure that the photographs do not get posted onto their highly respected websites. It was diplomatically worded, but got the message across loud and clear all the same.

Once this was done, Riya called their friend Sreeja. Though it was almost one in the morning, Sreeja answered on the second ring with a clear "Hello?"

"You awake?" Riya asked without caring either way.

"Riya?" Sreeja's voice held a note of surprise. "What's up? Is anything wrong?"

"We need your help," she said briskly. "Shalini's gotten herself into an icky situation."

"Really?" Sreeja's voice was completely alert now. "What happened? What has she done now? Is Sanjana causing any trouble?"

"No, nothing like that. As much as I hate to say it, she's innocent in this instance," Riya said hastily. "An ex of hers is threatening to release some photographs of their time together to the company and social networks on the internet," she quickly explained the stop-gap measures they had taken to manage the situation. Once she was done, Sreeja let out a low whistle.

"That's pretty slick work in such a short period," she sounded impressed. "What do you want me to do?"

"What can we do to prevent the photographs from hitting our company network?" queried Riya, her tone betraying the anxiety she was trying so hard to hide. "Can we run a blocker program or something?"

"I've got something better in mind," replied Sreeja thoughtfully. "Don't worry. I'll ensure that those photos aren't released by electronic means. If this creep decides to mail them by post or courier, my putting up electronic walls and barriers would be in vain," she cautioned.

"Don't worry about that," said Riya with a confidence she was far from feeling. "That end will be taken care of. Can you come to office tomorrow?"

"Sure thing," she said without hesitation.

"Around eight? I'd like to get this over with as soon as possible."

"Sure," said Sreeja with a yawn. "Will Shalini be coming in as well?"

"No, she has to go to Bangalore for the campus recruitment drive," said Riya regretfully. "I'd have liked her to be there, but she has a chance to defuse this bomb once and for all from there. So it's just you and me tomorrow."

"No issues. Good night then."

"Good night, Sree," she responded. "And thanks a ton."

"That end has been tied up," said Riya, turning to face Shalini once she ended the call. "We've done all that we can for now. Let's catch some sleep. How are you getting to the airport in the morning?"

"Derek's picking me up at five-thirty," she replied. "Oops! I haven't done any packing yet!" she squeaked.

"Relax," Riya smiled at her. She dragged the other girl into her bedroom, grabbed a suitcase from the top of her closet and laid it on the bed. Then clothes for three days were pulled out and stuffed into the suitcase, followed by lingerie, footwear and toiletries. The suitcase was slammed shut and then the backpack was filled with all the papers Shalini needed to carry, along with her laptop and tablet. The entire exercise took exactly fifteen minutes. "See?" she smiled. "All packed up!" She started to leave, but Shalini obstructed her path.

"Not so fast," she drawled. "How did it go with Anup?"

"Really?" she retorted sardonically. "You want to discuss that *now*? With the shit hitting the fan with regards to your personal life?"

When Shalini did not budge, she sighed. "Alright. Nothing happened. We finished dinner as soon as we could after you left, then we went to his place as planned, where he showed me his studio, which was great by the way. Then we looked at some of his paintings which I believe belong on the wall of a prominent art gallery. Then we drove around for a while before he dropped me at home."

"That's it?" Shalini was dubious. "You just ate, saw paintings and drove around?"

"Forgive me if my activities seem so boring and unexciting to you my dear *friend*, but I was worried about you," she remarked acidly. "Not exactly the right frame of mind to be in for romancing."

"And if I hadn't freaked out, you'd have had a nice romantic evening?" Shalini asked sarcastically. "Give me a break. Let's not kid ourselves here! You were just looking for an excuse to cut and run anyway. And as for any overtures on his part, they would be cut off at the pass, isn't that correct? At least he's smart enough to realize that and play the game by your rules and take the friendship route."

"Drop it Shalu. I have never cut and run!" Riya said through gritted teeth. The warning was unmistakable, but it was wasted on the other girl, who could be thicker-skinned than an elephant when she chose to. "Don't push me!"

"I'm not!" she cried indignantly. "I only want you to come out of your self-imposed exile where romance is concerned. What's the harm in trying at least?"

"It'll happen when it happens," she responded philosophically. "For the moment, we're friends and I'm fine with that. I'm sorry if that doesn't meet with Your Majesty's approval. Now if you'll excuse me, I need to get some sleep."

"Fine!" said Shalini, giving up for the time being. "Good night." Then her tone softened, "And thank you for everything. I really appreciate it."

"Don't mention it," Riya said shortly and let herself out of the apartment.

Shalini shook her head sadly. She hadn't meant to piss off Riya, but talking about relationships with her was like standing on a ticking time-bomb.

CHAPTER 23

Though it was a Saturday, Riya did not have the luxury of sleeping in and woke up by six-thirty, feeling like she had been rolling down the Niagara Falls without a barrel the whole night. She had gotten over the slight altercation with Shalini the night before. She was used to her friend's ways by now. She was tired to her bones, but there was no hope of getting any rest and relaxation that weekend. There was much work to be done, and all she wanted was to roll over and go back to sleep. But with a force of will, she pushed herself out of the doldrums as she got out of bed, trying to clear the cobwebs from her mind and be ready to tackle the latest challenge which had been thrown her way. She wished she could sleep in and enjoy the weekend like any other normal person, but she couldn't afford that luxury. Shalini's mess had to be straightened out and it could not be done from her bed. She quickly showered and got dressed in a pair of gray trousers and a yellow shirt with cap sleeves which made her look both professional and stylish. When she was finished getting ready, she checked her smartphone and found that Shalini had texted her just before boarding the plane a few minutes ago.

En route 2 Bangalore. Derek's wit me. C u in 3 days. Tc.

She quickly replied, wishing her luck with both the office assignment and the personal one, asked her to call when she landed and went into the kitchen to make some breakfast. She decided to make bread pakoras and carry some for Sreeja as well. It took her twenty minutes to finish frying the last piece of pakora. Quickly, she ate some, alternatively sipping steaming hot coffee from her favorite mug. The rest was wrapped in aluminum foil and placed in her handbag. She then grabbed her car keys, locked the front door and went down to the parking lot.

It was early morning and a Saturday as well, so traffic was very light. She drove swiftly and reached the office premises at ten minutes to eight. Her car seemed to be the only one in that section of the parking lot that morning, which was not a big surprise. Being alone in the huge building till Sreeja or someone else showed up would be freaky, but it wasn't really a problem. She had done it before and was not afraid to stay alone. Besides, it wouldn't be for long. She quickly entered the building, swiped her card and went to the fifth floor, which was almost completely deserted except for the one person she most certainly did not want to see. She wrinkled her nose in displeasure and tried her best to keep out of the way.

"Where's Barbie, Ken?" Rajesh Tiwari asked snidely.

Riya did not bother to respond, since she had not been addressed by name, and kept walking towards her cabin.

"I'm talking to you!" he snapped, annoyed at being blatantly ignored.

Still she did not respond. The guy needed to learn some manners and Riya wasn't in the mood to deal with any of his nonsense that morning. There were far more important matters occupying her mind. Just as she came to her cabin, she found him standing at the entrance, blocking her way.

"Answer me," he snarled.

"What do you want to know?" she snapped back. Politeness was wasted on people like him.

"Where's Barbie?"

"Who?" she asked, deliberately looking clueless.

Rajesh let out an angry sigh. "Your friend Shalini."

"Oh!" Riya pretended to search in her pockets. "Sorry," she sang out. "I don't carry her around."

"Stop trying to act smart."

He was starting to get on her nerves, and she had to forcibly restrain herself from launching into an all-out verbal assault. "It's really none of your business where she is, but I'll tell you just to get you off my back. She's gone to Bangalore for co-ordinating campus recruitment. Now will you please move out of my way?" she asked, as patiently as she could. "I've got plenty of work to do and I don't have even a single extra moment to waste on you."

"Sanjay from Projects has gone to Bangalore for the same purpose. Why wasn't I selected to go along?" he complained.

"Go ask the management," she snapped, finally losing her patience. "I don't make such decisions."

"And the management, and by that I mean Shashi Kiran, doesn't make such decisions without consulting the both of you!" he bit out.

"I honestly don't know what you're talking about," she sighed in exasperation.

"First, you sweet-talked him into re-assigning Sanjana and now you're queening it over the rest of the company. And the only person who could have kept you in your place is out of the way!"

"You mean Sanjana?" she tried not to smile. "She could have kept us in our places? Please don't make me laugh Rajesh."

He looked at her, the malevolence clearly spilling out of every pore of his being. "And now," he continued, as if she had not spoken at all, "the three of you are planning something big. But she'll find out what it is and then you'll all go down together."

"Rajesh, a word of advice," she said, pretending to be sincere. "You'll do well to stay away from her and please stop listening to her conspiracy theories. Stick with her and you'll only land in unnecessary trouble."

"You're nobody to preach to me," he said icily. "And you know nothing about Sanjana! So don't go around talking nonsense about her."

"Suit yourself," she shrugged. "Now, if you'll please move out of the way..."

"Why is Sreeja, the Queen of Nerds on our floor?" he asked suddenly.

"Rajesh," Riya heard Sreeja's mellifluous voice behind her and turned to smile at her friend. "This is an office, not a concentration camp. Anyone can be in any floor if they have some work there."

"What work brings you down here today?" he was still looking and sounding irate and was digging himself into a nice big hole without realizing it.

"That doesn't concern you," she smiled sweetly. "And watch your tone with me. Pulling rank isn't really my thing, but with you, I find nothing wrong in doing so. I'm junior vice-president, Encryption Technologies. So I'm miles above you in the hierarchy. What has put you in such a *cheerful* mood so early in the morning anyway?" she asked, looking between the two of them.

"Miss High and Mighty's mere presence is enough to sour anyone's mood!" he growled.

"Seriously?" she asked, opening her eyes as wide as they would go. "But I always find that I'm in a better mood after being with Riya."

Muttering something unintelligible under his breath, he left the two girls alone and walked away. Sreeja looked inquiringly at Riya, who just shrugged. "This place is filled with all sorts of crazies," she said. "He just likes to pick a fight with whoever is available I think." Sreeja just shrugged and waved him off.

"Good morning by the way," she said with a warm smile. "How's our friend holding up?"

"Yeah, a good morning to you too, Sree," Riya responded with equal warmth, her earlier bad mood forgotten momentarily. "She's doing much better than I expected. Madam has decided to take this creep head-on and I appreciate her attitude, I really do. I just want her to be careful, that's all."

"Well, she was never one to grovel," laughed Sreeja. "And don't worry about the office network. I've been here for some time now and set everything up. No one can sneak anything in without my knowledge. I have set it up so that all incoming and outgoing mails have to be routed through Encryption, meaning me and Radhika. I have not let the rest of the team in on this. The fewer people who know about this, the better. Besides, I can trust Radhika with my soul. Can't say the same for certain other members of the team," she said in a clear, musical voice.

"Thank you, Sree," said Riya, relieved. "Radhika's in today?"

"Yes, she came in when I asked her to," she responded. "She's a good kid, very talented and hard-working."

"Yes, I know."

"Where's the heroine of this saga now?" queried Sreeja.

"She should be landing in Bangalore right about now," she replied, looking at her watch, which showed that it was eight-fifteen.

"Good. I don't want her getting all hyper and sitting on my head," laughed Sreeja good-naturedly. "And one suggestion. Please appraise Mr. Shashi Kiran of the situation. If the creep decides to send the photos by post, then he shall be able to take better damage limitation measures than us."

"Point noted," said Riya. Just then, her smartphone rang. It was Shalini. "Yeah?" said Riya into the phone.

"We landed at Bangalore," Shalini announced.

"Good," said Riya. "Sreeja has everything under control here."

"Can I talk to her?"

"Sure," said Riya, handing over the mobile to Sreeja.

"Sree," said Shalini in a voice filled with relief and gratitude. "A zillion thanks for everything. I owe you big-time."

"Yes you do, munchkin," laughed Sreeja. "And I'll hold you to it when the time comes. For the moment, stop worrying and get some work done. Oh and talk to Mr. Kiran as soon as possible."

"Is that really necessary?" Shalini asked hesitantly.

"Absolutely," reiterated Sreeja firmly. "Only he can do damage limitation if this creep sends physical copies of the photographs by mail or courier. So promise me you'll talk to him."

"Will do," she agreed reluctantly with a sigh. "Catch you later."

"Sure. Have a good trip." She handed the phone back to Riya.

"Will you talk to Mr. Kiran?" Shalini implored. "I can't look him in the eye while telling him all this."

"Don't worry," said Riya soothingly. "I'll be with you. He needs to hear it from you."

"I don't want him to see any of those pictures," Shalini said quietly.

"Relax," said Riya calmly. "He's not the judgemental type and if we don't tell him, the post cannot be monitored."

"Do you think Sudarshan has an ally on the inside?" Shalini asked.

"You've been reading too much detective fiction," said Riya, smiling into the phone. "Where's Derek?"

"Taking a conference call from one of his clients," said Shalini.

"Okay," said Riya. "Now listen to me. I need you to concentrate on the campus exercise first. Let Derek do the digging. Once he comes back and tells you what he's found out, call me and we'll come up with the best course of action. I don't want you going to fight him with all guns blazing from the get go. Let's be subtle."

"I don't think subtlety is going to help us in any way In this instance," said Shalini moodily.

"Subtlety always helps," Riya said reassuringly. "Now remember. Keep your cool and don't do anything rash."

"Sure grandma," said Shalini, and Riya could hear the smile in her friend's voice. "Besides, I don't think Derek will let me do anything stupid."

"Yes, he'll keep an eye on you," grinned Riya. "And when Mr. Kiran comes in, I'll call you so you can explain everything to him."

"Fine," Shalini sighed. "It'd be much easier to do that over phone than if I'm looking straight at him I guess."

"You were the victim of a psychopath. He won't think any less of you because of this, Shalu. You know that," said Riya calmly. "Just relax."

"I'll try," she retorted. "Catch you later."

"Stay out of trouble," she warned before ending the call.

She turned to find Sreeja with a broad smile on her face. "What did I tell you?" she asked. "Hyperimaginative and paranoid as ever!"

"Some things never change," Riya sighed dramatically.

"Why don't you come down to my floor?" suggested Sreeja. "We can have a cup of coffee and you can see for yourself what security measures I have taken."

"Sure," agreed Riya. "I have nothing to do here till Mr. Kiran gets in."

"Great!"

"What time did you come in anyway?" she asked curiously.

"Around six-thirty," replied Sreeja. "Radhika came in around seven."

"I'm sorry," Riya apologized sincerely.

"For what?"

"For ruining your Saturday for—"

"Stop it right there," Sreeja interrupted. "Every person is entitled to their privacy. When that's being threatened, we as human beings do what we have to do. And Shalini's a good friend, albeit a quirky one."

"Still," Riya persisted. "It was not fair on our part to impose on you like this and requesting you to use company resources to block out personal troubles."

"Keep prattling on," said Sreeja. "But I won't listen any more." By then they had reached the second floor where the Encryption section was located. They bought a cup of coffee each from the vending machine and went into Sreeja's cabin. Radhika Pandiaraj, Sreeja's young colleague joined them. Both of them explained what had been done to route all official communications through Encryption and Riya looked pleased when they had finished.

"I can't thank both of you enough," she said warmly. "You have managed to do so much in such a short span of time."

Radhika smiled self-deprecatingly. "It was nothing," she said shyly. "Sreeja told me it was to protect Shalini. I admire and respect her a lot."

"Thank you all the same," she smiled. "But I have one question. What if the photos are mailed to any other branch of the company?"

"He'll go up against a wall," replied Sreeja, having anticipated the question. "Encryption for the company's India operations is wholly controlled from Chennai. This is the hub. The senior vice-president at HQ has been told that one of the employees is facing an external threat. I haven't given him any details, but he knows better than to ask me. There's no need to worry. Nothing can get past us to any branch within India. And I sincerely doubt that he'd want to send the pictures anywhere else other than Chennai."

"No," agreed Riya. "His objective is to embarrass her. That can only happen if she and people known to her get to see the pictures."

"That's my assumption as well," said Sreeja.

"Good," sighed Riya. Her smartphone rang just then and it was Shashi Kiran telling her to come to his cabin right away.

"He's in earlier than I expected," commented Riya after ending the call. She stood up and bade goodbye to the two women, thanked them once again and left the cabin.

When she reached Shashi Kiran's cabin, she peeped in to make sure he was alone and went inside. "Good morning sir," she greeted with a smile.

"Good morning," he said jauntily. "Shalini has landed safely I hope?"

"Yes she has," Riya replied. Then sensing the opening she had needed to bring up the photograph issue, she pressed on, "We have a problem. Or rather, she has a problem."

"Oh?" his tone was instantly concerned. "Is she facing any trouble with the travel arrangements or accommodations? The staff at the hotel have been apprised of her special requirements. Is she having trouble despite that?"

"Nothing so mundane," said Riya with a slight smile. Then her face turned sober. "Nasty blasts from her past have come back to haunt her."

"Explain," he said laconically.

Riya drew out her smartphone and dialed Shalini. "I think you should hear it from her," she said in answer to his raised eyebrow.

Shalini answered with a soft hello. "The boss is here," said Riya without preamble. "Tell him." Then she put the phone on speaker.

"Good morning sir," she said hesitantly.

"Good morning. Have you landed safely? Accommodation is satisfactory I hope?" he asked solicitiously.

"Everything is fine," she answered. There was a pause, then she said, "I'm in trouble."

"What sort of trouble?" he asked patiently.

"I really didn't want you to get in the middle of this sir," she said apologetically.

"Spit it out, Shalini," he said curtly. "Then I'll decide how best to resolve it."

"The guy I was dating in college almost raped me once and was psycho enough to shoot pictures of me in that sorry state. He is now threatening to send those sordid photographs to the company and social media," she said in a rush.

"For what?" he asked in a deceptively calm tone. The phrase "almost raped" did not go unnoticed by him and he was holding on to his temper with great effort. Shalini? Almost raped?

"Blackmail," she said simply.

"When did you get to know of this?" he asked, still sounding calm.

"Yesterday night," she replied.

"So why wasn't I notified immediately?" he demanded into the phone, the veneer of calm finally cracking while staring daggers at Riya.

"We thought—" she began.

"Apparently, that's the one thing you *didn't* do!" he snapped.

"Sir," Riya said calmly. "We more or less took care of the social networking front and Sreeja Ravishankar has—"

"So you saw it fit to tell Ms. Ravishankar right away, but delayed telling me!" he fumed.

"Sorry sir," Shalini said in a choked voice. "I wanted to keep you out of it for as long as possible. If those photos—If you—I thought I could never face you again if—"

"Shalini," he said in a soft, gentle voice. "This is not your fault. You're the victim here. The one mistake you made was dating this psychopath. Even that can be attributed to poor judgement, nothing else. A youthful mistake. You don't have to feel ashamed for someone else trying to violate you then and use those photos to violate your privacy now. None of us are sanctimonious enough to say that we have never made mistakes in our lives."

"Thank you sir," she managed to croak, sounding as if she was about to burst into tears.

Shashi turned to Riya. "Tell me what all has been done so far." There was a note of calm authority in his voice.

In a few short sentences, Riya explained what all had been done and who else were involved. Shashi gave her a faint smile when she concluded.

"Good job," he complimented. "Now what do you want me to do?"

"In case he sends the pictures in physical form," began Shalini.

"Got the point," he said before she could go any further. "We can't monitor the mail traffic completely. However, I think if this guy wants to send anything to the company, he'll choose to send it to someone high up in the hierarchy. So the incoming mails of all members of top management can be monitored closely. That's the only thing I can do."

"I think that's all we can do," said Riya practically. "If, despite all our efforts, he still manages to sneak in something...?"

"Then we'll send an official mail to all employees stating that someone out there is on a deliberate smear campaign to sully the reputation of our employees. Today it's Shalini, tomorrow it could be someone else, it's our duty to be vigilant and report any untoward incidents, and more to that effect," he said firmly.

"Don't worry Shalini, every problem has a solution. We just have to find it," he spoke reassuringly into the phone.

"She and Derek Mathews are going to try and find a way to defuse this problem from the source," said Riya.

Shashi sat back and studied her intently. Finally he said into the phone, "I hope you know what you're doing, young lady. And where does Derek Mathews fit into the picture?"

"We, uh, are dating," Shalini replied.

"I won't ask anymore," he said, sensing her embarrassment. "But just be careful. And don't worry about anything. We'll do what we can to prevent it." With that, he ended the call.

"How do you people know Mathews?" he asked Riya.

She shrugged. "He lives in our building. Top floor. From what I can see, he's completely bowled over by Shalini, though for the life of me, I can't figure out why!"

Shashi's face bore a look of amusement at Riya's last few words. The words may have sounded unflattering, but he knew otherwise. "Ah! Well, no surprises there. Will he be able to help her out with this?" he queried.

"Yes," she said without hesitation. "If anyone can help her sort this mess out, it's him. Plus, he has got a cool head, which is more than can be said about Shalini."

"Good. Now getting back to our project, I have gone through the latest changes you have made to the project proposal and feasibility study and I like it. However, these are points I wish you to include," he said, handing over a USB drive. "The changes are all highlighted in red."

"Why didn't you just mail this to us, sir?" she asked, looking quizzically at him.

"Problem with internet connectivity since last night in my neighborhood," he explained. "That's why I asked you to come in today. I hope it'll be rectified by today evening."

"Okay," she said. "I'll try to incorporate the changes and finish it before I leave for Hyderabad tomorrow."

"Good luck with that," he smiled. "Go home now."

"See you sir," she smiled warmly back at him. "And thank you for everything."

CHAPTER 24

Shalini ended the call with Shashi Kiran and took a few moments to compose herself. The call had not been as awkward as she had feared. Her boss had not been judgemental at all and had put her at ease. A small smile of relief was playing on her lips. With herself, Riya, Derek, Sreeja and Shashi Kiran after him, Sudarshan really did not stand much of a chance. In fact, this small army was too much for a person like him. He was going to go down and stay down for the count. She was determined to ensure that.

A car from Derek's company had come to the airport to pick them up. They checked into different rooms in the hotel at which InfoSoft MicroTech had arranged accommodation for her and met up for breakfast in the hotel's restaurant once Shalini was through with her phone call.

"Are you sure you don't want to let your family know about this?" he queried.

"I'm positive," she said with an affirmative nod. "I'm in no mood to deal with their judgemental lectures and sermons on how bad and sinful I must have been to have landed in such an unholy mess."

"Wow!" he whistled. "They can be that bad?"

"Oh they can be worse, especially my mom. She's intolerable when she gets into one of her holier-than-thou moods. At such times, I can't stand to be around her. I have no intention of telling them anything unless it becomes absolutely and unavoidably necessary."

"Do you wish to visit the flat your family owns here?" he asked.

"No."

"Alright," he smiled. "So that means once your work at the college is finished, I'll have you all to myself."

"I guess," she smiled back. "But we still have the nuisance of Sudarshan to take care of."

"That will be handled, I'm sure," he said cockily. "He's just an irritating fly and like one, he'll be squashed."

"Aren't flies supposed to be swatted away?" she asked coyly.

"Not this one," he retorted. "He has to be squashed with no chance of resurrection."

"Good to know!" grinned Shalini.

"I shall go straight to my office after breakfast," went on Derek, his tone growing serious. "I have made an appointment to meet with Rakesh Mitra at eleven."

"He lives in Bangalore?" she queried.

"No, fortuitously, he's here for a few days on business, which works quite well in our favor."

"You'll be going to Mitra Software from your office?" she pressed, wanting to know all the details.

"No, Rakesh is coming over to my office. Incidentally, we have some RFPs we need to discuss. And he has some other commitments later on in the same area, so it's more convenient for him."

"Where's your office?" she asked.

"indira Nagar," he responded. Changing the subject, he asked, "And where is the flat your family owns in Bangalore located?"

"Koramangala."

"Fantastic location," he smiled.

"Will you take me to your office sometime?" she asked out of curiosity.

Derek smiled enigmatically. "I'm hoping one day you'll work there."

"Are you trying to poach me, Mr. Mathews?" she demanded with an arched eyebrow.

"Most definitely," he grinned back at her. "Though not for a while yet. Now finish your breakfast. We've got quite a day ahead of us."

"How can I forget," she sighed, then hit a button on her talking wristwatch. It was almost nine-thirty and she needed to be at the college by ten.

"Shall I drop you off at the college?" he asked, standing up.

"No," she said. "The company has arranged a cab to take me and the others to and from the colleges. But thanks anyway."

"Will you be alright on your own?" his concern was obvious.

"I'm a big girl Derek," she smiled, touched that he cared enough to ask.

"I know," he gave her a chaste kiss on the forehead. "Just take care of yourself, you hear? I'll see you in the evening, hopefully with some good news."

"I'm counting on it," she responded.

They went outside, where Derek's chauffeur brought his car around. He waved quickly to Shalini before the car took off. She was soon joined by Sanjay Prabakar and Deepak Krishnan, both in their early thirties, who had accompanied Shalini to Bangalore. "When are we getting picked up?" Sanjay asked her. He was a stocky man of medium height with a prematurely receding hairline.

"Any moment now," she responded. Just then, a cab pulled up in front of them and the cab-driver got out.

"Ms. Shalini Samuel from InfoSoft MicroTech?" he queried.

"That'd be me," she said. "Come on, our ride is here."

Using the cane, she expertly manoevered herself into the backseat of the cab. The two men followed her inside. The ride to the first college was made in silence. When they reached the campus, the placement cell co-ordinator greeted the two men warmly and looked askance at Shalini, noticing the cane.

"Is anything wrong, Mr. Seetharaman?" she queried.

"Ahh," he quickly recovered. "I was told a Ms. Shalini Samuel would be joining us."

"I'm Shalini Samuel, HR co-team lead," she said calmly, extending her hand.

"Of course, of course," he was flustered. "I'm sorry miss, but we didn't know—"

"Mr. Seetharaman, I'm the HR representative for today's selection process. Unless you have a problem with that, I suggest we begin the proceedings," she said in a clipped, official tone. She had no patience for dealing with people with narrow minds incapable of entertaining r accepting something apart from the set norm.

"Shalini, you don't have to be so curt," chimed in Deepak, a tall, thin man with the pasty complexion of someone who spent most of his time indoors. "He was just clarifying something."

"I don't have time for this," she rounded on him. "Mr. Seetharaman, please show us where you have made the arrangements."

"Sure, ma'am," he said hastily, turning and leading the trio down the hallway into a room used by students for making audio-visual presentations. "We can have the interviews here," he informed them. "You can also use it as your command center. Will it be sufficient?" he asked, directing his question to the two men.

It was Shalini who answered. "Yes, now if you'll show us where to place the materials we brought, we'll be ready to start."

"Y-yes ma'am," he stammered. "This way please."

They soon connected Shalini's laptop with the projector screen and opened the file containing the presentation about the company they gave before every campus selection process began. Once this was done, they got out all the items needed for the day ahead. The trio was soon joined by the college principal and senior professors. The company would be opening an office in Bangalore soon and this mass recruitment was aimed at filling new vacancies which would arise as a result.

They were halfway through tabulating the results of the written test when Shalini's phone vibrated. The voice alert told her it was Derek. She went out to the corridor and answered the call.

"Hello?"

"I've got some dirt," he said with suppressed excitement. "Really juicy dirt."

"Yes?" Shalini asked cautiously. "How juicy?"

"His departure involves his conduct towards some of the ladies in the company, one young programmer in particular," he went on.

"Why am I not surprised?" she muttered. "Sometimes I wonder what madness overtook me the entire time I went out with him. Maybe I was possessed or something."

"Relax. It happens to the best of us," he said comfortingly. "We'll talk when you get back."

"Sure," she said. "See you later Derek."

By lunchtime, candidates who would undergo final round of interviews in the afternoon were identified. They began interviewing them soon after their lunch break and the provisional list of selected candidates was mailed back to Shashi Kiran in Chennai. By the time they were ready to call it a day, it was almost seven in the evening. Sanjay and Deepak were picked up by the cab arranged by the company while Shalini climbed into Derek's waiting BMW.

"Hungry?" he queried.

"Mmmm. Tired and hungry," she responded wearily, laying her head on his broad shoulder.

He held her around the waist and pulled her closer. "We'll go back to the hotel so you can shower and rest a bit before dinner. We'll order room service," he offered. There was a secret smile on his face she didn't quite understand.

"Fine," she murmured. "I want to know everything you found out."

"All in good time," he crooned comfortingly, tightening his grip around her waist.

They exited the elevator in the fifth floor, where they each had separate rooms and walked into Shalini's room. The lights had come on when she had opened the door using the key card and she stood open-mouthed, staring at the spectacle before her.

The entire double bed was covered with flowers. Fragrant jasmine was interspersed with red roses. The small breakfast table in the corner was artfully arranged with white linen, candles and roses. She turned to Derek, who was sporting a wide grin. "Wow!" she said. "Are we celebrating something? Is it your birthday?"

"Nope," his smile became broader. "And yes, we're celebrating something. Tonight's the one-week anniversary of us becoming a couple."

"Awwww. That's so sweet," she could feel a grin spread across her own face. "Thank you so much!" Impulsively, she threw her arms around his neck and kissed him on the lips. He was surprised, as Shalini had never actually initiated kisses between them, but had only responded to his advances, He was also thrown off-balance by her sudden move for an instant, but recovered quickly and responded to the kiss with ardent fervour.

Abruptly, she pulled back, looking deeply embarrassed. "Sorry," she whispered. "I didn't mean—"

"Don't be sorry," he growled and pulled her into his arms and started kissing her properly. He sat down on the bed, dragging her down with him. One of his hands started caressing her generous bosom, gently at first, then more firmly. His mouth moved down to her neck while his hand fumbled with the buttons of her shirt. She wanted to pull away, her mind screaming it was too soon, but for once, the voice of reason was suppressed and she gave in to the kiss, enjoying sensations she had never experienced before. Though he had kissed her several times in the last week, this was different. There was more pressure, a sense of urgency even. His lips moved back up to claim her mouth once again while his hand had managed to unbutton her shirt halfway. Her breasts were now tantalizingly visible through the black lacy bra she was wearing.

Derek's lips were soft against her own, coaxing gently until she parted them and gave him full access. His tongue was inside her mouth, exploring, searching, giving and demanding all at once. His kisses were gentle at first, but became more intense as the long-held need in him for her increased. Her pulse quickened as she felt him caress her nipple through the thin material of her bra. Her initial hesitation was gone now as she put her arms around his neck and pulled him closer, deepening the kiss. For some inexplicable reason, even though they had been going out for only one short week, Shalini felt as if she had known Derek her entire life. She trusted him completely, and that was saying something, as Shalini normally took her own sweet time in giving someone her trust. She shifted so that Derek could have access to her other breast. As the kiss intensified, his hand on her breasts grew more frantic as he stroked, caressed and sqeezed gently yet firmly. Her arms tightened further around his neck as he took them both deeper and deeper. They had kissed several times before, but this was different, more intimate, more possessive.

When they finally pulled apart, both of them were breathless. "That was—" began Shalini.

"Wow!" said Derek, finishing her sentence. He put his finger on her lips. "Shhh. Please don't say you regret it, because I most certainly don't. Things may be happening a little faster than I thought, but I'm not complaining."

"No Derek," she said with a smile. "I do not regret it and I'm most definitely not complaining. I would happily go to bed with you tonight, but the timing is all wrong. I don't think I would be able to concentrate on much with the Sudarshan issue still hanging over my head."

"You could never disappoint me, sweetheart," he said, placing both hands on her shoulders and looking intently into her soft brown eyes. "But I do get the point. Much as I want to go all the way with you, tonight's not the night."

"My head is too clouded with issues," she explained.

"I understand perfectly well, pretty girl," he smiled at her.

"You know," she said blushing a little. "I've kissed only one guy before. And it felt nothing like how I feel when I kiss you. And this," she smiled, "was the best kiss yet!"

Derek's mouth tightened. "It makes me sick to think that slimeball had his hands all over you. It makes me want to rip him into little pieces. He never deserved you, princess."

Shalini hung her head. "It makes me sick to think how stupid I was," she said quietly.

Derek tilted her chin up to face him. "Don't let's think about him or anyone else now. It's just me and you and this moment." He leaned forward and kissed her once more. This time, his kiss was fierce and demanding, yet held an underlying tenderness that made Shalini feel more sure of herself while kissing him back. Finally they pulled apart and he gently smoothed back her hair and buttoned up her shirt. "Go and shower," he said softly. "I have already instructed the restaurant to bring up our dinner at eight."

"You think of everything," she smiled, still a little breathless from the kiss.

"Yes I do," he smiled back at her. "Get used to being looked after and pampered, princess."

"Be careful what you wish for, because I might get used to all this attention and expect you to pamper me all the time!" she grinned.

"It'd be my pleasure to look after my girl," he laughed.

Giggling, she pulled out some clothes from her suitcase and walked into the bathroom and quickly showered and got dressed in a comfortable pair of sweatpants and polo shirt. "You're beautiful even when you're under-dressed," he commented cheerfully.

"Thank you," she said. "You do say the nicest things."

"They're all true, pretty girl," his smile broadened. "Dinner's here. Let's eat."

As they dined on cream of tomato soup, *tandoori* chicken, *naan*, *mutter-paneer* curry and chocolate mousse, Shalini began to unwind and told Derek about the events of the day. He was annoyed to hear about the way the placement co-ordinator had treated her.

"Great job of putting him in his place," he complimented her. "But I wonder what sort of jerk he is."

"I have to deal with people having such attitudes quite frequently," Shalini said matter-of-factly. "Understanding and maturity are commodities in short supply when it comes to dealing with a person who's not like them either physically or mentally."

"Yes," he agreed. "People forget how unpredictable life can be. Anything can happen to anyone and their lives could be changed forever in the blink of an eye." Shalini nodded, agreeing completely with that sentiment.

"So tell me what you found out about the scum I had the bad taste to go out with while I was temporarily insane," she said, swallowing the last spoonful of mousse.

Derek became instantly serious. "He seems to be a bad lot," he said "And I'm glad you're no longer involved with him."

"So am I," she said fervently.

"He was fooling around with three women while he was at Mitra Software," began Derek. "Two of the affairs fizzled out, but the third one got really serious."

"Meaning?" asked Shalini.

"The lady in question got pregnant," he replied. "A young girl named Tulasi Subramaniam, fresh out of college. Single."

"He seems to have lost all sense of morality," observed Shalini. "What happened after that?"

"Apparently, the girl demanded that he marry her and he had refused saying he was already married and couldn't leave his wife, who had just given birth to their child. The girl attempted to kill herself by consuming pesticide."

"Oh dear!" she paled visibly. "He has gone from bad to worse! What happened then? Did she survive?"

"Fortunately, her roommate found her and got her admitted in hospital. The quick action saved her life. However," he paused, "the suicide note she'd written clearly implicated him. Then somehow, the note got suppressed and the girl withdrew her case, but she told the company bigwigs all that had taken place before submitting her resignation. He was quietly asked to resign or else face dismissal on disciplinary grounds. He took the easy way out."

"So how did he manage to get another job?" queried Shalini. "I mean, if they checked his references..."

"Mitra Software did not want a scandal, so they simply told his new employer that he had left the company for personal reasons."

"So if they get to know the real reason..." Shalini mused.

"He'll be destroyed," finished Derek.

"Let's do it," said Shalini.

"I'm with you, whatever you decide," said Derek sincerely. "But think twice before you decide to go down this road. I suggest you sleep on it and we can discuss it further tomorrow, along with the legal implications."

"Alright," Shalini agreed reluctantly.

"You know what I can't figure out?" Derek asked.

"What?"

"How a strong, vibrant young woman like you fell for a dirtbag like him. Don't get me wrong," he added hastily. "I'm not judging, just curious. From what I've heard about him so far, he seems to be nowhere in your league. I'm having a hard time imagining you with someone like him."

Shalini was lost in thought for a few moments. "I think I was in love with the feeling of being in love," she said at last. "That's the only way I can explain why I decided to take leave of my senses for that period in my life. I was feeling alienated and lonely in an environment in which I felt out of place. My family and I weren't getting along very well for a variety of reasons and I was missing my closest friend. None of these is any excuse for plain stupidity, but they all added up as a recipe for disaster and drove me straight into the arms of the wrong guy." She smiled ruefully. "Mind you, I'm not trying to justify my actions. It's just that under different circumstances, I wouldn't have even paused long enough to give him the time of day."

Derek smiled, visibly relieved. "It's good to know," he said. "So you needed a shoulder to lean on and he was conveniently around. And then he decided to take advantage of your vulnerability."

"Exactly," she agreed vehemently.

"And now he wants to get back into your life through threats and coercion," he continued.

"It'd seem so," said Shalini.

"Well, he can try all he wants, but it'll happen over my dead body!" he exploded, letting out some of the pent-up emotion he'd been feeling all day. "I'll be damned if I let him harm a single hair on your pretty head."

Shalini couldn't help her smile. "Thank you," she said. "But I think we can manage a bloodless coup if we play our cards right. And once this nuisance is out of the picture, we can get on with our lives. We have too much to do to waste time on this worthless creep."

"Well said, my beautiful, adorable Jhansi ki Rani," he smiled. Then he pulled her into his lap and they started to kiss with a burning passion. When his mouth came down to her neck and his hand came down to her thigh, she moaned and whimpered with pleasure. Finally, with a monumental effort, they pulled apart.

"I better get going," he groaned, moving her gently from his lap. "If I stay here any longer, we might end up taking this all the way."

"Maybe we should," said Shalini, with a mischievous gleam in her eyes.

"Are you serious?" he asked, incredulous.

"Of course not!" she laughed. "I was just yanking your chain. We both know the timing is all wrong."

"Yes," he agreed with a smile, running his hand through his curly black hair to make it look presentable.

"So see you in the morning?" she queried.

"You bet!" he grinned before pulling her into his arms once again for a quick kiss. "Good night princess."

"Good night Derek," she smiled. Once he left the room, she locked the door, turned off the lights and climbed into bed.

CHAPTER 25

Shalini had just started to doze off when her mobile rang. The voice alert recited a series of digits. It was the same number from which Sudarshan had called her the night before. She debated letting the call go to voice mail, but decided against it, took a deep breath to compose herself and attended the call.

"Hello?" she said, making her voice sound deliberately more sleepy than she really was.

"Hello, Shalini darling," said a raspy, mocking voice. "Did I wake you?"

"First of all," she said slowly and clearly, "don't call me darling. Ever. And second, yes, you did wake me. I don't appreciate being woken up at odd hours by strangers."

"I'm not a stranger," he cried out indignantly. "I'm your—"

"As far as I'm concerned, you're a stranger, not to mention a would-be rapist. So if you have something to say, state your business. If not, hang up and never call me again."

"Awww, come on, you don't mean that," he mocked her, deliberately drawing out his words.

"Yes I do."

"Fine. So have you given any thought to my proposition?"

"Proposition?" she snorted. "Blackmail you mean."

"Call it whatever you want," he continued. "Have you decided to do the right thing?"

"If by the right thing you mean telling you to take your threats and go screw yourself, then yes," she retorted, trying to keep her voice as calm as possible.

"You're making a big mistake!" he snarled. "Those photos. I could ruin you! Bring you to your knees!"

"Those photographs could at the most cause me embarrassment, but they won't ruin me!" she shot back coldly.

"When I'm done with them," he said, sounding enraged, "they'll make you look like a—"

"Don't you have anything better to do than making threatening phone calls to a girl who has made it abundantly clear a long time ago that she wants nothing to do with you?" Shalini interrupted his tirade, not wanting to listen to him calling her names.

"You'll have something to do with me if you wish to preserve your pure and pristine reputation!" he snapped, sounding bitter and cruel. He was starting to slur his words and Shalini suspected he was probably drunk off his ass.

"You're mistaken in your assumptions, Sudarshan," she said, her voice quiet but assertive. "I don't intend to get involved with you ever again. I don't care what ace you think you have up your sleeve. I'm not giving in to your crazy demands. Besides, if you send those photos anywhere, I'll get hold of Julie and ask her to corroborate my statement about how the photos actually came to be. The world is not kind to men who plot violent crimes against women and then try to blackmail them about it. That's all I have to say to you. Now deal with it and leave me the hell alone!" she spat out angrily, disgusted with him and at herself for ever having known him at all.

"You'll live to regret those words!" he snarled venomously.

"Yeah, well, we'll see about that," her tone was frigid.

Not wanting to listen to any more of his threats and nasty words, she disconnected the call. Her hands were shaking with a mixture of anger and nervousness by then, but she refused to let herself feel fear.

She took a few shaky breaths, trying to calm down. Her heart was beating too quickly as a result of adrenaline. Shalini got off her bed and opened the balcony door. The cool night air did little to cool off her emotions, but it felt soothing against her skin nonetheless.

With Sudarshan, she had put on a mask of bravado and acted as if she wasn't worried about any possible repercussions that might arise if the photographs were released, but in truth, she was concerned. He sounded really vengeful and irrational. It was clear he would not take her rejection lying down. The relationship had been a huge mistake from the beginning and the end had been bitter and violent. Now she was paying the price for that single error in judgement. She just hoped that the price wouldn't be too high. He needed to be dealt with and it had to be done swiftly and in a manner which would discourage any such insane schemes in the future.

She thought of calling Derek, but it was already quite late and she didn't want to disturb him. Instead, she called Riya.

"Hey Shalu! What's up?" Riya sounded pleased to hear from her.

"Hope I didn't wake you," said Shalini.

"Nah. I was working on some changes to the feasibility study," she replied. "So how was your day?"

"Wonderful for the most part, with the exception of the last half an hour," said Shalini wryly.

"Why? What happened?" demanded Riya, noting the change in her friend's tone. "Did Derek Mathews try to—"

"It's not him," Shalini interrupted her. "And for the record, he's been wonderful."

"So what is it?" asked Riya.

"Sudarshan called," sighed Shalini.

"What now?" Riya sounded annoyed and exasperated.

"Still singing the same song. Told me I'm making a huge mistake and how he can ruin me with those photographs and so on," she replied, sounding eerily calm.

"Oh did he now!" snorted Riya. "Who does he think he is? Don't worry honey. All he's doing is digging himself a deep, deep hole. How did you respond?"

"I basically told him to go to hell," said Shalini. "Maybe I should draw up a map for him or something. You know, to help him find the way."

"Shalu," said Riya, a smile in her voice. "I have no doubt you told him off. But you don't have to put up a show for my sake. How are you, really?"

"Angry, nervous, concerned, but not afraid," said Shalini, sounding resolute. "Derek has given me the ammunition I need to fight back."

"Good. What kind of ammunition, exactly?" she asked with interest. When Shalini told her, she let out a low whistle. "That's quite enough to shut him up for good I think. What are you planning to do with it?"

"I'm leaning towards a direct confrontation," said Shalini thoughtfully. "Even though Derek doesn't seem to be a big fan of the idea."

"Just be careful while doing it," Riya warned. "And whatever you do, for God's sake don't do it alone!"

"Trust me Ri, I'm angry, but I'm not so blinded by rage to be reckless and foolish," she promised. "When I first told Derek about what I was thinking of doing, he told me to sleep on it and decide in the morning. Well, Sudarshan has helped me make my decision. I don't need to wait until morning to make up my mind."

"Fine," Riya exhaled. "Does Derek know about tonight's phone call?"

"No, I'll tell him in the morning."

"Alright. Good night honey. Try not to think about the situation and get some sleep."

"Will do. Good night."

CHAPTER 26

After talking to Shalini, Riya continued to work late into the night on Saturday and revised the feasibility study report according to Shashi Kiran's exacting instructions. Then, she tried to write some preliminary coding and ran test programs. The success of the project hinged on her ability to integrate Shalini's concepts into programmable code. This could prove to be tricky, but she was confident that it could be done. Her boss seemed to think so too. Now if only the ghost from Shalini's past could be exorcied! She needed her to concentrate all her energy on the project and the unexpected re-entry of Sudarshan into her life was complicating matters, not to mention a totally unwelcome scenario. She could live with Shalini taking time off to be with Derek, but Sudarshan causing her to waste precious time dealing with his lunatic blackmail schemes was intolerable. He was nothing but an annoying nuisance who was encroaching upon her friend's precious time. *Not to mention screwing with her mind*, Riya thought ruefully.

She wanted to see him go down for two reasons: one, she was never one to let anyone walk all over her or her friends and wanted to see him shown his place and two, she really needed

Shalini's time and attention to be on their quest to make a billion dollars. This strengthened her resolve to redouble her efforts to thwart his plans to damage Shalini's reputation. With this thought firmly etched in mind, she shut down her laptop and went to bed. Sleep did not come easily, however. She spent most of the night tossing and turning, imagining innovatively painful ways to punish Sudarshan, should he ever have the terrible misfortune of meeting her face-to-face. Finally, with an evil smile on her lovely features, she fell asleep in the early hours of the morning.

She woke up around nine on Sunday morning and quickly got ready. She had already gotten all the papers she needed to carry from the office, so she didn't have to drop in today. And all her packing was already done. She switched on her tablet and logged into her e-mail program.

There was an e-mail from Shashi Kiran, sent at 1 A.M, sitting in her inbox. She rolled her eyes heavenward. His internet connectivity issue had been resolved apparently and he was back to his usual workaholic ways. *The man would never change*, she thought in amusement and wondered if he ever slept. She opened it and it just said that on Wednesday, she and Shashi Kiran had to meet some important people. Riya replied that she would be ready and was looking forward to it. Then she noticed a mail from Anup with the subject line COLORS & MUSIC. Curious, she opened it.

He was inviting her to an art exhibition and classical music concert on Tuesday night. They were taking place at the same venue and the two of them could easily attend both. She thought for a second. She'd be getting back to Chennai on Tuesday afternoon and had to be prepared for whatever was expected of her on Wednesday night. Could she afford to take Tuesday evening off from the project to take Anup up on his invitation?

She wanted to, but was not sure if it would be possible for her to do so, then decided to throw caution to the winds for once and have a little fun. She replied that it would be her pleasure to accompany him.

Just as she was packing up her laptop and tablet in her backpack, Sreeja called and told her she'd pick her up around 12.30. She was waiting in the ground floor lobby by the time Sreeja drew up in a cab. The girls greeted each other warmly.

"Any word from Shalini?" queried Sreeja.

"Yeah, it seems Derek Mathews has managed to find out some things about the creep which can be used against him. That's the good news," she paused.

"Does that mean there's bad news as well?" asked Sreeja, surprised and a bit concerned.

"Well, Sudarshan had called her late last night, pretty much repeating all his threats," said Riya with a frown.

"Oh hell!" Sreeja sighed. "And I'm sure that must have put our friend in a fine mood!"

"She was angry and nervous," replied Riya. "But not afraid. Shalini's determined to take him down using the information supplied by Derek."

"Can't really blame her for wanting to do so. I just hope that in this fight against him, she has enough sense not to get caught doing something underhanded. Subterfuge and subtlety is called for here," said Sreeja, concern evident in her soft, mellifluous voice.

"She's not stupid," smirked Riya. "But if she gets carried away in her quest for vengeance or whatever, Derek will keep her from getting into hot water. He's a sensible man and must have dealt with many tricky situations in his business. Batting on a sticky wicket shouldn't be alien to him."

Sreeja agreed wholeheartedly with a vigorous nod, but she was smirking wickedly as she said, "Batting on a sticky wicket may all be very well, but has he actually dealt with Shalini when she has decided to assume the role of Avenging Angel? Do you think he's up to the task?"

"That," grinned Riya, "remains to be seen. And it will help him and us understand how well he can hold up under *real* pressure!"

Both the girls laughed heartily, then Riya's face suddenly turned sober. "All jokes aside," she said seriously, "I wish Shalini had shown better judgement in her student days and stayed well clear of this creep!"

"It can't be helped, Ri," said Sreeja sensibly. "We all make mistakes. The trick is to learn from them and become better and stronger. Shalini made a mistake by falling for this guy. Maybe she was taken in by his sweet-talking or whatever, and it has come back to haunt her. But it can be dealt with and I'm sure that when it's all over, she'll be wiser and stronger than ever."

"I know you're right," Riya let out a deep breath.

"Of course I'm right. I'm a genius, after all," reiterated Sreeja with a smug smile that also held warmth and understanding. "So just relax and let her take care of it. Shalini is bold and resourceful. Now that the initial shock has worn off, she's more than capable of handling the situation. We have done all we can to cover any contingencies that may arise. Just try not to worry."

"I'll try," Riya gave a slight smile.

"So we're visiting two colleges in Hyderabad?" Sreeja asked, deciding it was time to change the subject.

"A slight change of plans," said Riya, taking a moment to switch gears from personal to professional. "We shall be playing a support role to the Hyderabad team. Initially, we were asked to fly down because they were spread too thin, but now their schedule has been cleared and they'll be taking care of the nitty-gritties while you and I my friend, will just be part of the interview panel."

"Yippee!" Sreeja clapped her hands. "It's time we got some royal treatment after all!"

"I'm with you there," smiled Riya. "With the junior vice-president of Encryption on the panel, I think royal treatment is guaranteed."

"You'll be HR VP before you know it," said Sreeja reassuringly.

"Riiiight," drawled Riya. "You and I both know the only way to reach the top of the ladder in HR while still being in the twenties is if I start a company of my own."

"So why don't you?" asked Sreeja. "You and Shalini could turn anything into gold."

"Let's see," said Riya vaguely. Sreeja was a good friend, but the billion dollar project was not her secret alone to divulge. "And what about you? Are you going to continue working in the private sector?"

Sreeja shook her head decisively. "No, I want to work for or start my own think-tank within a year."

"My best wishes to you for that," said Riya with a smile.

"Thank you. And how are things between you and Anup Sharma?" Sreeja asked, curious.

"As well as could be expected. He's a good friend and fun to be with," replied Riya. "It turns out he and I have a lot in common."

"Good to know," Sreeja smiled, not pursuing the subject any further. The rest of the ride was made in a comfortable silence.

CHAPTER 27

Just as Riya and Sreeja were going through security check at the airport in Chennai, in Bangalore, Shalini and her colleagues had finished tabulating the results of the written test and the names of shortlisted candidates were put up on the bulletin board before they decided to break for lunch. Derek picked Shalini up from the college and took her to a small restaurant where they could get heavenly biriyani.

"I'm going to grow fat," she groaned. "For over a week now, it seems like I'm eating out all the time."

"Not quite all the time," he smiled. "And I don't see why becoming a little fat should bother you."

"Are you kidding?" she expostulated. "Do you have the slightest idea how hard I have to work to keep myself in shape? And I haven't been anywhere near a gym in the last one week! I think I should look like a giant balloon by now!"

"No, you're not looking like a balloon, not even a small one, I swear! So calm down," he said mildly. "At this rate, you'll hyperventilate! Just relax and enjoy the food."

"Damn, but this biriyani is sinfully delicious!" she smacked her lips to emphasize her point.

"I told you so," he sang out with a broad grin. "So what time are you likely to get off today?"

"Should be done by four-thirty, five at the latest. The shortlist is really short today."

"That bad, huh?" he asked.

"The quality has left a lot to be desired," she confirmed with a nod.

"I can totally understand," he reflected. "We faced the same problem when we conducted our own recruitment exercises. The employability of many students these days is questionable at best."

"Tell me about it," she agreed with a smile.

"So have you thought about how to proceed with the other issue?" he asked. He knew just what he wanted to do; break the neck of the sleazeball, preferably with Shalini stashed away safely somewhere, but the final call had to be Shalini's,

Shalini took a deep breath. "I have definitely decided to confront him face-to-face," she said quietly. "He called me again last night."

"What!" Derek looked flabbergasted. "When?"

"Sometime after you left," she explained as succinctly as possible what had transpired during the conversation.

"So why exactly did you wait this long to tell me about it?" he asked in a dangerously low voice.

"I didn't want to disturb you last night and today morning, we had to leave in a hurry," she hastened to explain, sounding defensive.

Derek exhaled a sharp breath as he tried to quell the fury growing inside him against the man tormenting the most important person in his life. "So how do you want to approach the uh, problem?" he asked in a calmer voice.

"Do we have an address for him?" she asked with a gleam in her eyes.

"I have the address from Mitra Software's records," he qualified. "Whether he's still living there or not is anybody's guess."

"We'll start there," she said grimly. "Once we come face-to-face, he and I are going to have a long—talk."

The manner in which the word "talk" was uttered was not lost on Derek. He looked at her sternly. "This 'talk' will happen in my presence," he said in a tone that brooked no argument.

"You've made that perfectly clear on more than one occasion, but I think it'd be best if I—" she started.

"Shalini," he warned.

"Fine," she gave in. "You can come with me. All said and done, I guess it would be better if you accompany me."

"Good," he smiled. "We'll go straight after you're done at the college."

"Alright," she nodded.

Derek dropped her back after lunch, promising to pick her up as soon as she was ready to leave. She waved till the car rounded the corner, then she went back into the interview room, smiling and thinking to herself how lucky she was.

The rest of the afternoon flew by. Only a couple of candidates came up to scratch and by four-fifteen, she had e-mailed their names to Shashi Kiran. Then, she called Derek to let him know she was done for the day. Ten minutes later, she received a text saying he was waiting outside.

"I'm leaving," she announced to Sanjay and Deepak. "The cab will be here at five to take you to the hotel and then the airport."

"Aren't you coming back to Bangalore with us?" Sanjay queried.

"No, I shall be returning tomorrow evening," she clarified. "I have got a few personal errands to take care of. See you guys in office on Tuesday. Thanks once again for all your help and co-operation." Her tone was warm and cordial, but the look in her eyes made it perfectly clear that further questioning would not be welcomed.

Deepak started to say something about taking advantage of a business trip to take care of personal duties, but a warning look from Sanjay made sure that the words died on his lips. They bade goodbye to Shalini, who quickly and carefully made her way out of the college building.

CHAPTER 28

Derek was waiting in the visitors' parking lot. He had told the chauffeur to take the day off as he wanted to drive Shalini around himself. When she walked into view, he went to meet her halfway and they walked back to the car together. Once again, he opened the front passenger's door for her, which won him a wry smile.

"So where does he live?" she asked, cutting straight to the chase once he was settled in behind the wheel.

"You don't beat around the bush, do you, princess?" he shook his head and smiled indulgently. "As per Mitra Software's records, he's supposed to be residing in Kalasipalayam."

"Oh? That's close to where my friend Anita lives. She's in Richmond Road," she said.

"Good then. Let's check the address out first. I hope to God he still resides there. Once we're done, we'll drop in on your friend."

"No, we'll drop in on her before," said Shalini decisively.

"Any particular reason?" he asked, looking bemused.

"She's a lawyer, a really good one," replied Shalini. "If we indeed decide to take the coercion route, I want to know what the legal ramifications and repercussions are likely to be."

"Wouldn't it be simpler to tell the police?" asked Derek. That was not what he wanted, but if it would keep Shalini out of mischief, he was all for it. "Once they know his track record, they wouldn't hesitate to take him into custody for blackmail."

Shalini however, was having none of it. "Yes, but what purpose would that serve?" she argued. "Even if my name is kept out of the media, what's the guarantee he'd give up all existing copies of the photographs along with the memory chip? He'll get out and find a way to come after me once again."

"If the right kind of pressure is applied—" began Derek.

"I know you can probably wield some influence over the police and come to some arrangement," she cut in. "But that would be only temporary. And this fellow is slippery as an eel. No," she shook her head. "I want this over and done with once and for all."

"Shalini, this is a huge risk," he tried to reason with her.

"I know," she breathed out. "And I quite understand if you don't want to get involved any further."

"That's not what I meant!" he said in a quiet, deliberate tone. Shalini could see that he was barely containing his fury. "I don't want you to do something when your emotions are all over the place, which might land you in hot water. When will you understand that I LOVE you, Shalini?" he exploded, banging his fist against the steering wheel, finally giving vent to his pent-up rage and frustration.

"And when will you understand that I have to close this chapter of my life once and for all so that I can move forward with you!" she shouted back, her eyes stinging with unshed tears. "If you're ever hoping to hear those words from me, we have to put a stop to this once and for all! My way is the only way," she was trying very, very hard to keep her tone level and her eyes from watering.

Derek glanced at her out of the corner of his eye. She looked pale and her breathing was rapid. Without saying a word, he manoevered the car into a quiet side-street and killed the engine, then turned around and took her hands in his. "I'm sorry, princess," he said gently. "I didn't mean to yell at you."

"Do you have any idea how hard it has been for me to trust you enough to give this relationship a chance, Derek?" she asked in a barely audible whisper.

"I know," he said quietly. "I can see that in your eyes. I know that you were attracted to me as much as I was to you, but I could see you were holding back. I didn't approach you for the last couple of years because I didn't want to scare you off. But recently, I saw that you were softening, so I decided to give it a shot. I saw how unsure you were on our first date and how much you've grown to trust me in the last few days. Enough to," he took a deep breath before continuing, "to let me in to such a huge extent and reveal so much about yourself. That's precious to me, princess."

"Sudarshan took away my ability to trust people, especially men," she said in a calmer voice. "If he hadn't broken me so badly and left me feeling worthless, you wouldn't have had to wait for this long to ask me out. I want this monkey off my back. I want," she paused, searching for the right word. "I want closure."

"And I want you to have it," he said sincerely, squeezing her hands. "I just don't want you to get into trouble over it, that's all. He's not worth it."

"I know," she said, looking intently into his eyes. "But sometimes, you just have to do what has to be done and leave the rest in destiny's hands."

"You're right," he conceded finally, unwilling to tear his eyes away from hers and unable to say no to the earnestness in her beautiful face. "Whatever you want to do, I'm with you all the way."

"Thank you," she said with a small smile. "You don't have to do this, you know."

"Shut up before I decide to lecture you and give you a piece of my mind. Trust me, you won't enjoy it," he threatened with a laugh, starting the car and reversing it. Shalini laughed as well and her mood lightened considerably. She called and informed Anita that she and a friend would be dropping in shortly, then she told Derek the address.

Presently, they pulled up in front of Anita's apartment building, headed up to the fourth floor, walked down the corridor and rang the doorbell. The door was opened by a slim, pretty girl in her mid-twenties with a cute little child in her arms. "Hi Shalu," she greeted warmly, leading them into the living room. "And who's the gorgeous hunk?" she whispered into her friend's ear.

Shalini blushed to the roots of her hair as she introduced them to each other. "Anita, this is my boyfriend Derek Mathews. And Derek, this is my best friend Anita Manoj."

"Hold on," said Anita, placing the little girl in a walker. "You have a boyfriend? Since when?"

"Since last Saturday," admitted Shalini, looking at the floor as if she found the tile pattern very interesting.

"And you waited for this long to tell me?" Anita sounded annoyed. "Look at me, dammit!"

"I was going to tell you—" Shalini began.

"When?" she shot back sarcastically. "Not a single word over the phone in all this time and now you're appearing at my doorstep with a boyfriend I know nothing about!"

"May I interrupt?" Derek asked calmly.

"This doesn't concern you!" she shot at him, staring daggers at Shalini.

"Anita, Shalini has told me a lot about you—" he tried once again.

"And she has told me nothing about you!" Anita fumed.

"Keep quiet. You're not helping!" Shalini hissed at Derek. She turned to Anita. "Nitu, come on. Are we going to stand here and fight about who did or did not say what? Don't you want to know why we're here?"

Anita took a deep breath. "Sit down both of you," she said finally, indicating the three-seater leather couch and taking a seat on the single-seater opposite. "I'm still mad at you though," she said to Shalini, her voice much calmer now.

"I know Nitu and I'm sorry, okay? I was waiting for your visit next weekend because I wanted to tell you in person. I thought I owed you that much."

"I'll get over it," said Anita, smiling for the first time since Shalini had broken the news.

"Good, because I need your advice, and I can't afford to have you pissed off at me," she smiled back.

"Shoot," said Anita, walking into the kitchen and returning in a few minutes with a tray of snacks and juice.

"Sudarshan called me on Saturday," began Shalini.

"The creep you used to date some years back?" she asked, staring at her friend in astonishment. "Was he attempting to crawl back into your life after all these years? He must have some nerve, considering the fact that the last time the both of you met, he had been attempting to force himself upon you."

It was Derek who replied. "That's one way of looking at it," he said with barely contained fury.

"Stop talking in riddles and spit it out," said Anita impatiently.

"He has some photographs from that last encounter. You know, when he had ripped off my clothes and stuff. He has done something to those pics and now he claims they look totally different and compromising. He's threatening to release them on to social media and to my workplace as well," said Shalini in a rush. "Unless…"

"…you agree to crawl under the sheets with him," Anita finished.

Shalini nodded, "Bang on."

"And you being you, I'm guessing that you don't want to go to the police," said Anita.

Shalini shook her head firmly and proceeded to tell her friend about all the preventive measures and damage limitation efforts they had taken so far. She also told her what Derek had found out about Sudarshan.

"Again, knowing you," said Anita when Shalini had come to the end of her recital, "I'm guessing you want to use all this dirt to chop his balls off and hand them back to him on a platter."

"Again, bang on," said Shalini.

"Are you a lawyer or a mind-reader?" queried Derek, looking amused.

"Oh I'm no mind-reader," Anita smiled back. "It's just that I've known her nearly all my life. We grew up together. I can predict her reactions from across oceans and continents if it comes to that."

"Well Ms. Clairvoyant, how much legal trouble will I get into if I go through with this?"

"Nada," said Anita without hesitation.

"Explain."

"If you have to get into trouble, he has to press charges. And what charges would he press? 'Oh there was this chick I used to fool around with and once almost managed to rape, and I just managed to click some pictures of that encounter when I thought I had overpowered her and when I tried to blackmail her with them, she turned the tables on me. So please do something about it and protect me from her villainous actions?' Do you realize how absolutely ridiculous it sounds?"

A wide grin spread across Derek's rugged features and Shalini burst into laughter, relief washing over her like a tidal wave. "So I can go ahead with the plan?"

"Yes, but do make sure that he doesn't have any sort of recording device or CCTV cameras aimed at you when you're threatening to stuff his balls down his throat."

Shalini grinned and nodded, turning to Derek. "Do you know anyone who can ensure that he hasn't hidden any surveillance equipment around his place?"

"Sure do," said Derek with an easy smile. "A very dear friend of mine is a private detective. I'm sure he can handle it quite easily. But I don't think we need to worry because the last thing Sudarshan would expect is for you to come charging after him like a raging bull. But we'll play it safe. I'll get Ramkumar to come along with us once we have confirmed the address."

"So it's only going to be a scouting mission today?" Shalini asked, looking disappointed.

"Yes," he said firmly. Turning to Anita he said with a smirk, "You, madam, are quite a dangerous woman."

"Never forget that," she grinned wickedly. "You ever so much as make one wrong move with her, it'll be *your* balls which will be served for breakfast!"

"Christ Almighty!" Derek expostulated. "What did I do to get entangled with a bunch of beautiful, dangerous young women?"

"You fell in love with the gang's mascot," Anita grinned diabolically as Shalini smacked his arm playfully.

"Oh yeah, that's right," said Derek with an exaggerated sigh. He stood up and looked at Shalini. "We better get going, princess."

"Sure," she said, getting to her feet and hugging Anita. "It was good to see you, dear. Tell Manoj we're looking forward to your visit next weekend."

"Sure will. Be careful, Shalu and keep me posted," responded Anita. "It was a pleasure meeting you Derek." They shook hands warmly. "I look forward to seeing you next weekend when I come to Chennai."

"Likewise, Anita," he responded with equal warmth.

CHAPTER 29

"You're what?" Shalini cringed as Riya's voice screeched into her ear through her smartphone.

"You heard me the first time," said Shalini with the calm of a zen master.

"Have you lost your mind?" she shrieked. "Please tell me you're not drunk or high," her friend pleaded.

"None of the above," she replied in the same quiet tone. "I told you I'm taking him down. I meant every word I spoke and now it's time for some action."

"Shalini…" her voice trailed off.

"What?"

"When you said you wanted to confront him directly, I thought you meant something more subtle, like showing him you don't care what he does or implying that you too have an ace up your own sleeve. But out-an-out blackmail? How wise is that?"

"Counter-blackmail," Shalini corrected.

"Yes, whatever. Is Derek on board with this venture?" she queried.

"He was reluctant at first, but I think Anita convinced him."

"Honey...,"

"Don't worry, I won't be reckless or stupid," she tried to assure her friend.

"I'm not worried about that," Riya sighed. "What about the fallout? He won't take too kindly to getting outsmarted by you, you know."

"Well, tough luck to him," said Shalini, still sounding eerily calm. "I'm done taking bullshit. It's time to dish some of it back where it came from."

"And Anita is absolutely sure there will be no legal repercussions?" she asked, changing tack.

"Yes, unless he presses charges, and somehow, I can't see him doing that. He'll be digging himself a nice, deep grave if he goes down that road."

"Alright," said Riya reluctantly. "But no unnecessary heroics, you hear?"

"Got it," said Shalini crisply.

"And one more thing," said Riya. "Inform Mr. Kiran of what you're planning to do. Better that he's made aware of this insane venture before it gets off the ground than after it happens. And it'd be better he hears it from you than me." Then the line went dead.

Shalini sat staring at the display of her smartphone, contemplating Riya's final words. Then with a deep sigh, she used the voice command to call Shashi Kiran.

He answered on the third ring. "Shalini," he said tersely, without bothering with a greeting. "Give me the rundown. Don't hold anything back."

"Good evening sir. The recruitment—" she began.

"I have received your e-mails," he interrupted. "And I'm pleased with the work you've done. But that's not why you're calling, so spill."

Shalini took a moment to gather her thoughts, then she proceeded to tell Shashi Kiran all that Derek had learnt and what they planned to do with the information they now possessed. "He must be aware that if this ever gets out, he's ruined. And my friend Anita says it's quite alright. From a legal standpoint, it's not likely to lead to any problems. And if he decides to complain to the authorities, she says he doesn't have a leg to stand on."

"She's right," Shashi agreed. "Normally, I wouldn't recommend this course of action, but on this occasion, you're right. This fellow is dangerous and needs to be taught a lesson. But promise me that you will be absolutely careful while doing it."

"I promise, sir. Too much is at stake here and I can't afford any wrong moves. Derek's accompanying me."

"Let me talk to Mathews," was all he said in response. Shalini silently handed the smartphone to Derek, who raised a brow at her questioningly. Shalini shrugged in reply.

"Hello Mr. Kiran, this is Derek Mathews," he said in a clipped, official tone. "Yes, of course... I'm sure... I'll make certain she is... No, not at all. As a matter of fact, I have a vested interest in making sure this situation is handled... Thank you Mr. Kiran. Goodbye." He killed the call and handed the phone back to Shalini. "You're very lucky," he said quietly, looking intently into her mesmerizing brown eyes. "He's an amazing boss."

"I know, He's more than just a boss," she smiled. "What did he say?"

"Told me to keep both eyes on you, asked if the information was accurate, ensure that you don't get carried away and lose your head and..." his voice trailed off as he smirked knowingly at her.

"And?" Shalini prompted.

"And told me to ensure the 'low-life' is knocked out and stays down for the count," he finished.

"I thought he'd say something like that," she smiled softly.

"He's a good man," commented Derek.

"He is," she agreed. "Shall we go now?"

"Yes," he said, turning the key in the ignition. They drove a little farther up the road and after a couple of kilometers, turned left into a side street. The apartment building in front of which they came to a stop seemed well-maintained, but it had a run-down look to it. There seemed to be no one at the security booth, so they drove straight in and got out of the car.

"Are you sure this is the place?" Shalini asked doubtfully.

"Yes, I'm sure," he assured her.

"But it seems so... inelegant," she finished, for want of a better word.

"Maybe he has come down in life," he said with a smile. "Come on, let's go and find out if he still shacks up here."

They headed into the building and found that the elevator was out of order, so they took the stairs to the third floor and rang the doorbell of 3A.

"But the address says 3C," Shalini hissed.

Derek signaled her to be quiet. The door was presently opened by a plump, middle-aged woman who peered at them curiously. "Sorry, if you're selling something I don't want it," she said rudely.

"Ma'am," said Derek patiently. "We're not salespersons. We just got back from the U. S and are trying to track down a friend of ours who lives in this building, but we have forgotten his door number and he isn't answering his phone. Can you help us?"

"What's your friend's name?" she asked suspiciously.

"Sudarshan Lakshmipathi," said Derek, fingers crossed.

"Oh, him! He used to be in 3C here, but has moved to 5B now. The owners wanted the apartment back," she said without hesitation. The lady was obviously fond of gossip and keeping track of her neighbors' movements.

The young couple thanked her and quickly headed towards the staircase. "Now what?" asked Shalini.

Derek thought for a few seconds. "I'll go and see if he's home," he said at last.

"How?" asked Shalini. "Are you going to knock on his door on some pretext?"

"Shalini..." he was lost for words. "The business community calls me a rising star in the advertising industry. I didn't get to be successful by being naïve and stupid."

"I'm sorry," she said immediately. "I didn't mean—"

"Never mind," he said briskly. "I'm just going to snoop around surreptitiously."

"And if he's home?" she pressed.

"Then I'll call Ramkumar and we'll get this over with tonight," he said decisively.

She took a deep breath and said, "Okay." Derek squeezed her hand reassuringly before bounding up the stairs.

He was gone for about fifteen minutes, which felt like hours for Shalini who was pacing back and forth nervously in the third floor lobby. She heaved a huge sigh of relief when she finally saw Derek coming down the stairs.

"He's out somewhere," he said, answering her unasked question. "But his neighbor said in the morning, he usually leaves for work around eleven. We'll come back early tomorrow morning."

"Oh I wish this thing wouldn't drag on so!" she sighed. "I want to leave it all behind and move on with my life, dammit!"

"Just bear with it one more night, princess," he said soothingly as he put his arm around her slim waist and pulled her close to him and they started walking down the stairs.

"I'll try," she smiled up at him, but the smile did not quite reach her eyes.

Derek helped her into the car and climbed in behind the wheel. He then leaned forward and took her into his arms. "Don't worry," he murmured into her hair as he buried his nose in it. "Tomorrow, all this will be behind us and you'll finally be mine."

"I'm yours already," she murmured into his chest, which was rock-hard from regular workouts.

"Hmmm," he murmured. Finally, they pulled apart and he was rewarded with a genuine smile from Shalini which made her look radiant and ethereal. The same smile which had captured the young entrepreneur's heart two years ago.

CHAPTER 30

They had dinner at a small, intimate restaurant on the way to their hotel and it was well past ten by the time they reached Shalini's room. "Goodnight princess," he said, lowering his head to kiss her gently on the lips. She tilted her head back, giving him easier access to her mouth while at the same time, she pulled his head down to deepen the kiss. What started as a gentle goodnight kiss soon became a full-blown expression of their burning passion for one another. He bit down gently on her lower lip, eliciting a soft moan of pleasure from her. Suddenly, he pulled apart. "You better go inside before I take you right here, right now," he growled.

"I seriously doubt that," she said between breaths.

"How can you be so sure?" he asked as he smiled and gazed into her soft brown eyes which were filled with heated passion for him.

"Because you're not the type to take advantage of a girl when she's feeling vulnerable," she said with complete conviction.

"Ahh. I'm happy to hear that, my love," he looked pleased.

"Come on in for a few minutes," she invited.

"I'd like that," he looked at her warmly. "It's been a long day and unwinding with you for a few minutes sounds good."

"Then get that pretty butt of yours inside," she grinned up at him, squeezing the said body part affectionately.

"Yes, Your Highness," he saluted and bowed smartly, which caused her to go into a fit of giggles. The thought that he could give her such uninhibited happiness warmed his heart. She was a truly remarkable young woman.

Once she had shut the door behind them, they stood staring into each other's eyes. Neither spoke a word. Instead, he grabbed her roughly by the waist and scooped her into his arms, clamping his lips firmly down on hers. There was nothing gentle about the kiss this time. It was fierce and demanding and filled with all the desperate passion and longing he had felt for the last two years every time he had set eyes on her. For her part, she responded with equal fervor, opening her mouth to let him thrust his tongue inside. By the time they pulled apart and he sat down on the bed with her cradled in his arms, they were both panting. "That was some kiss, mister," she said at last, when she had managed to gulp some air into her lungs.

"Whatever princess wants, she gets," said Derek with a soft smile, his arms holding her to him gently.

"Well, I originally wanted to lay my head on your shoulder and whisper sweet nothings to each other, but I liked what happened just now even better," she said coyly, batting her eyelashes.

"So did I, honey, so did I," he said, smoothing back a few locks of hair from her forehead.

"You make me happy, Derek. Very happy," she admitted with a shy smile. "I never thought I would find such happiness with a man. Ever."

"I'm glad to hear that," he was genuinely touched by her honest admission. "My mission in life is to make you happy."

"Good," now she was just being cheeky, but he didn't mind that.

"You look very tired," he observed.

"You're right," she yawned. "I'm bushed."

"Off you go to bed," he said getting up. "Be ready to leave by seven tomorrow morning."

"Fine," she said, going to lock the door.

"And if he tries to contact you again, I want to know about it right away. You hear?" His tone brooked no argument.

"Yes," she said softly.

Derek could sense her apprehension. "Hey," he said, hugging her tightly and stroking her back. "It's going to be okay, princess."

"I hope so," she said, her voice somber. "Goodnight, Derek."

She changed her clothes, brushed her teeth and got into bed. Her mobile rang. *Oh no, not again,* she thought wearily. But the voice alert told her it was a call from her old college friend Chitra. Shalini hadn't heard from her in several months and wondered what she could possibly want at that hour. Frowning, she answered the call. "Hello?"

"Hello Shalini," said a hearty voice. "Long time no hear."

"Same goes for you," Shalini retorted. "How are you?"

"I'm good," said Chitra. "What about you?"

"Fine, thanks," replied Shalini. "So what's up?"

"Uh," there was an awkward silence.

Something in Chitra's tone sent Shalini into full alert. "Chitra?" she asked.

"I received a picture on two of my messenger apps about an hour and a half ago," she said in a rush.

Shalini went rigid. "Oh?" she asked cautiously.

"It was a picture of you," Chitra's tone was hesitant. "With Sudarshan. It was uh, not a very good photograph."

"I see," Shalini didn't know what else to say. The other girl was being very diplomatic and did not go into graphic detail. She did not have to. Shalini knew exactly what to expect in one of those photographs.

"Shalini, apparently, several others from our batch have also received it. I saw your warning on all my social networking pages, so I deleted it immediately and told the others to do the same. Do you know who's behind this?"

"Who do you think?" Shalini asked rhetorically.

"Sudarshan?" Chitra gulped. "But it was all a long time ago. Why would–?"

"Perhaps he has lost a few vital brain cells," Shalini exhaled. "Damned if I know Chitra. I haven't been in touch till he called out of the blue a few days ago. I wonder how he got my mobile number."

"I don't know," Chitra replied. "From one of the guys perhaps."

"Perhaps, but I don't really care how he got my contact number. But I do care that he's out trying to sully my reputation."

"I thought I should tell you," said Chitra.

"You did the right thing. Thank you Chitra," Shalini's voice was warm.

"What are you going to do about it?" queried Chitra.

"I don't know," Shalini answered vaguely. "I'll think of something."

"Take care Shalini. I think he's unstable. Just be careful," said Chitra.

The two girls had not been particularly close during their college days, but they were often teamed up together for group work and had always gotten along well. They had a mutual respect for each other and Shalini was grateful to Chitra for alerting her about the latest development in the soap opera her life had recently become. She thanked Chitra once again and ended the call.

Then she called Derek and quickly told him the entire story with a calm she was far from feeling. He listened without interrupting and when she was finished, asked how she was holding up.

"I don't know," she answered honestly. "The one thing I know for sure is that I hate his guts and wish that I could tear and rend him into little pieces."

"That's understandable," returned Derek, fighting to keep his own temper from boiling over. "Right now, I think I'm capable of breaking every single bone in his body!"

"He has gone too far," said Shalini, her calm façade finally cracking as her voice trembled.

"Yes, and we'll deal with it," said Derek reassuringly. "First thing tomorrow, we'll teach him it doesn't pay to mess with you."

"Can we make him stop?" asked Shalini, unsure for the first time since the drama began.

"Yes we can. After I called Ramkumar and told him everything, he has done some really good work. I finished receiving his update just a minute before you called. He has the girl's suicide note in his possession, and better yet, her former room-mate is willing to speak out against him if required," he said in a calm, self-assured voice. "Don't worry. We've got this in the bag. Do you want me to come over?"

"No," she said. "I'll be fine, but thanks for asking."

"Promise me you'll get some sleep," he pleaded.

"I'll try," she said. "Good night Derek."

"Good night and please don't worry Shalu. We'll take care of this. Together."

She believed it. This belief in him and herself finally helped calm her turbulent mind.

CHAPTER 31

Shalini lay awake staring at the ceiling for a while before finally falling into a fitful sleep. The next morning, she was woken up by the ringing of her smartphone. She cursed, knowing who it was, before answering the call with her eyes closed.

"'Lo?"

"Wake up," said a brusque voice.

"What do you want?" she barked back.

"Derek texted me that that jerk was out yesterday and you would be going to meet him today."

"So?"

"So rise and shine, love," came Riya's sarcastic voice. "You can't take him on while you're flat on your back now, can ya?"

"Oh shut up," she growled. Then she let out a loud sigh and told Riya about Chitra's phone call the night before. When she was done, Riya was silent for a long minute.

"He has proved once again that he's the lowest of the low," she said at last.

"That's the biggest understatement I've heard in quite a while," said Shalini sardonically. "If there's a point beneath low, he sure as hell belongs there."

"True enough. And how are you feeling, short stuff?" she asked with concern.

"Okay, I guess," said Shalini. "I didn't want anyone seeing those photos, but some have seen and I don't like it one bit. I just don't understand what he hopes to gain by doing this."

"Cause you to lose face," replied Riya. "How did your friend react to the photographs?"

"Fortunately, she had seen our warning on the social networking sites, so she deleted it without a second thought and told my other batch-mates to do the same," she said with a sigh of relief. "And my other batch-mates may not have been my biggest fans, but they're not malicious or spiteful enough to pass the picture around like candy. Besides, they're fond of Chitra and listen to her."

"Good. I appreciate her common sense and quick thinking," Riya pronounced. "But this fellow needs to be taught a lesson. Why don't you inform his employers about his earlier indiscretions instead of confronting him?" she suggested. "An eye for an eye."

"That thought crossed my mind too," admitted Shalini. "But what purpose would that serve? We need to get our hands on all existing copies of those photographs first. I don't want to be drawn into the muck any more than I already have been."

"Good point," returned Riya. "What about releasing the information after getting what we need? There's no need to act honorably anymore."

"You know what?" said Shalini decisively. "Till last night, I was willing to play fair. Photographs in exchange for my silence.

But after he drew first blood with the instant messenger shit last night, I have changed my mind. I'll get even with him, and then some. Trying to play mind games with me, is he? I'll show him who holds all the cards soon enough."

"Attagirl!" Riya said happily. "Will Derek agree?"

"I'm hoping he'll be cheering me on," she said with an evil, mirthless laugh. "Enough about me. What are you upto?"

"Sreeja and I are taking it nice and easy. We don't need to run around this time. All that's expected of us is to sit in the interview panel and e-mail back lists of provisionally selected candidates to Mr. Kiran."

"Lucky you!" Shalini said enviously.

"And I need you to take care of this and get your big, ugly butt down here so we can get back on track with the competency project," continued Riya.

"I want that too, Ri," sighed Shalini.

"I have run some test programs," she went on as if her friend hadn't spoken in between. "Initial results are good. We just need to figure out how to incorporate your concepts into the code."

"We will," Shalini promised. "Now if you'll excuse me, I have some derriere to kick."

"Keep me posted," said Riya before ending the call.

Shalini quickly showered and got dressed. By six-thirty, she called Derek and told him she was ready and raring to go. He laughed and within five minutes, knocked on her door. She was dressed in a fitted black shirt with cap sleeves over a black pencil skirt that fell just below the knees. Black high-heeled pumps completed the suave, deadly, confident look she was trying to project.

He let out a low whistle. "He doesn't stand a chance with you looking like that!" he laughed.

Shalini punched him lightly on the shoulder. "The intention is to intimidate, not seduce," she reminded him. Then with a wicked grin, she added, "Well, at least, not him!"

"Of course not!" he snorted. "You think I'd let you do that, even if it was all part of the plan?"

"No," she giggled. "I suppose you wouldn't! By the way, there's been a change of plans."

"Yeah?" he queried, looking expectantly at her.

"I'll tell you on the way. Come on, let's get going."

He drove while she explained what she wanted to do. "His latest actions have called for a change in plans," she finished. "I'm no longer content with just coercing him into giving us all copies of the photographs. I want to finish him off by sending the information we possess to his current employer."

Derek did not comment for some time. Then he looked at her and smiled. "I can't say I blame you for thinking on those lines. But are you absolutely sure you want to do this?"

"Yes," she said firmly.

"Fine, then answer one question for me, princess. Is this a strategic move or is it wholly motivated by a desire for revenge?"

"A little of both," she said honestly. "But mostly a strategic move. When going after an enemy, ensure that he's totally vanquished so that he doesn't come after you again."

"Alright," he smiled wryly at her. "I'm with you, Ms. Avenger."

They munched on some biscuits and drank orange juice which Derek had had the forethought to pack as he had no desire to let Shalini tackle Sudarshan on an empty stomach. He knew how irrational she could become if she was hungry. They arrived in front of Sudarshan's apartment building just after seven-thirty. Traffic had been light and they had made good time. He killed the engine and turned to face her. Taking her face between his hands, he leaned forward and gave her a long, deep kiss, sucking and biting her luscious lips. When they pulled apart, Shalini gave a contented purr. "What was that for?" she asked in a sing-song voice.

"For good luck," he explained. "And um, to mark my territory."

Shalini laughed. "You don't have to do that!"

"Yes I do," he said stubbornly. "You're mine. No low-life on Earth gets to threaten you and expect to get away with it!"

For the first time since the drama began a few days ago, Shalini actually felt sorry for Sudarshan. He did not know who he was dealing with and now had unwittingly managed to make a formidable enemy in Derek Mathews. *And the poor sucker didn't even know it yet!* She shook her head in wry amusement.

"Now remember," he warned. "NO VIOLENCE! We'll get in and out like civilized people."

"Yes sir!" she saluted smartly. "Where's this detective friend of yours?"

"Got here ahead of us and is waiting in the fifth floor lobby."

"Well then, what are we waiting for? Let's go!" she bounced on her feet impatiently.

He took her firmly by the arm and led her towards the building. Fortunately, the elevator was working today and they quickly got out on the fifth floor. A tall, stockily built man with a military bearing hurried towards them as soon as he saw Derek.

The two men greeted each other warmly and Derek turned to Shalini.

"Shalini, meet Ramkumar, my good friend and the proprietor of Quest Private Detectives. Ram, this is my girlfriend Shalini."

"Pleased to meet you, miss," Ramkumar said, extending a hand to Shalini. "I just wish the circumstances were different, more pleasant."

"Likewise," she smiled at him as she shook his outstretched hand. "And please call me Shalini."

"Sure, Shalini," he smiled back at her.

"Ram used to be an officer in the Army and has excelled in all his assignments. He has also undergone commando training. He decided to leave the army after five years and set up his own private detective agency. Now, he's one of the best in the business. We've known each other for a long time, " he finished with a smile.

"That's great! You sure do have friends in useful places," she grinned at Derek.

"And Ram, Shalini is—"

"I'd love to hear all about her, my friend," Ramkumar interrupted. "But first, let's take care of business." He turned and started towards Sudarshan's apartment.

"Sure Ram. You know what you have to do," said Derek, halting Ramkumar in his stride.

"Actually Derek, it has already been taken care of," Ramkumar said as he turned around to face the younger man.

"What?" asked Derek, stopping dead in his tracks. "You didn't!" he whispered. "Please tell me you didn't!"

"Of course I did," he said matter-of-factly. "I thought you were a smart guy, pal. Asking a guy to show us around his house so we can hunt for surveillance equipment would be ridiculous, not to mention illegal as hell."

"And breaking into his home isn't?" asked Derek sardonically.

"Not if he doesn't know," Ramkumar was unperturbed.

"Ram, if he gets to know…" Derek began.

"He won't. Not now, not ever," Ramkumar interrupted. "There was nothing inside. Besides, I'm not a novice to get caught doing something so elementary as this. Derek, please don't tell me how to do my job. If anyone else had said it, I'd have taken it as a personal affront. Just trust me. I know what I'm doing."

Shalini looked between the two men, astounded. "You actually broke into his flat?" she whispered.

"Yes, when he was out for a short while, probably to clear his head. It looked as if he was severely hung over," said Ramkumar patiently. Then he turned to Derek. "What do you say, man? Shall we get on with whatever this is?"

"Yes, let's get this over with," he said briskly, grabbed Shalini's hand and strode purposefully towards 5B.

CHAPTER 32

Shalini took an involuntary step back at the first sight of the man who had opened the door of apartment 5B in answer to the doorbell. Derek put a steadying arm around her waist without taking his eyes off his girlfriend's tormentor.

The man he was confronting was tall and thin, almost weedy-looking. He had a small, unremarkable face with hard, dark eyes, bushy eyebrows, straight nose and lips blackened by regular nicotine usage. His eyes were red-rimmed, and Derek suspected it was due to the hangover Ramkumar told them about. All in all, he couldn't see what Shalini had once seen in him. *She must have been feeling REALLY lonely and friendless to have fallen for this piece of trash,* he decided. *Oh Shalini, he so didn't deserve to know you at all. Your normally astute judgment about people must have abandoned you completely for the duration you were dating him. And he was touching you. God oh God, this scumbag never deserved to so much as come near you, leave alone put his filthy hands on you,* he raged within himself.

Sudarshan looked uncomprehendingly at the two men until his eyes settled on Shalini, who was staring back at him, fiercely defiant. He initially looked shocked, then a slow, demonic, malevolent smile spread across his face. Shalini did not back down, however. Fury emanated from every pore of her being. She glared at him, daring him to make the first move. Both parties stood staring at each other without moving for what seemed like an eternity.

Derek sensed the tension in the air and stepped forward. "I'm Derek Mathews, Mr. Lakshmipathi. I believe you're acquainted with my girlfriend, Ms. Shalini Samuel." He was fighting hard to control his own anger and act civil.

Sudarshan finally took his eyes off Shalini, focusing on Derek. "Girlfriend?" he repeated, sounding surprised, as if such a possibility was beyond comprehension.

Derek's mouth tightened, but it was Shalini who answered. "You thought I'd be mourning your loss for the rest of my life, slimeball?" This earned her a self-satisfied smirk from Sudarshan, confirming that that was exactly what he had been thinking.

Derek squeezed her waist warningly. The message was clear: don't push him too far too early. But the message seemed to be lost on Shalini who was overcome with a cold fury on seeing the smug look on the face of the man who had caused her so much heartache and agony and almost managed to destroy her ability to trust another man. *Almost, but not quite.* She longed to smack the look right out of his face, but held back. First things first.

Ramkumar could sense the tension hanging thick between the two parties and decided he had seen enough. He was aware of the situation and the thought of someone using a young woman's past to blackmail her did not go down well with him. He had two young daughters and knew exactly what he would do if anyone tried to blackmail any of them ever in their lives. He stepped forward and said in a deceptively mild tone, "Mr. Lakshmipathi, why don't we go in and discuss this like adults?"

"And who's this bodybuilder?" Sudarshan asked snidely. "Are you doing both of them now, Shalini honey? Could have fooled me with the holier-than-thou act you put up while we were together," His tone was cruel and mocking. "Even after a good beating, you managed to keep your precious chastity intact, didn't you? Looks like all that has changed now."

Decorum and self-control be damned, thought Shalini as she took a step forward, her arm raised and ready to slap him, her face twisted with rage. Derek pulled her back and held her tight against him, though he was itching to take a swing at this sorry excuse for a human being himself. "No," he hissed into her ear. She tried to break free, but his hold was unrelenting. Turning to Sudarshan, he said in a cold, hard voice, "We can do this outside where your neighbors can see and hear or we can be sensible and take Ram's suggestion and discuss this inside. Your choice. Either way, you will not address Shalini in this disrespectful manner anymore." Derek didn't think he was capable of holding on to his own temper if this idiot kept this up, much less keep Shalini in check. His fists itched to hurt him in the worst way possible. Derek hated violence of any sort against women.

"Let me go!" Shalini cried out suddenly. "There's nothing further to discuss with him! Words won't do! It's a mere waste of time! Let my fists do the talking!"

"Bring it on!" Sudarshan was breathing hard. He couldn't believe the way she was behaving. The sweet, shy, compliant girl he remembered was nowhere to be found, her place taken over by this fierce wildcat with her claws unsheathed and ready to rip into him. He had thought the threat of exposing the photographs would bring her to her knees and make her submit to his demands, but he had not anticipated her taking him head-on and fighting back. It was as if the girl he had once known had never existed at all. It was hard for him to accept that she had simply been going through a rocky phase in life and hadn't quite been herself when they had dated years ago. He was sure she must have heard about the photograph he had sent the previous night via instant messenger, but there wasn't a hint of apprehension or fear in her eyes, only anger. He couldn't understand this sudden turn of events. For the first time since the whole thing had begun, he started to feel a little uneasy.

"Let me go!" she screeched once again, trying to break Derek's iron grip.

"Shut up Shalini!" Derek snapped, turning her around in his arms and glaring down at her. She looked shocked at his sudden harshness. She turned pale and started biting her lower lip nervously. Feeling her nervousness, his features softened a bit. "Calm down," he said in a much gentler voice. "Screaming is not going to do any of us any good."

"Mr. Lakshmipathi..." Ramkumar's tone was insistent.

Sudarshan sighed and went inside, leaving the door open for the others to follow him into the apartment. Things were definitely not going according to his plan at all.

The living room was shabby, as if it hadn't been cleaned for a long time. Newspapers were strewn all over the couches and coffee table, which in turn were coated with a film of dust. The trio looked around gingerly before deciding to sit on three plastic chairs which looked relatively less dirty than the rest of the furniture. Shalini had regained her composure by then and did not need to be restrained by Derek anymore. The initial shock had worn off and her cool, methodical brain had kicked in and she was contemplating the best and most effective course of action to take.

"May I know what this is all about?" asked Sudarshan, attempting to look innocent and failing miserably.

Derek looked at Shalini, who gave him an imperceptible nod. "A few days ago," he began in a cold voice, "my girlfriend received a phone call from you."

"So?" Sudarshan asked smugly. "She was my girlfriend first. I had a right—"

"No!" Derek snapped angrily, cutting him off. "The keyword here is '*was.*' You had no business calling her, much less trying to blackmail her."

"Oh is that what she told you?" Sudarshan asked, his eyes wide. "I was only trying to work things out between us."

"Aren't you married, genius?" asked Shalini calmly.

"I'm in the process of getting divorced. I just thought I'd see if you're interested in getting back together," he was looking pleased with the way he obviously thought he had recovered his ground.

"Listen," said Derek in a deceptively calm voice. "Do you know who I am?"

"You said your name was—"his mouth fell open suddenly as realization dawned. "Not Derek Mathews, the advertising mogul?" his throat was suddenly dry.

"That's correct," said Derek, still in the same eerie, calm voice. "And the one thing I hate more than anything is people trying to waste my time and bullshit me. Especially people like you, Mr. Lakshmipathi."

Sudarshan was looking sick now. "Y-yes," he stammered out.

"So let's cut to the chase, shall we?" Ramkumar interjected, enjoying Lakshmipathi's obvious discomfort.

"Sure," he said woodenly. "What do you want from me?"

Shalini leaned forward. "You claimed to have in your possession some pictures you've apparently taken when you attacked me physically with the intention of sexually assaulting me assuming you had me at a disadvantage," she stated in a clear, calm voice. Neither her face nor her voice betrayed any hint of the turmoil in her heart as she uttered those words and the ghastly scene replayed in her mind. "And you threatened to release them to my employers and social networks if I don't come back to you and act according to your demands."

Ramkumar had surreptitiously started recording the conversation on his smartphone and a tiny recording device in his shirt pocket from the moment Lakshmipathi had opened the door and the recorder was still on and camera was still rolling.

"I had put the call on speaker and have witnesses to the conversation, so don't bother denying it," she lied smoothly.

"Yes, I did," he shot back, his tone defiant. "And I meant every word of it!"

Wonderful, thought Ramkumar. *Keep going, asshole.*

"And," she continued in the same calm voice, "two nights ago, you again called and uttered the same threats."

"Yes, so what?" he snarled.

"Then," she droned on, "last night, you sent an attachment via instant messenger to our batch-mates which contained one of these alleged photographs."

"Yes, and those photographs are real enough," he smirked. "How does it feel to be exposed, darling? Not feeling so pure and holy now, are we?" His tone was taunting.

"Great," said Shalini calmly. She deliberately ignored his taunts, though she longed to rearrange his facial features. "Now that we have established your intentions and the fact that you wantonly invaded my privacy without a shadow of doubt, we can move forward. Here are my demands: I want all existing copies

266

of these photographs plus any and all devices in which they are stored. Hand them over and we'll never refer to this incident ever again."

"Like hell I will," he snapped. "Those are my photographs and I'll do what I please with them!"

"Let me explain something to you," Derek interjected quietly. "If Shalini here decides to go to the police and press charges against you for attempted blackmail, you'll be ruined for life. And she can always file a defamation case against you and drag you to court for causing her humiliation. If you refuse to co-operate, I'll personally ensure that your life as you know it is over."

"Mr. Mathews," said Sudarshan, turning his attention to Derek. "With all due respect, if she had wanted to report this to the police, you wouldn't be here right now. Besides, why are you taking so much pains for her? Believe me, she's not worth it," he said with so much malice in his voice that Derek thought he was seriously unhinged.

Derek was close to losing his temper and breaking the other man's neck, but he restrained himself. "You have no right to address my girlfriend in a disrespectful manner. I think I already made that very clear. Now about those photographs."

"Forget it. I'm not handing them over!" he snarled.

"Very well then," he said, nodding at Shalini. "Go ahead Shalu."

"KVG Technologies," she began in a slow, deliberate tone, "will receive an e-mail tomorrow detailing the *real* reason you left Mitra Software. And a package too, for good measure."

Sudarshan was looking ashen. "I don't know what you're talking about!" he cried out brazenly, "and I'm sure you don't either!"

"Don't I?" she challenged calmly. "Does the name Tulasi Subramaniam ring a bell?"

He was staring at her in horror. "You're bluffing," he whispered.

"Her former room-mate, Mythili Jeganathan, is willing to back us up," she went on coolly. Ramkumar had talked to the girl in question the previous evening after he had received Derek's phone call and the e-mail containing all the relevant information, and she was on board with the plan if it came to that.

Sudarshan's head was spinning. They were telling the truth. He could see that now. Shalini was cool and composed and seeing her unruffled made him snap completely. "Do what you want!" he cried out. "You can prove nothing! I'll publish those pictures wherever I can and you'll be ruined! Your rich, hotshot boyfriend here will then dump you like a hot potato! Then you'll have no choice but to come crawling back to me!" his insane laughter resonated around the apartment.

Shalini shook her head sadly. "What did I ever see in you?" she wondered out loud. "And for the record, yes, we do have proof. The note Tulasi wrote before her attempted suicide is in our possession, and if needed, we'll get in touch with the young lady and convince her to come out with her story in public."

Ramkumar said quietly, "Mr. Lakshmipathi, if the truth behind your departure is made public—and I'm sure Mr. Mathews, with all his media connections can make that happen quite easily—you'd be ruined for life. He doesn't care about Ms. Samuel's past or those photographs. He knows how to handle a scandal. We're here only because we don't want Ms. Samuel to lose her peace of mind over this unfortunate episode that happened so long ago. If you continue to refuse to hand over what we want, then believe me, the media blitz we're planning will bury you in your own bullshit so deep that you can never rise again." All this was said with the best impassive expression Shalini had ever seen. Every word was true. Derek could organize a smear campaign in the media any time. It was only her desire to avoid publicity and save her family embarrassment and awkwardness that was holding him back.

"Dude, she's not worth all this," he pleaded, turning to look directly at Derek.

"Let me be the judge of that," said Derek coldly.

"Are you going to hand over the stuff or are we going to sit here all day debating my worthiness?" Shalini asked sarcastically. "We don't have all day, you know. And our time is much too precious to be wasted on you. Too much has been wasted already, I think."

"Can't we come to a compromise?" he pleaded.

"I'm not interested in any compromise with you," she snapped.

"I'm sorry for what I said the other day," he went on doggedly, digging himself an even deeper hole. "I won't use those photographs anywhere."

"And you expect me to believe that after the stunt you pulled last night? News flash: I don't trust you, jerkface. You can take all your empty promises and shove them up where the sun doesn't shine," she spat scornfully.

He sighed, running a hand over his face. "Fine," he said at last.

"Good. Ramkumar will accompany you," Derek informed him in a tone which brooked no argument.

Ramkumar rose from his seat and accompanied Sudarshan into one of the bedrooms. Derek turned to Shalini. "Good job, pretty girl. I'm proud of you."

"Well, I almost lost my head over all the ugly things he was saying earlier," she admitted sheepishly.

"Well, good that I restrained you," he smiled.

"You snapping at me brought me out of it," she admitted.

"I'm sorry about that, but I had to do it," he said apologetically. "I don't like yelling at women, leave alone the love of my life, but the situation called for it and I had no choice but to do it."

"No harm, no foul," she smiled understandingly.

"He's wrong, you know," he said suddenly. "You're worth it."

Tears sprang unbidden to Shalini's eyes. She did not know how, but Derek seemed to have an uncanny knack of picking up on her insecurities and reassuring her when she needed it. And this time, she hadn't even known it herself, but Derek had sensed it. She opened her mouth to speak, but at that moment, Ramkumar and Sudarshan came back into the living room.

"Got it all, Derek," said Ramkumar in a satisfied tone.

"You sure he didn't make any copies?" Derek queried.

"Well, I have checked his laptop, tablet and mobile and deleted everything. All flash drives and memory cards have been emptied and returned to Mr. Lakshmipathi here. So unless he has copies stashed somewhere else or given a copy to someone else, I have got everything."

Derek turned and looked at Sudarshan. "If you have back-ups anywhere else, now would be the time to come clean," he warned. "Because, believe me, if any of those photos ever go public or are found circulating in any media ever again, consider yourself ruined." His eyes bored into the other man's, radiating venomous fury and determination. Sudarshan had no doubt whatsoever that Derek would carry through with his threat.

He hung his head in shame and defeat. "That's the last of it," he said in a low voice.

"It better be," said Shalini coldly. "Else that e-mail and package would be in your employer's possession so fast you wouldn't know what hit you. I may even decide to file charges of assault and battery with the intention of rape. Julie can be counted on to testify. An eye witness account would damn you for sure."

He stared into her eyes. She stared coldly back at him. There was none of the fear and compliance he had expected to see in them when he had originally thought of this crazy scheme in a drunken haze. Staring back at him was a beautiful young woman made strong and brave by life's experiences who couldn't be intimidated easily or taken for a ride by anyone ever again. He sighed inwardly at his foolishness in thinking that she would be the same girl she used to be all those years ago. He couldn't shake off the feeling that he had made a terrible mistake by not holding on to her when he had had the chance more than four years ago. It was too late now, he realized. She would never be his again. Looking back, he could see that even back then, she had never truly been his. Though she had been close to him, she had always held something back. And she had never looked at him the way she looked at Derek Mathews now, eyes filled with yearning, respect and love.

"Goodbye Shalini," he said through gritted teeth, filled with jealousy and refusing to accept defeat gracefully. "And good riddance! You'll realize the mistake you're making by walking out on me soon enough!"

"Don't hold your breath," she shot back. "For all I care, you can go to hell and stay there till the end of time! And a small tip: if you ever wish to win a girl back, threats and blackmail are not the way to go," With that, she turned to Derek and said, "Let's go Derek. I'm hungry."

"Yes princess," he said with an indulgent smile. "Let's go."

With one arm firmly clasping her around the waist, he steered her out of the shabby apartment with Ramkumar bringing up the rear, a bulky folder clutched in his arm.

Sudarshan watched them go, feeling as if he had lost once and for all the one person who had mattered in his life. He had lost her due to his own spinelessness and inability to stand up for himself and for her all those years ago and now... She was gone forever, tucked safely in the arms of a man who'd do anything in the world for her. He shut the door and went inside to reflect on the sorry state of his life, wondering where his "brilliant" plan had gone so terribly wrong.

CHAPTER 33

Shalini let out a sigh of relief. "That went well," she commented as they walked towards the car.

"Yes it did," he grinned happily.

She turned to Ramkumar. "Thank you Mr. Ramkumar. We couldn't possibly have carried it off without you."

"No problem, Shalini," he said with a kindly smile. "Happy to help. And it's Ram."

"Of course," she flashed a broad smile at him.

He shook Derek's hand warmly. "Thanks for all your help, Ram," Derek said with a smile. "Your presence had the desired effect and smoothed things over for us. And the groundwork you carried out at such short notice was remarkable."

"You're welcome, pal," Ramkumar smiled. He could see that what existed between his good friend and the pretty young woman at his side was not a casual fling like the other relationships he had seen Derek get into over the years. This was something special. The guy was obviously in love with the young lady and from what he could see, the feeling seemed to be mutual. He hoped he was right, for both their sakes. Despite the age difference between the two men, Derek was one of his closest friends and a wonderful person. He deserved to be happy. Shalini Samuel may be fragile in appearance, but he could sense that every inch of her slender, five-foot-two-inch frame was made of steel.

Derek touched Shalini's face tenderly. "Let's go get some breakfast," he said softly. Then he looked at Ramkumar. "How did you get here, Ram?"

"I called a cab," he answered.

"Then we'll drop you off wherever you want," offered Derek.

"What, you're not going to pay me for my invaluable service?" he asked, feigning to be offended.

Derek saw through his friend, as he always had. "Alright," he laughed. "Name your price."

"A first-rate breakfast at a fancy restaurant would be enough to fill my stomach and soothe my wounded ego."

"Your ego?" asked Derek with a smile. "I don't remember wounding that!"

"Ah, but it's wounded all the same," Ramkumar insisted, trying hard to maintain a straight face and failing. Shalini was enjoying the friendly banter of the two men.

"Fine," Derek sighed in mock-resignation. "I know just the place. They have a multi-cuisine breakfast buffet."

"That sounds great. Let's go!"

Derek readily acquiesced as Ramkumar got into the front and offered to drive. The young couple climbed into the backseat and Ramkumar drove off. Shalini sank back into the plush leather seat and took a deep breath. "I'm very, very relieved and glad it's finally over," she said quietly.

274

"Yeah, me too," Derek agreed heartily.

"The things he said..." said Shalini with a shudder.

"Shhh," he put his arm around her waist and pulled her close. "It doesn't matter now, sweetheart. It's over."

She leaned her head against his chest and cried softly, the emotions of the last one hour finally catching up to her. The floodgates opened and tears of relief coursed down her cheeks. He stroked her hair gently and murmured soothingly. Finally, her tears subsided and she looked up at him with a weak smile. "Thanks."

"For what?" he asked, surprised.

"For helping me with this," she said, with gratitude shining in her eyes.

Derek shook his head. "If you'd thought even for one moment that I'd have stood by and watched you being blackmailed, you're so wrong. You're a strong girl and would have kicked his sorry behind all on your own, but you're my girl and ahh, well, it'd kinda my duty to lend a hand with the butt-kicking."

This made Shalini laugh. "Well, when you put it that way..."

He leaned forward and kissed her on the forehead, aware that he couldn't take it any further with Ramkumar in the driver's seat, who for his part was enjoying quite unabashedly the romance unfolding behind him.

"I have to call Riya and Mr. Kiran," she said, pulling out her smartphone.

Riya answered on the first ring. "Tell me!" she barked, without bothering with unwanted niceties.

"It's been taken care of," she said mildly.

"Well, duh," snorted Riya. "I expected no other outcome. I want details."

"And of course it cannot wait till I get back to Chennai," said Shalini.

"If you're smart enough to know that, why all this banal chitchat?" she snapped. "Get on with the story!"

Quickly, Shalini told her friend all that had transpired at Sudarshan's apartment just a few minutes ago. When she finished, Riya was quiet for a moment or two. "He would have never expected to find you at his doorstep first thing in the morning, breathing fire," she said at last.

"No," she agreed. "He must have expected me to kneel at his feet and grovel or something. Fat chance! I hope he takes the message and stays the hell away from me in future," she sighed wearily.

"I suspect he will," said Riya. "Cowards like him will thrive as long as their intended victims give in to their demands. The minute they fight back, these losers will not know where to run and hide."

"You're right," she said.

"So are you going to send the information to his employers?" queried Riya.

"Yes I am," she replied, looking at Derek. "But not right away. I'll wait for a few days, allow him to feel that his secret is safe and then send it."

"Good plan," said Riya appreciatively.

"I know," she grinned devilishly.

"Good girl."

"We're flying back to Chennai today evening. When are you getting back?"

"Tomorrow afternoon," said Riya. "I'll see you then, Avenging Angel."

"Alright Ri. Bye."

She then called Shashi Kiran, who listened intently to her narrative and said, "Good job," when she finished.

"Thank you sir," she said warmly. "I'm especially grateful for all your support."

"Don't mention it," he said with a laugh. "Now hurry up and get back here. Enough time has been lost and we need to concentrate on the competency module now."

"Yes sir," she said. "I'm looking forward to devoting my energy to it."

"Good," he paused, then continued, "I have some news for you."

"Uh-oh," she said, noting the change in her boss's tone. "What's it, sir?"

"Someone will be joining the HR team shortly," he said quietly.

"Huh?" she said, not comprehending his words and what they might imply. "So?"

"A manager has been transferred from Kolkata and while it won't affect your chain of command directly, he'll have his finger in the pie so to speak," he said almost reluctantly.

Shalini was silent for a long minute. "Are you there, Shalini?" he asked.

"Who's this guy?" she asked at last.

"Someone you know," he said mysteriously.

"Who?" she persisted. She did not like the way her boss was sounding. He did not sound happy with the new arrangement and she needed to know why. Shalini had a sneaky suspicion of where this was headed, but she needed to hear it from him.

"Alok Malhotra," he said at last.

Deafening silence greeted this announcement. He had just confirmed her suspicions. "Shalini?" he prodded gently.

"Are you freaking kidding me?" she finally exploded, which earned her a raised eyebrow from Derek.

"No," Shashi Kiran sighed. "I wish I was Shalini, I wish to God I was." •

"Does Riya know?" she asked, feeling deflated. All her euphoria from her victory over Sudarshan vanished.

"No, you're the first to know," he clarified. "I'll let her know straight after this call."

"You'd better, sir," she said fiercely. "She's not going to be happy about this, mind you. After all, Priya Vijayakumar is one of Riya's closest friends and the bastard tried to molest her and managed to get away with it! It was poor Priya who had ended up quitting for no fault of hers!"

"I know, but there's nothing much we can do at the moment," he said. "But don't worry. I'll take all steps to ensure that your work atmosphere remains as pleasant as ever."

"Don't make promises you may not be able to keep, sir," she said wryly. "We'll talk about this once we're both back in Chennai. Of course this has to happen just when we're planning something big! When is he joining?"

"Next Monday. And relax. I'll still be your boss," he tried to make light of the issue, but failed miserably as his heart was not really in it. The three of them made a great team and as far as he was concerned, this was an unwanted intrusion.

"Oh joy!" she squeezed all the sarcasm she could into those two words. "Alright sir, see you tomorrow. And thanks for the heads-up," her tone softened as she bade goodbye to Shashi Kiran.

It wasn't his fault after all. She was quite certain he'd have tried everything in his considerable power to stop this from happening.

She ended the call and rubbed her forehead. Her head was starting to ache. "Great! Just what I needed to hear!" she muttered angrily.

"Problem?" queried Derek.

"You could say that," she said sullenly. "And it's the understatement of the millenium. Oh by the way, I love you."

She said it so casually that at first, Derek thought he must have misheard her. Then as realization dawned, his mouth fell open. This he most definitely did not expect to hear, especially at that moment and definitely not in that flippant manner. But without missing a beat, he responded. "I love you too, princess. More than you'd ever know. You're always full of surprises."

End of Part 1